Chapte

A lison couldn't live her life without music. ~~~~~ ~ ~ that.
Whether elated or depressed and happy being down there, those songs were always there for her. The music groups she'd followed over the years, she could never be anything less than in love with them. The way they dressed, the way they spoke, and the music they made together as a group made her feel as though she were part of a gang, as if the people in those groups were her best friends, the circumstances of her life in Manchester meant a few of them actually were. Meeting people as she journeyed through life, she couldn't understand why they didn't love music as much as her. She'd ask them, and they'd always respond with a stock answer of "all sorts", the most generic, non-committal, devoid of passion response possible, and Alison hated it. She'd always say the same thing if they asked her: "Guitar groups signed to independent record labels."

Born Alison Wells in nineteen sixty-four and raised in Altrincham, her love of guitar music came from her Uncle Keith. They were very close; her first memory of him was sometime in the sixties. He arrived at their home carrying a box of seven-inch singles and his guitar case. He played in a beat group and played records at the social club around the corner every Saturday night. His guitar and ability to play it fascinated her; she would sit cross-legged in the lounge as he attached a new set of strings, listening attentively to everything he said.

"Don't ever think the groups on Top of the Pops are the only ones out there, Alison; other groups exist and play concerts, groups from round our way an' all. Keep your ear to the ground. Buy the music papers, so you know who's about. Go to concerts in town; it's not far."

He would say that to her every year when he gave her a birthday present, usually a gift-wrapped record. For her fourteenth, he gave her a seven-inch single, on the cover a black and white image of a boy playing a drum and the words *Joy Division*. He winked at her when he told her the group were local lads and were playing a concert in the city centre next week. After she'd listened to the record transfixed by this new sound from Salford, she wanted to see them play live. She even convinced her best friend to come with her, though telling their parents wasn't an option since both girls were still four years from eighteen. Alison knew that town at night was out of bounds, but she didn't care; she had to be there. Jimmy Smith was a fifteen-year-old boy from Stretford she met outside the venue before the concert started. They'd met briefly once before; they fell in love that night. They shared birthdays, and it freaked her out. Jimmy said it was because they were meant to be together and were part of the same soul. Alison loved that.

Now in September 1999, as a thirty-four-year-old woman, she stood in the open plan living space at the back of the Highgate home she shared with her husband Simon for the last four years, staring at the back of the album cover in her hands.

Strangeways, Here We Come, the cover is a bit worse for wear around the edges; she'd bought it on release day twelve years ago when The Smiths had split up. She knew for the rest of her life, this group would remind her of Jimmy, her boyfriend from the age of fourteen but now her ex-husband. She hadn't seen him in nearly five years, but it didn't matter.

It always felt like *The Smiths* were *their* group.

Jimmy grew up on King's Road in Stretford, living next door to *Morrissey*, his sister and his mother. In May 1982, he watched *Johnny Marr* arrive at the *Morrissey* home, and they were introduced. They were both eighteen and played the guitar; they had common ground to talk about and got on well. Jimmy knew *The Smiths* had formed before anyone else.

They say good things never last. *The Smiths* split up after five years. Jimmy and Alison divorced after sixteen. She shook her head, baffled at how quickly time passed, carefully dropping the needle onto the record's outer edge. A soaring voice and bouncing piano came from the speakers, loud enough to make her happy but not wake her husband.

Hello, I am the ghost of troubled Joe.

She stood for a moment in her pyjamas and dressing gown gazing at the vinyl record spinning around before turning and walking toward the bi-folding glass doors across the back of their home. She loved Saturday mornings; it allowed her to listen to the music she loved. Simon didn't share her taste in music anyway. There was something special about being alone downstairs in the house, with the freedom to listen to her records.

Alison was a freelance professional photographer, and she'd intentionally left this weekend and all of next week free; she needed a break after a four-day corporate shoot in Canary Wharf. Whenever she was home, she would listen to music, check through photographs, prepare invoices for clients, or do the housework. She would only listen to *The Smiths* when

Decades

Steven Anthony Lomas

Ukiyoto Publishing

All global publishing rights are held by

Ukiyoto Publishing

Published in 2023

Content Copyright © Steven Anthony Lomas

ISBN 9789360168681

www.ukiyoto.com

For JoJo.....and for Tony, Ian, Martin, Rob, Pete, and Mark, I'll never get the chance to thank you personally.

Watched from the wings as the scenes were replaying
We saw ourselves now as we never had seen
Portrayal of the trauma and degeneration
The sorrows we suffered and never were free.

Contents

her husband was at work or in bed; his claim they are depressing irritated her because she didn't see it that way. She felt *Johnny Marr's* music was uplifting and celebratory, not depressing. She'd often wonder if I'm hearing this music differently from everyone else.

With a mug of tea in her right hand, she unlocked the doors with her left. With a gentle push, they slid open completely, allowing the music from the large speakers in the lounge to reach the furniture on the decking. She stepped out there and put everything onto the table, the white cordless telephone, this morning's newspaper, her cigarettes, lighter and a clean glass ashtray.

She brought her mug of tea to her lips and took a drink before placing it on the table and sitting down on the weatherproof, cushioned wooden chair. Lighting a cigarette and taking her first drag of the day, sitting for a moment thinking as she exhaled all that cigarette smoke, she smiled.

It was a calm and sunny September morning with barely any movement in the tips of the large conifer trees at the back of the garden. The first song faded, followed by loud alerting electric guitar chords introducing: *I Started Something I Couldn't Finish,* the second song on the album. Alison smiled, remembering when Jimmy would play that song on his guitar at home, in the flat they shared in the centre of Manchester. The white cordless telephone handset began ringing. Alison answered after three rings.

"Hello?"

"Hi, is that Alison Smith?" a female voice asked.

"Yes, but it's Alison Wilson. I've remarried. Can I help you?"

"Oh, I see. Well, it's Farley Hall Hospital looking after a patient called Jimmy Smith. We can't trace any of his family, and your name was on his records."

Jesus Christ, just as I'm thinking about him! She thought, taking a much-needed drag on her cigarette and then putting it in the ashtray. Her heart started racing; she didn't know what to think. Jimmy's in hospital. Oh my God, what's happened? She worried.

"What about his mother?" Alison asked.

"She died five years ago, apparently."

"Oh no. Not his mother as well," Alison sighed, knowing the divorce had hit her hard.

"What's wrong with him? What's happened?" she continued.

"All I can tell you over the telephone is that Jimmy has been in a car accident and is in a long-term coma, but he's stable. He regained consciousness a few days ago, hence the call."

"How did this happen?" Alison asked, concerned.

"I'm sorry, I can't say, but if you visit us in person, the consultant can explain."

"Where are you?" Alison wondered; Jimmy had flown to America after the divorce.

"Cheshire. I can give you travel directions if you like?"

A moment of silence. Alison was thinking, wondering, thankful she'd booked next week off.

Regardless of what Simon says, this is Jimmy, and I've got to go.

She asked for the address, wrote it down and ended the call by promising the nurse she would be there on Monday to see the consultant. She threw the handset onto the wooden table; it bounced once and landed on the newspaper. Dropping her face into her hands, she wept, the next song on the album had just started playing, and the haunting sombre sound of *Death of a Disco Dancer* perfectly suited the desperate situation she felt she was in. Mixed emotions about the whole thing, the knowing but not really knowing, Jimmy, her childhood sweetheart in trouble, the man she'd wanted to spend her entire life with. Sixteen wonderful years together and everything ruined by the last one. She would give anything to erase what had happened.

She ate breakfast for the next two hours before her husband came downstairs. Then she sat out in the garden, only coming indoors to make a mug of tea or change the record she was listening to. She only listened to *The Smiths*; all she could think about was Jimmy.

Alison smoked cigarettes, drank tea, and ignored the morning paper on the table. She wanted to listen to that music and stay in the past, think about Jimmy and all those happy times she'd shared with him. She watched a lone magpie land on the decking next to her, making her frantically look around the garden for another.

One for sorrow, two for joy, one for sorrow, two for joy.

Where was that other fucking magpie, she thought, frustrated and terrified. The symbolism of this lone magpie on the decking spelt the worst for Jimmy.

She didn't want the divorce when it happened five years ago.

Jimmy *wanted* to leave her. Yet now it seemed he needed her more than ever.

Chapter 2

An early morning mist rolled slowly across the Cheshire countryside, covering the landscape in a thick white translucent fog. Driving along a quiet country lane, Alison kept her dark blue saloon under thirty; visibility was reduced to only a few yards. The road ahead was unknown. The state Jimmy was in was unknown. She hated not knowing, ignorant of what had happened to him. Stepping into a situation where she didn't have all the details really knocked her confidence.

They say you never forget your first love.

Alison had spent the last five years trying to forget about Jimmy.

Her husband Simon didn't want her to leave London and drive up here just to visit her ex-husband in a hospital. Despite a heated argument yesterday morning, she booked a hotel room in Manchester and left to head north after lunch.

Now it was Monday morning approaching nine o'clock. After a brief breakfast at the hotel, Alison had almost made it to the hospital. She eased her foot from the accelerator, changing into first gear, slowing her car as she approached the entrance. She indicated left, pulling off the country lane onto a long tree-lined driveway. She could make out Farley Hall through the mist in the distance. As a freelance photographer, she had visited halls like this to shoot weddings, but this was her first visit to a hospital inside a place like this.

At the end of that long driveway, through the slight opening in the driver's window, she heard the crunch underneath her tyres as the road surface changed from tarmac to gravel. She parked in front of the hall, pulled the handbrake and switched off the engine. Taking a deep breath, she checked her makeup in the rearview mirror and stepped out of the car.

She worried as she began walking slowly towards the entrance. Worried about Jimmy. Worried about being here. Despite him being her ex-husband, she didn't hate him. Despite the anger at the time they split, Alison couldn't be like that about Jimmy. She was trying to convince herself she'd made the right decision coming here before she had to convince her husband over the telephone later.

As she carefully tried to negotiate her way across the gravel forecourt, she immediately regretted wearing her best black pencil skirt and heels. She stopped walking, turned, and pointed her key at the car, which bleeped and locked as the indicators flashed. She continued walking towards the entrance, her heels finally finding the solid, stone steps, but her heart sank. A modern sign fixed above the 18th-century stone arch of the doorway, silver lettering against a black background:

FARLEY HALL HOSPITAL FOR BRAIN INJURY REHABILITATION.

Brain Injury? What has happened to Jimmy? She worried.

Her usual self-assured and confident demeanour was knocked sideways. Alison thought for a moment, standing underneath that sign; she didn't tell me anything over the telephone on Saturday; the nurse had referred to it as Farley Hall, and now I know why.

She had a sinking feeling in the pit of her stomach; it made her unsteady on her heels as she wobbled into reception. Alison approached the young blonde receptionist dressed in white standing behind the large white desk, her pure white dental smile obvious under the bright lighting.

"Good morning. I'm here to see a patient, Jimmy Smith."

"Hi, good morning, if you'd like to take a seat."

The receptionist smiled as she picked up the telephone receiver, gesturing with her other hand towards the seating.

"Thanks," Alison responded.

Sitting down, she began taking in her surroundings; everywhere was white and clinically clean, contrasting with a wide dark oak staircase leading upstairs covered in deep royal blue carpet, expensive seating, and a stack of glossy monthly magazines on a solid oak coffee table. She looked at the circular wall clock as white as the receptionist's smile, watching the red second-hand tick towards nine o'clock as a sharply dressed middle-aged man came down the staircase. Neatly trimmed brown hair, thick eyebrows, clean shaven, good looking, dressed in black trousers, highly polished black shoes, an expensive-looking shirt, and tie with gold cufflinks at each wrist, he approached Alison smiling as he greeted her. The smell of him wafted across her nostrils, subtle but incredible. Now that is an expensive aftershave, she immediately concluded. She stood to greet him, a man exuding intelligence, confidence, and money, she thought.

Mr Davies, lead Brain Injury Consultant.

"If you'd like to follow me, Mrs Wilson?"

She stood on the spot, refusing to move and follow him, that well-spoken voice sitting perfectly with his demeanour. He reminded her of Stephen Fry.

"Has Jimmy got brain damage, Mr Davies?"

The consultant stopped his strident walk and turned to face her. He sighed, mouth closed, as he exhaled slowly through his nose.

"I'll explain everything in my office."

Alison shuddered at that statement. This was much worse than she thought.

Upstairs she followed the consultant into his office. He offered her the seat on the side of the desk facing him. She looked around the office; it was a room entirely in keeping with this 18th Century building; stained dark oak panelling around the walls, Georgian sash windows, an expensive-looking desk between her and the consultant, the room gently lit from above by modern spotlights recessed into a lowered false ceiling. It felt odd to her to be sitting there. The nurse on the telephone said they couldn't trace Jimmy's family. She knew he didn't have any family left, and refusing to visit him because he was her ex-husband wasn't an option. After sixteen years together, she had to come. Mr Davies leaned forward from his high-backed, black leather chair and began to explain.

Alison made eye contact.

"Jimmy was hit by a stolen car that mounted the pavement where he was standing. As a consequence of the impact, he suffered a focal brain injury with multiple cerebral contusions and hematomas. His brain was bleeding, causing a build-up of pressure."

Alison placed her hand over her mouth. Despite being divorced from Jimmy, the news still shattered her. She was close to bursting into tears, and the consultant could see that.

"What? How did this happen?" Alison meekly asked.

"The accident happened in America. He's been in a Philadelphia hospital in a long-term coma. When he regained consciousness, he was flown back to England and came to stay with us here on the first of this month."

"Long-term coma? How long?"

"Four years and five months."

That response felt like a kick in the stomach. In shock and absolute silence, she looked at the consultant. Embarrassed, she broke eye contact. With tears in her eyes, she focused her gaze through the window at the tarmac driveway she'd just driven down.

"Four and a half years! When did the accident happen?" Alison squealed feebly.

"March ninety-five. Do you know his family? We can't trace them. Here," Mr Davies said, passing Alison a box of tissues.

The consultant hadn't expected such a tearful reaction from Alison; it was her ex-husband, after all. He decided that she didn't need to know Jimmy's full diagnosis at this stage; this woman was clearly hurt enough.

"Thank you. I don't think he has any family left. His father died when Jimmy was two years old. His sister died young, and his older brother died in the Falklands. It was the nurse who rang me on Saturday morning and told me his mother had died."

Alison put the box of tissues on the desk in front of her, pulling one out and wiping her eyes, attempting to compose herself in front of the consultant.

"I see. When did you divorce?"

"Five years ago. The end of ninety-four. We were together sixteen years. How is he now?"

"He's not good, but he is improving."

"Can he move around? Can he talk?"

"Well, he was very confused when he was admitted to us. He still is. He's weak, and his movement is quite restricted at the moment. He's also struggling with speech."

"Will he get better?" Alison asked, quite confused.

The consultant paused for a moment, leaning back into his chair. He thought carefully before proceeding.

"Difficult to put a timescale on how quickly and how well Jimmy is going to recover. Recovery periods vary greatly from patient to patient. These things take time, Mrs Wilson."

"I see. Can I see him? I could do with some air first, though."

"I understand this is shocking news for you. Jimmy's room is close to the rear entrance of the hall downstairs. You can exit the building through that rear door and sit in the gardens. Take some time out to process this before you see him."

"Do you think Jimmy will know who I am?"

"Well, having closely monitored Jimmy with our psychiatrists for the last two weeks, it has become apparent he has poor memory recollection. Almost total memory loss."

"What? You mean he won't know who I am?"

"Well, he *may* remember you. Just don't be too shocked if he doesn't."

"Oh," Alison sighed.

This was going to be difficult.

Alison forced a smile before turning and opening the office door, wondering how, if at all, she could help Jimmy.

#

Chapter 3

As Alison sat on one of the wooden benches in the gardens, she lit her third cigarette and looked at her wristwatch. Time had drifted by as she'd sat there gazing into space, unable to focus her mind on anything other than Jimmy. She'd been at the hospital for an hour, and the news had hit her hard. Surveying the gardens around her, realising she was out there alone, tears began to stream down her face. She couldn't help herself; they just came flooding out of her, her mind full of questions and uncertainty. What the hell could I say to Jimmy after all this time? Would he even know who I was? She had to pull herself together for Jimmy's sake. With a tissue, she wiped the mascara streaming down her cheeks before checking her face with a small compact mirror she had with her. Everything the consultant had said reassured her Jimmy was in the right place. This was a specialist hospital. This was a building, as old as it was, filled with consultants, doctors, and nurses. It was their job to rehabilitate people with acquired brain injuries, people like Jimmy.

Alison saw Mr Davies appear at the rear entrance, so she put the tissues and compact in her bag, walking over to join him at the doorway. They made the short walk together along the corridor. She stopped to take a deep breath before stepping into the room, treading carefully behind Mr Davies, instantly taking in everything she could see.

Jimmy was sat up in bed, a thin cream-coloured tube protruding from one of his nostrils, fixed in place to his face with translucent medical tape. His arms over the bed covers and down by his sides. A grey plastic peg on the index finger of his left-hand measures his pulse. An intravenous drip was attached via a needle into the back of his right hand, secured in place with that same translucent tape. Her eyes followed the clear, flexible tube from the needle in the back of his right hand into an inverted bag of fluid using gravity to slowly administer the drugs they were giving him. A table on wheels that could be swung around over the bed lay two slim A4 children's books. To her right, a huge window took up most of the wall giving the patient an uninterrupted view of the gardens. To her left is an ensuite wet room and toilet.

He turned his head in the direction of his visitors.

At that moment, they made eye contact.

For the first time in five years.

Alison felt sick to the stomach; the shock of seeing Jimmy like this stopped her in her tracks. She stood a few feet from him, placing her hand over her mouth to hold back the tears. Her heart sank, her legs wobbled, and she swayed slightly as they made eye contact. He looked so thin, the blue pyjama top just hanging off him. She could see the outline of his legs under the bedsheet. She looked down at his ankles, past his knees and up to his thighs; the outline of his limbs didn't widen. He was just skin and bone. He was silent; he was still; he didn't move. She made eye contact with him again, and he smiled, which melted her heart.

A smile means recognition, doesn't it?

"Are you OK this morning, Jimmy?" Mr Davies asked.

He looked at the consultant and then looked at the table.

"Do you want your books?"

Jimmy nodded. Alison watched Mr Davies move across to the side of the bed, moving the table over Jimmy's legs, assisting him by carefully lifting his right arm from its resting position onto the table. It was heartbreaking for her to witness.

The consultant turned to her; he could see she was upset.

"As I told you, he's very weak. A lot of our patients use these books to help them."

"I see," Alison replied meekly.

She didn't know what else to say. She wanted to scream.

Fuck! Fuck! Fuck! Jimmy, I can't handle seeing you like this!

It broke her heart to see her childhood sweetheart lay there in silence, completely disabled and unable to speak. Jimmy pointed specifically to the word 'who' as he nodded to Alison. She saw what he was doing and moved closer. Smiling, she put her hand on his leg over the bedsheet and her hand completely wrapped around his thigh; his leg felt completely devoid of flesh and muscle. The consultant saw what she was doing, and he offered her a reassuring smile.

"I know it's shocking; patients lose a lot of muscle mass in such long-term comas."

She heard the consultant but ignored him, focusing all her attention on Jimmy.

"Jimmy, it's Alison. You remember me, don't you?"

Seeing him so helpless, a man she'd always turned to for love and support, cut her up inside. She was fourteen years old when they met and fell in love. Now, as a woman in her thirties, she'd remarried and moved on, but it didn't stop her from hurting inside seeing Jimmy like this.

As Alison looked on, he moved his right hand across the table to an opened children's book of the alphabet.

Seeing her again, hearing her voice, he'd obviously remembered something.

First, the letter 'E', then 'L', then 'V', then 'I' and finally 'S'. He smiled at her as he pointed out the next word one letter at a time. First, the letter 'C', then 'O', then 'S'.

"Elvis Costello!" Alison announced, smiling at Jimmy.

He started crying when he stopped pointing out letters and relaxed his right arm.

"Oh, don't cry, Jimmy," she pleaded.

"Jimmy sang the song *Alison* by *Elvis Costello* to me on our first date," she said, dabbing his face with a tissue from the small packet from her handbag.

"Really? When was that?" Mr Davies inquired.

"A long time ago. September seventy-eight."

"Could I have a quick word with you in the corridor Mrs Wilson?"

"Sure, call me Alison. Won't be long, Jimmy."

Jimmy smiled at her as she turned and followed the consultant out of the room into the white-walled clinical corridor.

"I'm so pleased we were able to trace you, Alison. How long are you planning on staying?"

"I'm driving back to London tomorrow. I only booked the hotel room for two nights."

"Well, I think we've just witnessed Jimmy's first real memory recollection."

"Really?"

"Yes. He obviously remembers you. His memory loss isn't total if seeing you can bring out a memory like that."

Hearing the consultant say that made her mind up. She couldn't leave Jimmy alone like this, with the possibility of her presence unlocking more of his memories. He needed her; she knew that. All the anger she'd kept with her after the divorce just dissipated away. Only Alison could help him, and she understood that; she just hoped Simon, her husband, would understand later when she rang him from the hotel.

"Right. I'll book my hotel room for another night," she announced, pleased to be in control of her time commitments as a freelance photographer.

"If you're sure, that would be great. With no family to speak of, no one else can help him remember. Did you and Jimmy listen to music much in the past?"

"Oh yes. When we were teenagers, all our pocket money went on records and concert tickets. Why do you ask?"

"Well, music is so evocative in terms of helping people recall memories. It could help him a great deal."

"Really?"

"Oh yes. In fact, I would recommend you play him the music you enjoyed listening to together. I think it will help trigger his memories. Perhaps tomorrow. Today could overwhelm him."

"I understand."

"OK. Well, I'll leave you with him, Alison and go check on my other patients."

"Thanks again, Mr Davies."

"No, thank you for coming to see Jimmy; you're helping him already."

The consultant smiled at Alison before turning and walking up the corridor.

She stood and thought for a moment. Even though she now knew what had happened to Jimmy, it didn't make it any easier for her to deal with. She'd never met anybody with a brain injury. It worried her what she could be letting herself in for.

This is Jimmy though, all those memories, all that music, all those happy times, I can't run out on him now, she thought before nervously walking back into his room.

Sitting down in the chair next to his bed, there was silence as Jimmy just gazed at her. Alison was aware it was not absolute silence, becoming conscious of the hum and repeating bleeps from the machines he was hooked up to.

"Can you remember any of the times we spent together?"

She looked down at his right hand, finger pointing to a word. 'Some', which shocked and surprised her.

"Mr Davies said you had total memory loss."

Jimmy shook his head, and it worried Alison; she knew then that his memories hadn't been completely wiped out. The divorce wasn't a happy period for anyone involved. She didn't want him to remember that for his health and well-being.

"You remember us being together?"

He pointed to a phrase in the book opened on the table.

'Yes'.

"Great. Let's remember the good times; it'll help you get better," Alison suggested.

Jimmy mouthed 'OK' with no sound, not even a whisper.

"I was worried you wouldn't recognise me."

He was smiling at her, but she couldn't look him in the eye. Instead, her eyes focused on the heart rate monitor beside him, bleeping with reassuring regularity. A nurse entered Jimmy's room, and Alison took it as her cue to leave. She just didn't want to be there.

"Jimmy, I'm leaving. I'll come and see you tomorrow."

She quickly kissed him on the forehead, picked up her handbag and raced out of the room, gone before he had a chance to question why she was leaving. On her way out of the hospital, she ignored every nurse she ran past. Outside she quickly unlocked her car, got in and found her *Elvis Costello* cassette in the glove box. When she'd rewound the tape to listen to *Alison,* she'd started crying again. She hadn't listened to that song in years. She started the engine and raced up the driveway away from Farley Hall. She left the tape running and listened to the whole album, driving aimlessly around the country lanes of Cheshire, intentionally avoiding major roads, avoiding people, avoiding the present. She couldn't unsee what she'd just seen, eradicate from her mind the image of Jimmy lying helpless in a hospital bed. She knew this music would remind her of how he used to be in the past, instead of the helpless individual he is now.

Crossing the countryside, Alison put a considerable dent in her pack of twenty cigarettes listening to that album. Music, by association, inevitably took her back to being fourteen years old, living with her mother and father in Altrincham. Back to a time in her past when she fell in love with Jimmy Smith, aged fifteen, from Stretford.

#

Chapter 4

September 1978.

Jimmy Smith had walked up Oldham Street in Manchester a few times as a child. Always during the day, always with his older sister or mother. Tonight, at almost nine-thirty on a windy Tuesday night, the street looked completely different. Worryingly different. It was dark. It was cold. It was sinister. It was frightening. Jimmy had celebrated his fifteenth birthday eight days ago, and his best friend Simon was still only fourteen; they were too young to be in the city centre at night, but they had a reason to be there. To get into the music venue around the corner and watch *Joy Division* play a concert. Making forthright strides along the pavement, walking much faster than usual, this street was devoid of people but still frightening. Every shop along the street was covered by metal shutters which would rattle, bulge and flex as the wind got behind them, as if a wild animal was trapped inside trying to ram its way out through the shutters and pounce on them.

The only thing that slightly placated Jimmy's fear was Oldham Street, an arrow-straight road with no corners for anybody to hide behind and jump out and rob him or his friend. Manchester city centre was a desolate and dangerous place at night in the 1970s. This was their first time in the city during darkness.

"Fuckin 'ell Si, I'm not sure about this, mate."

"Stop shittin' it; we'll be right. Steven's takin' tickets on the door; we'll get in."

"I know, but we might get jumped."

"Will we fuck! Calm down; we'll be there in a minute."

When they found the place, they had half an hour to kill before *Joy Division* were due onstage, deciding to sit down on some concrete steps in a raised doorway down a side street that gave them a good view of the venue entrance. Jimmy pulled out his glasses case from his coat pocket, retrieving a joint. He put the illicit cigarette to his lips and lit it with the cigarette lighter he had with him. Reni, their friend from school, had introduced them to cannabis; his two older brothers smoked it a lot. They sold Jimmy two ready-rolled joints on his way home from school last Friday. Jimmy and Simon were always together when they smoked it, always away from home outdoors somewhere, usually under the monkey bridge because it was so close to where they lived in Stretford. They made a rule up, which they always stuck to "Four an' on", four drags on the joint and then pass it on. As Jimmy pulled as much smoke as he could into his lungs, Simon complained.

"Fuckin' 'ell Jim. Don't take massive pulls, man! There'll be nowt left for me!"

"Chill out. Here y'ar mate," Jimmy responded, passing him the joint.

"Look, Jim. Girls!" Simon exclaimed.

Jimmy looked across the road at the Band on The Wall, noticing two girls about their age walking toward the venue. One girl was instantly recognisable to him, and his heart began thumping.

Without thinking, he shouted, almost screaming, at the top of his voice: "Alison!"

She turned and looked over in their direction. She was smiling.

Jimmy ran across the road to join Alison on the pavement outside the Band on The Wall. She stepped away from her friend, and he stood directly in front of her. It had been 354 days since he'd last seen her at a *Warsaw* concert in Salford he'd attended with his older sister. She smiled back at him with warmth and recognition; it gave him butterflies.

"Jimmy, it's you. Are you OK?" Alison asked coyly.

"Yeah, I'm fine."

"I never thought I'd see you again," she purred

"Really?" Jimmy said, questioning her.

He glanced at Simon, talking with Alison's friend, ensuring they were sufficiently distanced from his first conversation with Alison. He didn't want to mess up and say the wrong thing, knowing this could be over before it had a chance to begin. Maybe she hadn't felt it as much as he had when they met briefly last year? Maybe she was playing her cards close to her chest? Perhaps he was simply afraid of ridicule and being laughed at by Alison and her friend? He just wasn't confident talking to girls.

It was a quiet night in Manchester city centre, hardly any cars or buses had driven by, he knew if he spoke softly, Simon and Alison's friend wouldn't hear.

Jimmy leaned toward her and openly admitted:

"I guess because ever since I first saw you, I haven't stopped thinking about you."

"Aww." She beamed back at him as someone would toward a kitten or baby. It made him think she was making light of something he'd put so much thought into.

This moment happening, their first proper meeting.

Fate, Jimmy felt sure it had played a hand.

It had taken almost a year for him to see her again, yet he still felt it was meant to be. More so, now she was standing before him. She was even more beautiful than he had imagined or remembered.

#

Jimmy took his coat off for them both to sit on, laying it down and lining up on the grass. They sat close together underneath the bridge. Alison was looking intently at what he was doing as Jimmy flicked a flame from the lighter and lit the end of the joint between his lips. Taking one short pull, he ingested the smoke. He heaved a satisfying exhale and turned to pass her the joint.

"Ere y'ar, don't suck in too much smoke. Do little pulls, or you'll end up coughing."

"Right, OK."

She nervously put the joint to her lips and inhaled gently.

She let out a couple of small coughs.

"Have another drag. A bit of a bigger one. Watch the end of the joint glow; you'll see if yer gettin' a good drag that way."

Though still fairly new to it, Jimmy was a 'seasoned smoker' compared to Alison. He was terrified she'd hate it. The teacher was afraid of the pupil, though already he valued Alison far more than he valued a recreational drug. Far more than he valued anything or anybody, really. One night together, he still felt they were destined to be together.

Jimmy smiled as he watched Alison put the joint to her lips, for a fourth time drawing in her cheeks as the end of the illicit cigarette glowed. Exhaling all that smoke slowly, she lay on Jimmy's coat next to him and silently passed him the half-joint that was left.

Gazing at Alison, he put the joint to his lips and took four more drags before stubbing it on the grass. He settled alongside her as she lay on his coat.

The teenage lovers looked straight up at the bridge's underside in absolute silence. A silence that Alison decided to break.

"Do you listen to the radio much, Jimmy?"

"Dance, dance, dance, dance, dance to the radio," Jimmy sang out, mimicking Ian Curtis, then laughing as the sound of his voice hit the underside of the concrete bridge and reverberated back at them both. He turned his head to look at Alison, their eyes met, and they both exploded into giggles.

As Tuesday night became Wednesday morning, they still had tears streaming down their faces; the pent-up excitement of this loud and joyous laughter took a long time to subside. As they lay on their backs next to each other, Jimmy watched their chests rise and fall as Alison rolled over onto him and lay her head on his chest. He knew tonight would end badly, being out this late on a school night. He just didn't want it to end. Alison would be late home and in trouble with her parents. Jimmy would be seriously late home and in serious trouble with his mother.

"Joy Division are different, aren't they, Jimmy?"

She lay there pressing up close to him and resting her right arm across him.

"Oh, aye. I love 'em. They're my favourite group."

"What's Ian like? Where did you meet him?"

"He's lovely. Our Vicky took Si and me to Liverpool on the train this summer. We went to a place called Eric's. When we finally found it, we saw a car parked outside and Ian was sat in it on his own. Our Vicky knocked on the car window, and he got out so we could have a chat with him. I was buzzin' coz he remembered me from the Salford Tech gig."

"Wow, no way. It's amazing he remembered you. Is Vicky your sister? What did you talk about when you met Ian?"

"She is, yeah. I can't remember what we talked about. I was surprised how softly spoken he was for a singer in a group."

Alison lifted her head, and they looked directly into each other's eyes.

"Do you want to see me again, Jimmy?"

She fell into his arms, not really expecting an answer. He moved his head slowly forward, passionately kissing her. They held each other close, their appreciation of time melting away.

They separated after a while for air before Jimmy asked her.

"Do you know the song Alison by Elvis Costello? I heard it when he was on Tony Wilson's show last year. I love it. It made me think meeting you was fate, to be honest. Is that sad?"

"No, it's not sad. I've never heard the song; you'll have to play it for me sometime."

"Yeah, I will. No point arranging anything just yet, though. We're both gonna be in trouble at home; me mam's gonna go barmy."

Jimmy glanced at his watch to check the time. It was almost 1am. The best night of his life so far would shortly be coming to an angry and inevitable end.

"Shit, we'd better get you home. It's one o'clock in the fuckin mornin'."
They both jumped to their feet as he grabbed his coat from the ground.
"You don't have to walk home with me, you know. I only live two minutes walk from here. I'll be fine. Get yourself home."
"Maybe yer right Ali."
"Hey. My parents hate that. I'm not allowed to let anybody call me that, you know."
"Oh, I'm sor......"
"...but you can. If you like?"
He looked at her and smiled. The time they'd spent together this evening made him feel it *was* fate. They kissed again. Slowly and passionately, the early morning minutes ticked away.
"I've gotta go," Jimmy said, parting their embrace.
"OK, Jimmy. Best of luck with your mum."
"Hey, best of luck with yours too. See ya."
"See ya."
They both walked slowly backwards away from each other. Neither of them wanted to turn away and end their first night together.

#

Chapter 5

The first thing Alison did when she arrived at the Midland Hotel was book her room for another night. She hadn't eaten since lunch at the hospital, so she sat in the restaurant for an evening meal before heading to her room. The first thing she did was switch on the shower and get undressed. Standing underneath the shower head in the steam-filled ensuite, she felt mentally and physically drained. Thinking over what had happened to Jimmy, her body warmed by the rapidly running hot water, thankful she'd booked a smoking room, she felt stressed. What a day. For the last five years, she'd lived happily with her husband Simon in London, never once thinking she would see Jimmy again. What a way for him to come back into her life. Yet the way he'd looked at her today convinced her he had no memory of why they'd divorced. What can I do to help him? Other than playing him some of the music we used to listen to together and see if that helps him remember? She didn't know what else she could do. How do I tell Simon I'd rather spend more time with my ex-husband than come home? She could only hope he would understand. Thoughts of tackling these problems pervaded Alison's brain as she dried herself.

Dressing in one of the hotel's expensive white towelling robes, she flopped backwards loosely onto the bed. She lay for a moment, motionless on her back, devoid of energy, staring at the ceiling. She thought about the tears she'd shed in the car driving around Cheshire, a cathartic release after the shock of seeing Jimmy today. I don't hate him; I could never hate him, and I can't let him down now. Fuck, what is Simon going to say? I need a fag. She thought as she lay there.

Reaching the bedside table, she grasped for her packet of cigarettes and lighter. She took one from the packet, put it between her lips and lit it. She took a long drag, picked up the telephone receiver and as she exhaled placed her cigarette in the ashtray on the bedside table. She'd promised her husband to ring him from the hotel after she visited the hospital and after he'd arrived home from work. She was loyal to him regardless of the unexpected phone call on Saturday morning. She dialled her home number in Highgate, it connected, and she listened to it ringing, waiting for Simon to answer.

"Hello?"

"It's me."

"Hi, you OK, love?"

"Yeah, I'm fine."

"How's Jimmy?"

"Not good."

"Why? What's happened?"

Alison paused; this was difficult for her. Jimmy and Simon had been best friends since infant school until the divorce. Like the only two survivors of a train wreck, Alison found herself drawn to Simon on the rebound, and they married the following year.

"Christ, I don't know where to start, babe. He was run over by an idiot in a stolen car."

"Fuckin' hell. Where? In town?"

"No, he flew to America when we split, remember. It happened over there.

"Right. When?"

"March ninety-five."

"Ninety-five? What's he been doing for the last four years?"

"He's been in a coma; he only came out of it a few days ago."

"What?" Simon asked, genuinely concerned.

Silence. She wished he'd come up here with her; having to tell him over the phone was hard.

"I know. Horrible, isn't it."

"A coma for four years? Fuckin' 'ell."

"He's in a bad way, babe."

"What did he say to you?"

"Nothing. He can't speak. He can barely move."

"He can't speak?"

"No. Jimmy's got brain damage," Alison sighed.

She lay on the hotel room bed holding the receiver to her ear; Simon didn't say anything. She reached over and picked up her cigarette from the ashtray, taking another much-needed drag. She knew he had something to say from the way she'd heard him sigh.

"Jesus Christ, that's shit that. Four years in a hospital in America, who paid for that? It's not free healthcare over there. Is Farley Hall private or NHS love?"

Fuckin' money, is that all he thinks about? This is your best friend since the sand pit, for Christ's sake! Alison thought as she exhaled, placing her cigarette back in the ashtray.

"I don't know, do I. All these questions. Jimmy can hardly move or speak; who cares."

"Well, I don't wanna get stung with a massive fuckin' bill when Jimmy gets discharged."

"I'll ask Mr Davies tomorrow. I didn't think to ask; it was so hard seeing Jimmy like that in that state. I hated it," she said, her voice quivering with emotion.

"Hey babe, don't cry. He's in the right place, ya know." Simon reassured her.

She dropped the telephone handset by her side and, putting both hands to her face, she wept for a moment. She could faintly hear Simon's voice on the telephone.

"Hello? You still there, love?"

She sat on the bed and sighed, composing herself before breaking the news to him.

"Yeah, sorry. I'm not coming home tomorrow, babe. I've booked another night."

"You've what?"

"I've got to. Besides, the consultant said music really helps with people's memories, so I'm buying a portable CD player and some CDs in the morning."

"Right. Yer coming home the day after, though?"

"I don't know yet. I might stay all week."

"All week! You'll be celebrating your birthday up there then," Simon exclaimed.

"I know, but it's Jimmy's too, isn't it. Be good for his recovery."

"You reckon? I know he's in a bad way; just remember who you're married to."

"I could do without being up here, ya know," Alison lied.

Their birthday coming up was the first thing she'd thought of after that call on Saturday.

"What's the point in you staying up there all week?"

"For Jimmy's sake. The consultant asked me if I could stay longer; the familiarity of my voice and me just being there was helping. They warned me he could have total memory loss."

Alison thought better than to mention him, remembering that *Elvis Costello* song.

"He's gonna remember what happened, ya know."

"We'll cross that bridge when we come to it. I was just happy he recognised me."

"Well, you've known him for twenty years, love he was bound to."

"I guess so."

"Maybe I can come up and see him one weekend?"

"Yeah, maybe."

"That's bad that though, isn't it. Four years in a coma. No wonder he can't remember anything. Did the consultant say his memory would return?"

"They don't know. Each patient is different."

"Right. Are you not worried?" Simon asked.

"What about?"

"What if he remembers why you split up. He fuckin' hated you back then, ya know."

Absolute silence between them. As sad as it was seeing her ex-husband so weak and vulnerable, the only saving grace was that he didn't remember why they'd divorced. It had hurt Jimmy so much back then. It was something she was never going to forget. Something she was terrified he could remember.

"I'm just glad he's alive, babe. Don't worry about it."

"OK." Simon conceded.

She knew her husband wanted her home, now she'd been to see Jimmy, and they knew he was well cared for. In her mind, she shouldn't be away from Simon, from real life, from London and her photography career for this long, but her heart was calling out to Jimmy.

Alison ended the call by saying she would ring Simon again tomorrow night. She was exhausted. There was nothing to stay up for. Watching the television in her room seemed pointless. She took the ashtray and her cigarettes over to the hotel room window, sitting down on the armchair. She brushed away the white net curtain and opened the window a little, looking out at the G-mex. In the distance, she could just about make out the City Road Inn opposite The Hacienda, an area she'd walked through many times in the past. She thought about the jubilant night she'd walked hand in hand with Jimmy after seeing *The Smiths* at the Free Trade Hall. Or when she was with Jimmy and Simon when they walked back to Stretford together after seeing *Happy Mondays* and *New Order* at The Hacienda. She hadn't been in Manchester city centre since the split five years ago, but it hadn't changed all that much.

Alison stubbed out her cigarette in the ashtray on the bedside table. She set her alarm clock for seven and moved back onto the bed. She clicked the bedroom light off and shut her eyes. She was angry and upset at what had happened to her ex-husband, saddened it had happened to him. He had no one else. Whether she wanted to or not, she was obligated to help him. She had no choice; they'd been in love for so long. She owed it to him until he remembered why they divorced. If he remembers? She'd spent five years trying to forget it; the last thing she wanted to do was help Jimmy remember that.

#

Chapter 6

Alison was awake and in the shower before her alarm went off at seven, thoughts about Jimmy preventing her from sleeping. She walked over to Market Street after breakfast. She bought a portable CD player, headphones, small portable speakers, and a few of his favourite albums on compact discs. She didn't arrive at the hospital until ten thirty and went to see the consultant; the receptionist had told her he was in his office, so she shot straight upstairs to speak to him. After talking with Simon last night, she wanted to know about this hospital. Standing outside his office, she knocked on the door.

"Yes?"

Opening the door slowly, she entered his office.

"Alison, good morning; how can I help you? Sit down."

"Morning, Mr Davies; my husband asked me something last night," she said, sitting down.

"Really? What was that?"

"Whether Farley Hall is NHS or private. I didn't know."

"No, it's not NHS. It is private, yes."

"How come this hospital is in an eighteenth-century hall?"

"Well, it was sold to a Private Healthcare Trust by Viscount Farley when Lady Farley was involved in a car accident and suffered a brain injury. He sold the property to the Trust that rehabilitated her. The Trust that now owns Farley Hall. The Trust I work for."

"I see. So, who is paying for Jimmy's rehabilitation? For him to stay in this hospital?"

"Ah." The consultant said, smiling and standing.

He moved away from his desk and turned to face the window. With his arms folded across his chest and his back to Alison, he sighed, turning to face her as he began to speak.

"The cost of Jimmy's healthcare is taken care of. That's all I can say, I'm afraid."

"Taken care of? Who by?" she asked, concerned.

"I'm sorry Alison, I can't say. Client confidentiality. All I *can* say is all of Jimmy's healthcare costs have been paid. The third party who paid have insisted on anonymity, and I have to respect that as a healthcare professional," he said, sitting back down at his desk.

Alison was baffled; it seemed she would never know who had helped Jimmy. She felt deflated and frustrated and sighed deeply as her shoulders dropped.

"Is there anything else? Have you been to see Jimmy?"

"I wanted to see you first. I've bought a CD player and some CDs for him this morning."

"Oh, that's fantastic, Alison; that will help with his memories, I'm sure."

"Great. Thanks, Mr Davies," she said, smiling at him as she stood up, her large leather handbag over her shoulder, a lot heavier than usual with all those CDs, the player, and speakers.

"You're welcome, Alison," he said, returning her smile as she turned to face the door.

She left the office baffled and confused, making her way downstairs. All she could think about was who had shelled out all that money as she made her way along the corridor to his room. This was something Jimmy didn't need to know; he had enough to deal with, she thought when she walked in, and that smile of recognition from him was there again. She put the portable CD player, headphones, and speakers on the bedside cabinet at the head of his bed. She leaned over the bed and kissed him on the lips. My God, she felt sorry for him. Maybe it was the force of habit? Maybe seeing Jimmy again after all this time? Maybe it was because he was just so vulnerable and helpless, and she wanted to give him something, offer him hope in some way. She didn't know why she did it. Alison shivered and felt an almost electrical surge through her body. She pulled herself quickly away from him, feeling awkward and uncomfortable. She cursed herself for not kissing him on the cheek. They made eye contact, and both smiled; she knew he'd felt it too.

"How are you feeling this morning?"

He still could not answer, so he mouthed 'OK' without taking his gaze away from her.

"I bought a CD player and some of your favourite albums in town this morning. I bought headphones and speakers, so you can listen on your own to the music or with me. Mr Davies thinks the music you love will help with your memories."

Jimmy nodded and smiled. She pulled a chair next to his bedside and sat with him. She pulled out a book with photographs of *Joy Division*, laying it on the table next to the children's books, carefully lifting his right arm and resting his hand on the table.

"See these four lads Jimmy. They're called Joy Division. The first group you and I fell in love with. We met at one of their concerts."

She ensured she looked at Jimmy and not down at the book when speaking. She carefully scrutinised his face for any reaction to what she'd just said.

She turned the page and pointed at the next photograph.

"That's their lead singer Jimmy. He's called Ian Curtis. He's from Macclesfield. So is their drummer, but the guitar player and bass player are Salford lads."

Jimmy began to nod his head as she described the group.

"Are you nodding because you recognise them?"

The table was quite wide, almost as wide as Jimmy's bed. There was sufficient space on it to keep the Joy Division book open and one of his books with phrases and words written in bold, black type. He pointed to the phrase 'I think so'.

"Jimmy, that's wonderful. I remember when we first met, you and Simon already loved them. You told me Ian Curtis had telephoned your house once to tell you they were going on Granada Reports to play a song. Though I don't suppose you remember?"

Jimmy shook his head.

"That's OK. At least you recognise them in these photographs. It's a start, isn't it?"

He nodded. Alison looked down at her bag on the floor beside his bed. She pulled out the CD of the first *Joy Division* album she'd bought this morning, placing it on the table in front of him. His eyes widened, and a smile turned up the corners of his mouth.

"You recognise that picture, don't you. It's their first album. I know it doesn't say anything on the cover; it's called *Unknown Pleasures*. You love that album, Jimmy. Fancy a listen?"

He nodded, smiling at her. She stood from the chair and grabbed the portable CD player, putting in new batteries from a pack she'd bought this morning. She smiled as she put the disc into the player and placed the headphones over Jimmy's ears. She was happy she could help him, using music they both loved to try and help him remember. The familiarity of this music went hand in hand with his earliest memories of her. She hit the play button and sat on the chair, ensuring the volume level wasn't too high. She could faintly make out the song coming from the headphones, the drum introduction, the guitars, and the voice of Ian Curtis. It made her smile, watching Jimmy react to this song. He knew this music; she could tell by his reaction. He loved this music; she knew that.

I've been waiting for a guide to come and take me by the hand.

As Jimmy listened intently to the lyrics, he winced, struggling to clasp Alison's right hand in his. Looking directly into each other's eyes as the music continued to play, he slowly mouthed a sentence to her. She couldn't hear him, but she knew exactly what he'd said.

"Am I? Your guide?" she asked.

He smiled back at her hopefully.

"Yes, I suppose I am," she concluded.

Before the next song, Alison explained she was going for a bite to eat. He smiled and mouthed 'OK', lost in this music that was so familiar to him.

#

When she returned to Jimmy's room, he was sleeping; the album had finished playing, and the headphones over his ears were now silent. After carefully removing them and switching the CD player off, she sat and watched him sleeping.

Minutes passed, and she considered leaving him to sleep until his eyes suddenly blinked open, her face the first thing he saw. His mouth yawned open wide before slowly closing. She watched him as he tried to speak.

"Why?" Jimmy slurred, expelling saliva that began to dribble down his chin.

It shocked Alison to hear sound forcing its way from Jimmy's vocal cords.

"What is it, Jimmy? What's wrong?" Alison asked.

"Why... Do you... Come here?" He slowly managed to slur out a sentence. With a tissue she retrieved from her handbag, she leaned over him and dabbed around his mouth. Hearing his voice again with a soft vulnerability to it warmed her heart. She'd never expected to see him like this, so helpless and in need.

"That's the first time I've heard you speak in a long time, Jimmy. We were in love. We were together a long time. I had to come," she explained.

"When... did... we... meet?" He slowly managed to slur.

"A long time ago. When we were teenagers. At a Joy Division concert. I'll never forget it."

He nodded, smiling, and she felt he was enjoying her storytelling. Though she wasn't telling stories. She was describing facts. Memories he'd lost because of the accident.

"You spotted me outside before the concert. Your next-door neighbour Steven was taking tickets on the door that night. Otherwise, I don't think we would have got in; we were too young."
He looked up at her like a lost and innocent child. She looked back at him; he was trying to speak. She paused for a moment.
"How......old?"
"You were fifteen, and I was fourteen," she responded softly.
He remained fixated, gazing at her as she continued.
"After we'd seen the group play, you offered to stay on the bus and walk me back to my house in Altrincham. We followed the train tracks; you took your coat off and spread it out on the grass under the bridge for us to sit on. You always were the gentleman, Jimmy."
She paused and made eye contact with her ex-husband lying in the hospital bed. She noticed he was crying again as she described how he'd offered to escort her home. He'd obviously remembered it. She could see it in him from his reaction. Nobody knew this man as well as Alison.
"Oh, don't cry, Jimmy. I'm here now."
        She moved her right hand up to his face, her palm touching his moist cheek, her thumb wiping away the tear underneath his lower eyelid. She pulled her hand away, wiping his face dry and the wetness from her palm with a tissue before discarding it. She smiled at him. She didn't want him to feel down after what he'd already been through.
Alison could see he was making progress, but she knew it would take time, and it was only a small start. The tiny tip of a huge iceberg of memories, she was determined to help him thaw out. She felt she owed it to him. Who else could help him?

#

Chapter 7

L ate into the afternoon, Alison was still sitting by Jimmy's bedside. He'd fallen asleep again, and she was enjoying sitting there just watching him sleep peacefully. At least she could momentarily *pretend* there was nothing wrong with him until she was wakened from her daydream when a young nurse entered the room.

"How is he?" The nurse asked Alison.

"He's asleep. He drifted off as I was talking to him."

Alison stood up, picked up her bag and put it on the bedside cabinet.

"Hi, I'm Alison, Jimmy's ex-wife."

"Yes, I know. Hi, I'm Sarah."

"Does he usually sleep at this time of day?"

"I think seeing you again has exhausted him, to be honest." The nurse responded, checking the machines Jimmy was hooked up to, continuing to do her job.

"Are all people with brain injuries like this, Sarah?"

"Well, in my experience, the majority of patients get tired very quickly, but their injuries are as individual as they are. I care for people in here much worse than Jimmy."

"Really? Will his speech ever come back, Sarah?"

"Oh yes. It will take time, though. I've looked after other patients in here who initially struggled with speech, particularly those who were in long-term comas. A few of them got their speech back within the first few months."

"Good to know. Hopefully, I can help him with that. There's no one else can help him."

"Apparently, they couldn't trace any of Jimmy's family."

"He hasn't any family left."

"Really? That's horrible. Lucky, they tracked you down?"

"I'm glad they did. I've booked my hotel room for the whole week, so I'm here every day."

"Oh, that's great for Jimmy. Where are you staying?"

"The Midland in Manchester."

"You live in London, don't you?"

"Yes, Highgate. I'm from Altrincham originally. I've been living down there for the last five years. Since Jimmy and I split, really."

"It must be hard for you seeing him like this?"

"It is. We may be divorced, but I don't hate him."

After a moment of silence and nothing else to say, Alison felt the time was right to leave.

"Well, I think I'll pop to the café. Wait for traffic to die down before I leave," Alison said.

"Oh, I don't blame you. I'm working tomorrow, so I'll probably see you."

Alison leaned over Jimmy and kissed him on the forehead.

"Sleep well, sweetheart," she whispered into his ear.

"See you tomorrow, Sarah," Alison said as she left the room.

The light was fading by the time Alison drove away from Farley Hall. She'd spent the entire day with Jimmy. In the moments he was awake, trying her best to help him remember who he was. Describing her memories of a young Jimmy Smith, the places they would go together and the things they would do. Nothing was pulling her toward Manchester other than a long soak in the hotel bath. Driving around the Cheshire countryside country lanes gave her time to think alone. To contemplate what had happened over the last two days. Baffled that someone somewhere had paid for Jimmy to stay in a hospital in America for four years, never mind the cost of staying at Farley Hall. It must be thousands, and I'm sure Simon will be as confused as I am when I tell him later; she began wondering with absolutely no idea who it could be.

The car ahead stopped at the junction, suddenly arresting her from contemplation. She slammed her brakes on much harder than necessary, racing away from the junction along a quiet country road without thought for where she was heading. She'd loved Jimmy with all her heart for most of her teenage years and twenties. 'We're part of the same soul'. He would often say to her. Their birthdays were shared, born only one year apart. It convinced her Jimmy was 'the one'.

Since the split, she'd been in a relationship with her husband for the last five years. She loved Simon, but it was different. Jimmy was her first love, her teenage dream, but the split was her fault. There was no escaping that. Since then, she'd tried her best to bury any memories of Jimmy, yet now he was all she was thinking about. Jimmy Smith, aged thirty-six this coming Saturday, is a current resident at Farley Hall Hospital for Brain Injury Rehabilitation. He was thin and ill, but his face hadn't changed much in five years. Perhaps he was the only man she'd ever truly loved? Somebody she never really wanted to be divorced from. But at the time, she was hated in Stretford and Manchester. At least her parents in London welcomed her home.

Alison took the last drag on her cigarette and pushed the butt through the narrow slit in the slightly opened window. She thought about how Jimmy had reacted when he first saw her yesterday. His smile and affection toward her meant he couldn't remember anything. Specifically, the reason they'd split up. She cursed, wishing they'd never separated, before reaching for her cigarette packet on the passenger seat and lighting up another. She took a long drag, exhaling as she pondered the enormity of what was going on. Alison felt driven by love and many happy memories, but there was something she knew Jimmy definitely hadn't remembered yet. Something she couldn't hide from him forever.

#

On the Saturday morning of their birthdays, when Alison went into Jimmy's room not long after eight, he was still sleeping. She didn't want to disturb him, so instead went to the café to get herself a mug of tea. Sitting in her usual garden spot, smoking a cigarette, sipping her tea, she reviewed how much Jimmy had improved since Monday. With so few clouds populating the bright blue sky, the gardens were bathed in the early morning summer sunshine. Alison put on her sunglasses, the frames completely camouflaged by her dark brown, almost black hair. Very Jackie Onassis. She put her cigarette down in the ashtray, cradling her tea mug in her lap, pondering how she felt about this week.

When she rang Simon from the hotel last night, he had no idea who was responsible for paying Jimmy's hospital bills. With such a small family, nobody in Jimmy's life had that sort of money. She put it down to him meeting a wealthy woman in America on the rebound after the split, just as she had done with Simon.

She knew she should be driving back to London tomorrow morning, but she wanted to stay up here. Jimmy had been a part of her life for so long. She knew she couldn't give up on him. For her last two days with him, she'd focused on describing his teenage years on King's Road, intentionally avoiding more recent memories. She felt the less she mentioned the nineties, the better. She was shocked he couldn't remember where he'd lived as a child. She had her own recollections of Steven Morrissey and his family next door. She thought when she met Steven, he was unlike anyone she'd met. When she played Jimmy an album by *The Smiths* yesterday morning, he'd tried to describe his feelings on hearing those songs. He said it was odd because it felt like he was hearing the songs for the first time, but they seemed familiar.

The sound of *The Smiths*.

He asked her what they used to listen to before that group. She had to explain to him they were not together during that early period of the eighties. Alison's father had secured a high-profile job in London just before Christmas in 1979. Obviously, the whole family had to move from Altrincham to London. She told him about the time they first saw each other again when *The Smiths* played in Manchester. She had so much clarity in her mind about that night in The Hacienda in the July of 1983. It was where she was reunited with him. It was a night she was never going to forget. The way her heart had melted, her stomach in knots, that wobble in her legs making her feel unsteady on the dance floor. She was worried these memories could draw her toward him again.

Jimmy was always insistent in his hospital room that they listened together through the speakers. She could sense the music of The Smiths was helping with his memories. Still, she witnessed yesterday afternoon just how much it was frustrating him.

"I think I can remember. I just can't remember the details!" He slurred a loud scream.

Infuriated, he lifted both arms and smashed them onto the table over his legs. Alison's eyes widened in disbelief at Jimmy's aggressive outburst.

"Jimmy, what are you doing? You've got to try and relax. Your memories will come back, I'm sure," she reassured him.

"Put Smiths on," he commanded.

"OK, which album?"

"Live one."

"OK. It's in my bag, love. One sec."

Alison grabbed her shoulder bag and dropped it with some force onto the bed, right onto Jimmy's shins, without realising it. She immediately looked at him, gazing out the window, not flinching when she dropped the bag. A horrible thought went through her mind as she smiled at him. Has he no feeling in his legs? That can only mean one thing, can't it? What if? No! Don't! I need to speak to Mr Davies about this; for fuck's sake, don't ask Jimmy about his legs, she worried as she fished through her bag before pulling out the compact disc she wanted.

"Got it. Here. Have a look at the sleeve while I connect the speakers."

She pulled out the folded insert, opening it flat onto the table over his legs. Jimmy stared at the image; of fans fighting over Morrissey's shirt.

"Ali?"

"Yes, Jimmy, what's up?"

He began speaking slowly; Alison smiled and patiently waited for him to finish.

"Do you think Steven... named the group... because of me and my family?"

"Who knows? Maybe? We can ask him if we ever see him again? I'm going out for a cigarette Jimmy, won't be long, OK?"

"OK."

Sat in the gardens smoking a cigarette, all these thoughts drew her to a conclusion.

This is the worst birthday I've ever had. This is the worst birthday Jimmy's ever had.

What is there to celebrate? Will Jimmy ever move from his bed? Can he feel his legs? Is he paralysed? Oh God, that word; I hope it's only temporary. I need to speak to Mr Davies.

As she came to that conclusion, it planted an acorn, a thought at the back of her mind. Jimmy couldn't stay in this hospital forever and had no one else. She had to stop thinking like that; she would return home with Simon soon. She knew when she got back to her husband in Highgate, she could forget about Jimmy for a while, focus on work and pay some bills. Amid life in debt, etcetera.

#

Chapter 8

Hand in hand in glorious sunshine, Alison and Jimmy were walking barefoot along the white sands of a Caribbean beach. He was speaking eloquently as he strolled effortlessly alongside her. They stopped to kiss and embrace. She was confused. He looked so well. It was then she realised she was dreaming. It shook her awake, but she didn't move. There was barely any light in the bedroom. It was still dark outside. She knew it must be early, her husband still asleep. His alarm wasn't due to wake her until six. She lay motionless on her back in the bed next to him as she turned her head briefly to glance at the red digital display of her alarm clock. 4:11 AM.

She thought again about the dream that woke her, wondering if it could be a prediction for the future. She couldn't stop herself from romanticising, even in this semi-awakened state. She'd spent a week with Jimmy and watched him slur, struggle, and salivate when trying to speak. She was saddened because she knew he would never be able to speak as eloquently as he had done in the dream or in the past when they were together.

Awake but still motionless, she cursed herself for thinking of Jimmy as soon as she'd woken. She rolled onto her side to face her husband. The man in her life. He was fast asleep. She slowly relaxed onto her back and didn't move for fear of waking him. Thinking about when she left the hospital yesterday and said farewell to her ex-husband after spending an entire week with him, she'd driven away from Farley Hall after lunch, despite Jimmy's angry and tearful protestation. When she told him she had to leave and go back to Highgate, it was the only time she'd seen him upset during the whole week. It took her a long time to convince him she'd be back soon. He didn't understand why she had to go. His brain couldn't be patient; Mr Davies had explained that to her. Over the last seven days, he'd grown accustomed to her being there. Like a child who'd had his favourite toy taken away, he cried, asked why, and then sulked. She left him sulking in his room before briefly speaking to Mr Davies and driving away from the hospital. She'd promised herself she would be heading back to London by two o'clock in the afternoon at the very latest. When she eventually left the hospital, she navigated her car through several country lanes and B-Roads, before joining the M6 motorway and heading south. She drove in silence. She knew every cassette tape in the glove box would remind her of Jimmy. She didn't like the idea of listening to the radio either. She was in no mood to hear the forced, false happiness that daytime radio DJs seemed to exude. She was angry. Angry about why it had to be her ex-husband and childhood sweetheart, who was hit by a car, leaving him with brain damage and massive memory loss. Angry that they didn't talk more back in ninety-four and work through their problems instead of splitting up. Angry because she'd stepped into the open arms of Simon, on the rebound and all too readily. Now angry with herself for slipping sympathetically into caring for Jimmy. Being emotionally drawn toward him because of what's happened.

The morning light in the bedroom finally woke her. She'd fallen asleep again not long after the dream startled her awake. It was late morning, and Simon had left for work some time ago. After showering, brushing her teeth and running a comb through her hair, she dressed in casual jogging bottoms and a t-shirt, the mismatched underwear underneath not bothering her; she was home all day anyway. She made her way downstairs, wandering through the dining room of their large Highgate home towards the kitchen. She loved the house, falling in love with it when they viewed it in ninety-five. At the time, they both knew they were daydreaming. The house was perfect but way beyond their budget. In a sweeping gesture from her parents, they bought the place for her and her new husband, Simon. She was overwhelmed at the time and felt fortunate to live in a place like this in London. After the week she'd had, she allowed herself a day's rest before chasing any leads for photography jobs. Today was a day for putting things into perspective and thinking. She knew her only commitments were to tidy the house and prepare an evening meal for Simon's arrival. She made a cup of tea in the kitchen before moving into the lounge to listen to music. It was always the first thing she did if she was home alone.

She placed her tea mug on a coaster on the coffee table before standing in front of the tall storage unit next to the turntable and running her finger across the spines of the records in their collection. Her eyes were drawn to the thin spine of *Bummed*, the *Happy Monday's* second album. She gently teased the record from its cover and placed it on the turntable. Since leaving the hospital yesterday, she'd consciously avoided listening to Joy Division or The Smiths. She knew certain songs would always remind her of Jimmy and draw her closer to him. She had every right to try and 'switch off' her thoughts about him. After spending seven days helping with his rehabilitation, she felt she owed it to herself. She knew this record would stir her memories of Simon more than those involving Jimmy. Though not always happy memories where Simon was concerned. He never really 'got' *Morrissey* or *The Smiths*. He wasn't with Jimmy and Alison when they saw *The Smiths* playing at The Free Trade Hall in 1984.

Simon only went to see them live once, whereas Jimmy and Alison had been to more than fifty of their concerts. When the three of them saw *Happy Mondays* supporting *New Order* at The Hacienda back in eighty-seven, Simon found his group. People he felt he had an affinity with in Gaz, Shaun, his brother Paul, and Bez. People who lived fast and took Class A drugs, which was a slippery slope, Jimmy and Alison saw Simon in danger of sliding down. It led to arguments between the three of them. Jimmy and Alison, a pair of pot smokers themselves, saw how cocaine changed Simon. Neither of them liked it. They wanted to help him. That's what friends are for.

She spent the remainder of the day checking negatives, organising paperwork, and looking through her diary of pending photography jobs. She would occasionally rise from the chair at her study desk to play a different record or take a break from the paperwork and polish surfaces or vacuum floors. It was a cloudless, bright late summer day. There were shafts of sunlight in every room of the house. Diagonal rays of light ++were populated by sparkling, dancing dust particles that Alison had disturbed whilst cleaning. She broke for something to eat mid-afternoon and went into the kitchen to make a sandwich. After eating whilst sitting in the kitchen, satisfied she'd made enough of an impact on the housework, she ran a full load of clothes through the washing machine. She relaxed on the sofa with another cup of tea. She was thankful that her thoughts seemed more focused on what to prepare for dinner than Jimmy's. It was helping her, being away from that hospital and back in the familiar surroundings of her home. Seven days with her ex-husband was long enough. She needed home and normality. Even though she didn't want to admit it to herself, she was glad for a break from Jimmy.

Mr Davies had said to her last week:

"The best way to behave toward a person with a brain injury is with tolerance."

After the time she'd spent with Jimmy last week, she fully understood what the consultant meant. Witnessing for herself his anger, a man both mentally and physically disabled to what extent she still didn't fully understand. It seemed all the focus was on his brain injury and memory loss. She hadn't dared ask when he would be out of bed and walking again. She took her last swig of tea and stood from the sofa, shaking that brief thought of Jimmy from her system, before heading into the kitchen to prepare dinner.

#

Chapter 9

When Simon arrived home from work, Alison felt frustrated he didn't ask about Jimmy as soon as he walked in. He just dropped his suitcase and keys on the kitchen island, said 'alright, love' and raced upstairs before she had a chance to speak. After showering, changing, and opening a bottle of red wine, he sat at the table with her by seven. Now sitting in front of her, he finally asked about his friend.

"So, Jimmy didn't say much then?" Simon asked, pushing a forkful of food into his mouth.

"He can't. It was horrible watching saliva drooling out of his mouth as he tried to speak. You know what Jimmy's like. Well, what he used to be like," she said, gazing at nothing and slowly twirling her fork in her right hand.

"Yeah, it must be really frustrating for him," Simon sympathised.

"It is. I saw him get really angry a couple of times. That's not the Jimmy we remember, is it? He was the most chilled out of the three of us."

"Don't forget what that consultant said; a brain injury changes a person's personality."

"Yeah, I know. It's just hard to take. You've not seen him."

"No, I know. Maybe we could both go up and see him near Christmas? Stay at the Midland for a few nights. What do you think, babe?"

"Yeah, that'd be great. Christmas is gonna be tough for him."

"Yeah, I know. You want a top-up, babe?"

"Sure."

Simon poured the rest of the bottle into each of their glasses, smiling at the back of Alison's head; she was gazing across the room through the bi-folding glass doors into their back garden.

"What's up, love?"

She turned to face him before speaking, a real sadness in her eyes.

"Jimmy's memories are fucked. I'm not sure he's going to remember all that much?"

"You were with him all week. Did he not remember anything?"

"Well, he had a bit of a breakthrough. Well, Mr Davies called it a breakthrough."

"How d'ya mean?"

"You know I told him about the night in seventy-eight when the three of us first met."

"Yeah."

"He remembered carrying around his mum's old glasses case. Somewhere to put his joints, he used to buy off Reni's brothers."

"Oh aye, I remember that. Good that. I guess all his memories are still in there somewhere, and we've just gotta help him pull 'em out."

"The consultant said I should play him the music he loves because music is so evocative and the best way to help people remember past experiences, apparently. That's why I bought a CD player and a few CDs from town last week."

"Good idea. What CDs did you get?"

"Unknown Pleasures, Closer and all the Smiths albums. When I was describing us meeting up in seventy-eight at the Band on the Wall, he listened to Joy Division."

"Right."

"It really helped. He wrote that down about joints and Reni's brothers. He couldn't say it. Took him ages to write that sentence. He can barely grip a pen or move things with his hands, babe."

"Fuckin' 'ell. I hope he gets better."

"Well, his speech improved a little in the time I was there," she offered.

"God knows who paid his hospital bills in America," Simon said.

"I know. It'll be thousands."

"Well, he was there four years, so it's probably millions, love. The only people we know with that sort of money is your mam and dad. They wouldn't have paid Jimmy's bills, would they?"

"Nah, no way. Besides, they would have told me. I think he met a rich woman over there."

"You reckon?"

"Why not? Look as us two."

"Yeah, you're probably right," Simon agreed.

He paused briefly, then asked her.

"What if he remembers why you split up?"

Alison looked away from Simon; he'd made her feel very angry. How could he say that when Jimmy had been through so much? She slid her chair backwards, scraping it loudly against the solid oak floor as she stood up. Picking up both empty plates and stomping towards the open-plan kitchen, she shouted as she walked away.

"Fuckin' 'ell Si! That's you all over that init!"

"What?" He pleaded innocently.

With a raised voice from behind the kitchen island, she shouted at her husband, who was still sitting there.

"Jimmy's in a bad way, Simon. What the fuckin' 'ell are you worried about?"

Still seated, Simon looked across to the kitchen angrily at Alison.

"If he doesn't know why you split, what's stopping you two getting back together?"

Alison dropped the two dinner plates onto the kitchen island, high enough to make a loud noise and illustrate her anger. She strode forcefully into the dining room to respond to him, standing in shock in front of her husband and staring at him sternly.

"Are you serious?"

"Well, you might? You were together for years."

"So? He's physically and mentally disabled. We don't know yet if he'll ever walk again, and all you're worried about is if me and him will get back together?! I'm not gonna throw away five years being married to you on a romantic and nostalgic whim, am I!"

He felt humbled and slightly foolish, breaking the silence with a suggestion.

"Shall I open another bottle of red love?"

"Do what you want. I've had enough. I'm going for a smoke in the lounge."

She was bloody annoyed and hoped he understood that from her tone. Walking to the kitchen island to pick up her cigarettes and lighter, she turned to face him as he asked her.

"Did you not ask the consultant about his legs?"

"No."

"Why not?" He asked, looking puzzled.

"Because I'm fuckin' terrified he's paralysed!" She shouted, turning away, leaving him alone at the dining table.

Before Simon could respond, she stood at the glass doors at the back of their open-plan home, sliding them open and stepping out onto the decking. She sat down on the furniture outside, turning away from him and looking toward the large conifer trees at the back of the garden.

Simon felt humbled, subdued and a little foolish for asking the question. Through those opened glass doors, he could see the back of his wife's head surrounded by a grey cloud of smoke from the cigarette she'd just lit. He stood up and left the room, taking another bottle of red to the study. He didn't want to talk about the possibility his best friend could be permanently paralysed.

She came back indoors when he'd gone, and in the darkness of the lounge, she stood for a moment. After spending a week with Jimmy in the hospital and now being back home, it finally sank in, and she realised; he was a different person from the one who'd been a part of her life for the best part of two decades. And she really did mean the best part.

She flicked on the reading lamp near the sofa and stepped over to the coffee table drawer, where she kept her cannabis and rolling papers. Home for just over a day, and already we're arguing, she said out loud as she walked across the now empty dining area toward the kitchen.

#

Alison had two photography jobs booked for the remainder of the month. A lifestyle magazine fashion shoot on Wednesday, and on Saturday evening, she'd be photographing the launch of a new art gallery in Chelsea owned by a close friend of her father's. A man who was insistent Alison stays the night in a suite in his Chelsea hotel. Simon couldn't attend. He was closing a deal at work. She didn't have to worry about getting to Chelsea with her photography equipment; the hotel owner sent a car and driver to collect her.

When she finally got to her suite after the photography and socialising had drawn to a close, she rang home to speak to her husband. There was no answer. It didn't really surprise her all that much. She knew Simon and his team would have closed the deal at work and gone out clubbing to celebrate, she concluded.

"If he's doing coke, I'll kill him," she said out loud, alone in that hotel suite.

She knew there would be another heated argument about Class A drugs at home tomorrow. The last time he'd gone on a cocaine bender was also through closing a big deal at work. What infuriated her most, he didn't even ring her to say he was going out after work. Yet again, he had gone on a bender without ringing to let her know.

She intentionally switched her mind to thoughts of Jimmy. It had only been six days since she last saw him, and she wondered how he might be improving. Smiling, she switched off the bedside lamp, lay back in bed, and closed her eyes.

#

Chapter 10

A few days later, when Alison pulled onto the driveway after a trip to the supermarket, she left her shopping in the car when she heard the telephone ring. Something in her mind told her to race for the front door and answer it; she had a gut feeling it was important.

"Hello?"

"Hello, is that Alison?"

Instant voice recognition made her heart start thumping in her chest. She knew exactly who it was and feared the worst. Jimmy had been back in her life for only a week, but she still gripped the telephone receiver until her knuckles whitened.

"Yes. Is that Mr Davies?"

"It is, yes."

"What's happened?"

"Nothing to worry about. Jimmy's making good progress. However, yesterday morning he had such an aggressive and angry outburst we had to call hospital security to restrain him."

"You're joking."

"No, I'm not. During the outburst, he was screaming your name. There's been miraculous improvement with his speech Alison, and he's been asking for you since yesterday morning."

"Oh shit! Sorry. Right. I Need to come up."

"If you could manage it, we'd all appreciate it here. It was the reason for the call today. Jimmy's being difficult with the nurses. He's not eating. He seemed settled when you were here."

"Oh, don't say that I'm trying to avoid thinking about him."

"OK, leave it with me, Mr Davies. I can move some commitments I have down here and book myself a hotel room for next week."

"That would be wonderful, Alison. It will really help Jimmy and help us build on this sudden, sharp improvement he's had. As long as your husband is fine with you staying up here?"

"Oh, don't worry about him. He's always busy with work anyway."

"That's great, as long as you're sure?"

"Of course. I'll probably drive up on Sunday, but I'll ring you tomorrow to confirm, OK?"

"Sure. Thanks again for your support, Alison. Speak tomorrow. Bye."

"Thanks for ringing Mr Davies. Bye."

She put the receiver back in its cradle, her back slid down the wall in the hallway, and sat on the floor with her knees up and her head in her hands. What have I done? Another week with Jimmy. What am I doing? Simon will go mad; he won't want me to go, she thought as she sat there alone.

Whenever she thought, 'you're married to Simon; you can't help rehabilitate another man for weeks at a time', she always ended up with the same counterargument. But it's Jimmy. It's my way of repaying him for all the love and friendship he's given me over the years, she thought. She was convincing herself before she had to convince her husband later. She knew Simon would go berserk when she told him. Throughout the afternoon and until he arrived home, she went over the best way to break the news she was going away for an entire week again. Regardless of his reaction, she always intended to travel north to support Jimmy. She had one big photography job in her diary for next week. In the past, if something came up unexpectedly, she would ring her friend Tracy Aspinall, a girl she'd met and become friends with at a photography conference in London a few years ago. If either of them was in a tight spot, they would pass each other work.

Alison finished drinking her tea in the garden before returning indoors to telephone Tracy, who was happy to take the job on. She thanked her friend and then called The Midland, booking a room for a week. Six nights at the Midland and the cost of all the petrol she's going to use isn't cheap. She knew that would cause Simon's blood to boil this evening. Not his wife being away from home for seven days, but the cost of her trip to his wallet.

Fuck him and his obsession with money.

Since his career in advertising had taken off, Simon had changed. He'd become much more ruthless and a little emotionally sterile toward her sometimes. He'd been best friends with Jimmy since infant school; she couldn't understand why he wasn't fighting to come with her at all costs.

#

On most evenings, she would drink half the wine that Simon would glug his way through; tonight, she was keeping up with him. It was nerves, and she knew how he was going to react.

After dinner, they took their wine glasses and second bottle of red into the lounge. It was late evening and too cold to sit on the back garden decking.

"You skinning up, love? I'll put some tunes on."

"Whoa, not yet. I wanna talk to you. Sit down," she said as she patted the sofa next to her.

"Oh yeah, what's up?" he asked as he came and sat down.

"Jimmy's consultant phoned today."

"Why, what's happened?"

"Well, there's good news and bad news, babe."

"Right, OK," he was still smiling, which didn't reassure her.

"The good news is Jimmy's shown huge improvements with movement in his hands and arms, and he's getting the power of speech back, babe."

"Wow, really? That's fantastic news. What's the bad news?"

She didn't answer straight away. She opened the coffee table drawer and started to build a joint. She was going to need it. Simon had never loved cannabis as much as she did. As Jimmy had. He didn't share a joint with her in the evening, as she had done in the past with Jimmy.

"Well. What's the bad news?" He asked, with a mildly impatient tone.

"Hang on," she said, tapping the joint on the table and then putting it to her lips.

She lit the joint and took a long drag, inhaling large amounts of thick smoke, which she exhaled slowly as she began to explain.

"Right. Jimmy had an outburst yesterday morning. They had to call hospital security."

"Yer fuckin' joking?" Simon exclaimed in absolute shock.

"I wish I was. The consultant said Jimmy was screaming my name. He's been asking for me ever since he snapped yesterday morning. And he's refusing his food."

"Have you spoke to him on the phone?"

"No, I was thinking of travelling up there on Sunday?"

"What? No, we can't. I've that meeting with the Cadbury board of directors on Sunday, and you've got that photo shoot in Essex next week."

"I could offer that job to Tracy. I've given her work in the past if something's come up," Alison lied, having already passed the job to her.

"Yeah, I know, but a week at the Midland again? The cost of all the fuel yer gonna use? It's not cheap, is it! It's money we can do without spending, to be honest, love."

"Do without spending? Are you for fuckin' real! It's Jimmy. Si."

"Yeah, I know, but the three of us is in the past. Too much water under that bridge. You've not forgotten how he attacked me five years ago, have ya? That's what fucked our friendship."

"It's not fucked, is it? We didn't know this was gonna happen, did we? You just want enough money to spend on coke to shove up yer nose."

Simon stood up. He was getting angry now. He always did when she challenged his cocaine use. He began waving his arms, pointing his finger at her accusingly.

"Literally, *pot* and fuckin' kettle, love. How much money do you spend on that shit?"

She stood to face him, square up to him. Simon had, and never would, hit her, but they have recently had some pretty volatile shouting matches.

"Not as much as you do on that stuff. Cocaine for rich people. We're not rich people. My Dad bought this house for us. And I spend less on weed than you do on booze, don't I?"

"Yeah, I know, but..."

"But nothing Simon. I'm travelling up on Sunday."

She didn't ask him. She told him. She was going to stay in the north. Help Jimmy when he needs her the most. He'd never needed her as much as he did right now.

"Yer not."

"Simon, I am. You've got work to keep you busy, and I know what it's like at your place. You, Phil, and Ian take *anything* at work as a reason to celebrate. Go out and hoover up a few lines."

"So what?"

"See, you're not even denying it, are you? There's so much coke flying about between you lot in advertising; I'm amazed you get any work done."

"Bollocks."

"No, Simon, it's not bollocks, and I'm driving up to help Jimmy on Sunday."

He stomped away to leave the room, not before having the final say as he reached the door.

"Fuck off to Jimmy then. See if I care."

He slammed the lounge door firmly shut. She heard the front door slam with much ferocity and his car start outside. With an intentional screeching of tyres, he raced away.

Imbecile, she thought as she put her joint in the ashtray and walked over to her vinyl collection. His attitude had made her even angrier than she'd expected. She wanted to listen to *Fade in/Out* by *Oasis*. Her go-to group if she was pissed off and wanted to scream. She played the record at a loud volume. Fuck the neighbours. Right now, she didn't care.

She stood up to shout along with Liam.

Get on the roller coaster; the fair's in town today.
You gotta be bad enough to beat the brave.

As the night ticked over into morning, she continued to listen to music. He was in the study drinking; she could hear his TV set in between the songs she was listening to. She smoked another joint before falling asleep on the sofa, stoned.

It was pitch black when she awoke with a start. She looked at her watch. It was four o'clock in the morning. Whatever time Simon had gone to bed, he'd left her asleep on the sofa. What's the point in waiting until Sunday? I should pack and go now? I'm awake. Fuck it. She thought as she crept upstairs in the very early hours of Saturday morning.

#

Chapter 11

It was still dark outside their Highgate home when Alison dropped her suitcase in the boot of her car and slammed it shut. Too early to telephone the hospital or the hotel and change her room booking. After waking so early this morning and the argument last night, her mind was made up. If nothing else, at least setting off early meant missing most of the traffic.

She sat in the driver's seat and started the engine. Fuck it, she thought as she put her car into first and drove away. She was still furious with Simon because of his attitude towards Jimmy. They'd been best friends for years, since well before seventy-eight when she'd met them.

As she idled along the empty high street, she was choosing music for the journey. It was always the first thing she did when she got in her car. She was heading north again with two songs on her mind as she drove down desolate and empty streets towards the motorway. Two songs she knew would make her think of Jimmy because she knew he loved them Two songs she had on tape in her glovebox. Two songs with absolute relevance in their titles and lyrics. Two songs she loved. *Flying North* by *Thomas Dolby* and *Hit the North* by *The Fall*. She lit a cigarette, and as she joined the motorway, listening to *Mark E. Smith's* unique vocals, she smiled as she remembered going with Jimmy to see the group play at *The Hacienda* in eighty-four.

Despite her early start, it was after seven, and the sun rose when she reached Birmingham. The traffic was building and beginning to slow her down. She knew there was still a drive of two hours in this traffic. When she eventually reached the last stretch of the M6 motorway, the morning rush hour was in full effect. It was almost nine when she finally reached the hospital.

She pulled into the car park, locked her car, and walked into reception. The girl on the desk recognised her, and Alison asked to use her telephone to ring the hotel. The girl who answered the telephone at the Midland was happy to start the booking today. Alison informed her she would check in by five today at the latest.

The receptionist rang his office, and it didn't take Mr Davies long to arrive downstairs in reception. Though he was shocked, he'd not expected to see her today.

"Alison, hi! I thought you were ringing to confirm, not actually showing up here today?"

"Morning, Mr Davies, it was a last-minute thing. I was struggling sleeping last night anyway, Simon's focused on a big job at work at the moment, so I thought I may as well travel up this morning. I left home at five," she lied, convincing him it was her husband's focus on work, not his attitude, that had driven her to flee the nest so early in the morning.

"You must be shattered?"

"Yeah, a little. I'll be OK when I've had a cup of tea and a couple of cigarettes."

"OK. Well, Jimmy's awake and being difficult. Refusing breakfast. Refusing to cooperate. I'd like a brief chat with you in private if possible? Before you go and see Jimmy."

"Sure, no problem."

She followed the consultant upstairs to his office. He played her the video footage of Jimmy's outburst. She sat there dumbfounded and concerned. At no point in her life had she witnessed Jimmy behave this way; it was shocking for her to see. It made her fear what Jimmy could be capable of, should he regain his strength fully in the future.

When she left his office with the consultant, and they made their way downstairs, he had to begin his rounds. Now she wanted a mug of tea, a smoke and time to think about what she'd just seen. They shook hands and smiled at each other before parting ways. Mr Davies along the corridor towards the patient rooms, and Alison headed for the cafeteria. The CCTV footage shocked her; she forgot to ask about Jimmy's legs.

Something was undeniably calming about that spot in the gardens behind Farley Hall. The thoughts she'd had whilst sitting there smoking a cigarette, sipping tea, and ingesting circumstances. Her mind wandered through the years she'd spent with Jimmy. No desire to leave anything out, no matter how small a detail. Fully aware that any one of her tiny inconsequential memory recollections could spark Jimmy's memories back to life.

Once she'd finished contemplating, she stepped through the rear entrance to the hospital. Walking along the corridor, she heard Jimmy shouting even before she got to his room. She stepped inside, and there he was, as the consultant had described. Being angry. Refusing to cooperate. She recognised the frustrated nurse with him as Sarah, whom she'd met the last time she was here.

"Hi, Jimmy," Alison proudly announced.

Despite the long journey and very early start, she'd made a huge effort to look her best for Jimmy. To look appealing to placate him. Jimmy and the nurse looked up from their quarrel to see Alison standing inside the doorway in full makeup, dressed in a smart black trouser suit and heels. She'd changed her clothes and sat outside the hospital's driveway entrance in her car.

"Alison!" He shouted, this time with arms outstretched, craving a welcoming hug.

As she walked toward him, her heart was beating much faster than the clip-clop of her heels on the room's solid floor. She said good morning to the nurse and, leaning over the bed, she hugged Jimmy. As she held onto him, she wanted to praise him for how much he'd improved.

"Jimmy, you're doing much better than the last time I saw you. You're speaking much clearer now. That's terrific. Isn't it?

She pulled away from him to gauge his reaction to what she'd said.

"I suppose so."

"You suppose so? Come on. You're getting better. I can have a proper conversation with you now. See if we can unlock some more of those memories. What d'ya think, darling."

The praise she was giving him, coupled with referring to him in that way, triggered the tears to flood out of him again.

"Oh, Jimmy. Don't cry. I'm here now."

"Where did you go?! Why weren't you here?!" He exclaimed with a tearful gravelly tone, raising his voice in frustration.

"Oh, Jimmy. I have a life in London with Simon now, but it doesn't mean that I don't care about you. It just means I can't be here all the time, that's all."

"Who's Simon?"

"Don't you remember Simon? Your best friend for most of your life?"

"Oh, Simon, yeah. Why are you married to him?"

"I started seeing him after me, and you split up. It's complicated, darling. Sad times. Let's remember the happy times first, yeah?"

"Yeah, OK," he responded. His smiling face was covered with a moist sheen of tears, obvious to Alison under the bright medical lighting. She took a tissue from a packet, dabbing his face dry, and Sarah, the nurse, immediately noticed Alison's positive effect on him.

"How about having some breakfast, Jimmy?" She asked him.

"Yeah, I'm hungry."

"Great stuff. I'll put some music on quietly while you eat. OK?" Alison suggested connecting the speakers to the CD player and putting them on the bedside cabinet.

"Yeah. The Smiths!" Jimmy exclaimed.

"Definitely, Jimmy," Alison responded, smiling at him.

"What was their first one? Put that on."

"OK darling, good choice," she said, putting the CD in the player and hitting play.

Jimmy, at last, began to eat his breakfast without protest, anger, or aggression. The nurse was visibly taken aback by this change and immediately left to find the consultant.

The opening drums of *Reel Around the Fountain* brought the little plastic speakers to life, and Alison sat in the chair next to Jimmy's bed.

As that first song continued, she smiled when she realised how long it'd been since she last heard this album. She really loved it.

It's time the tale were told,
Of how you took a child,
And you made him old.

A Child.

She thought about the video clip she'd just seen as she watched him eating breakfast. Now she was beginning to realise how the brain injury changed him. The confident, intelligent, and eloquent Jimmy Smith is gone. Now a man exhibiting the behaviour and naivety of a child.

The child.

She'd not talked about or thought of him for over three years. Neither had her husband. She cursed herself inside for allowing a song lyric to make her think about something she'd spent years trying to forget. Some days are easier than others. These things you never really forget. You just bury them and hope they go away.

\#

Chapter 12

Jimmy had nodded off. He was fast asleep.

"I must be boring him," Alison said.

"Of course not. TBI patients get exhausted really quickly." Sarah, the nurse, explained.

"TBI?"

"Traumatic Brain Injury."

"Ah, of course."

Jimmy sleeping soundly felt like a good opportunity for Alison to grab some lunch.

"Sarah, I'm going to pop into the cafeteria while he's sleeping."

"OK, no worries."

Alison left his room, making her way down the white-walled corridor beginning to look so familiar to her. She'd not gone too far when she bumped into Jimmy's consultant.

"Alison, hi. I'm glad I've bumped into you."

"Hi."

"I've arranged a meeting with everyone helping rehabilitate Jimmy. Monday at two."

"Oh, that's fantastic."

Alison considered asking about Jimmy's legs but thought better of it. I can't ask him here in the corridor. What if Jimmy's permanently disabled? I can't handle that on top of his brain injury. Anyway, by Monday afternoon, I'll know everything, she thought as she stood with the consultant.

"I'm in my office until four today if you need me for anything."

"OK, thanks," she said, smiling as she walked away from Mr Davies.

Strolling happily toward the cafeteria, she was impressed by how much Jimmy's movement and speech had improved since the last time she saw him. After she'd got herself a mug of tea from the café, she sat in her usual spot in the gardens contemplating the meeting on Monday. She sat only yards from where he lay, promising herself she would try her best to help him. She knew why seeing him again affected her because she'd never really stopped loving him. Or did she feel more drawn to Jimmy this week because she'd driven angrily away from her husband in the pitch-black early morning? Yet, when she'd arrived here and looked into Jimmy's eyes again, her heart fluttered, her stomach in knots. She'd felt it so much in the past.

It had been three very productive days for Alison in helping Jimmy remember the past. She'd intentionally focused on that earlier period of their relationship, avoiding any discussion of the nineties and the time when they split up.

#

Alison wasn't expecting the traffic she faced when she left Manchester on Monday lunchtime. When her car skidded to a stop on the gravel forecourt of Farley Hall, it was almost two. She'd wanted to arrive before the meeting was due to start and cursed herself for not leaving the hotel earlier. When she walked as briskly as she could in her heels into reception, the girl on the desk gestured her straight upstairs.

"Sorry, unexpected traffic hold-ups."

"It's OK, Alison, they're upstairs in his office; I'll let Mr Davies know you've arrived. Go on up." The receptionist said, picking up the telephone receiver.

"Thanks."

When she entered the Consultant's office, everyone involved in Jimmy's rehabilitation was sitting along one side of a large oval, dark oak table.

"Hi Alison," Mr Davies said, standing to greet her.

"Sorry, I'm a little late. Unexpected traffic."

"Oh, we wouldn't have started without you. Take a seat, I'll introduce you to everyone."

Alison sat at the side of the table nearest the door where she had just entered, facing the four medical professionals. She assumed three women and one physically fit male to be Jimmy's physio. As the consultant introduced them, they each nodded hello to her.

"Alison, this is Trudy Turner, the clinical psychiatrist whom I work closely with on Jimmy's rehabilitation. Sitting next to her is Alan Metcalfe, Jimmy's physiotherapist. Next to him is Adrianna Churchill, Jimmy's speech therapist. Finally, sitting next to Adrianna is Kath Archer, Jimmy's dietician."

"Hi, everyone, and thanks for all that you're doing for Jimmy. He seems to have made such an improvement since I was last here," Alison said, smiling as she returned their greetings.

Immediately the smile on her face dropped as the psychiatrist gave her a serious look.

"Yes, he has Alison. However, you need to appreciate the difficulties someone with an acquired brain injury can have." Trudy Turner explained.

"Well, he's obviously very poorly."

"Yes, but whenever people meet Jimmy in the future, they'll be unaware he has an acquired brain injury. Knowing him means we understand his behaviour and the things he says. We can pre-empt something from happening."

"His behaviour?"

"Yes. I've been working with people with acquired brain injuries for the majority of my career. I help lots of patients' families come to terms with the changes in their family member's behaviour."

"Oh, I see. I've never met somebody with a brain injury."

"Well, in simple terms, Jimmy could be impatient, frustrated, opinionated, and speak inappropriately in social situations. He has lost the understanding of how his behaviour and the things he says impact other people."

"Oh, I see," Alison responded.

"People with acquired brain injuries don't look disabled. This is why we term brain injury; the 'hidden' disability."

There you go, she used that word, disabled. Alison thought, feeling the time was right.

"Is Jimmy disabled, though? What's up with his legs? When will he be strong enough to come out into the gardens with me?" Alison asked hopefully.

The quick look Mr Davies gave Trudy Turner told Alison everything.

This wasn't going to be good news. She could sense it from their demeanour.

"Unfortunately, Jimmy has sustained some spinal damage in the accident. This only became apparent to us once he'd wakened from the long-term coma. His physical strength will return in time, but unfortunately, Jimmy is paralysed from the waist down. He will never walk again."

Paralysed? Fuck. No. Not Jimmy.

She could feel her heart and soul drop when the consultant said that word. She had hoped any paralysis would only be temporary. Still, she now had to resign herself to the fact that Jimmy would need a wheelchair for the rest of his life. To all intents and purposes, he looked 'normal'. He didn't look disabled. However, he *was* physically disabled. He couldn't walk; he couldn't run. He could never jump around and have fun. It broke her heart.

"Is there no way he will ever walk again?" She pleaded.

"No, I'm afraid not, Alison," Mr Davies said.

"We have to try to focus on the positives." Trudy Turner interrupted.

"Positives? Are there any?" Alison asked.

"'Of course. For a patient to be classified in a persistent vegetative state and begin recovering as quickly as Jimmy has, it must be celebrated. If we focus solely on the loss of the use of his legs instead of focusing on what he can do, it won't be good for his state of mind."

"Sure, I understand that. It's just a bit shocking for me to take in," Alison confessed.

"I know, but each one of us in this room is here to help Jimmy," Mr Davies said sternly, smiling reassuringly at Alison.

"And to help you help him," he continued, smiling at Alison.

"Yes, I know."

"And don't worry, the cost of his electric chair has also been taken care of."

"I assume by those who wish to remain anonymous?"

"Yes."

Obviously, Alison paid close attention to everything said during the remainder of the meeting. Still, Jimmy's leg paralysis was at the forefront of her mind. She was the only person he had for support; it would be life-changing for her too.

What choice did she have? He had no one else. Alison would be out of character to leave the hospital this coming Sunday and absolve all the responsibility she felt she had for him.

It's not my problem. We're divorced. She couldn't be like that.

The voices in the room became just noise as her mind started to wander. She thought about the life they'd spent together, the things Jimmy had said to her in the past.

We're part of the same soul.

We share the same day of birth.

We're part of the same soul.

He was right. The only reason he'd stopped saying that to her was because they'd split up. Yet now, he had no memory of it happening, no knowledge of the divorce. No hatred in his soul because of something she'd done. Despite this, she harboured a fear he would remember one day.

Chapter 13

Handbag over her shoulder with a large tea in a cardboard cup with a plastic lid in her right hand, Alison walked away from the cafeteria distraught. She'd spent over an hour in that meeting room and been completely overwhelmed. She needed to listen to music to deal with the emotions inside her. She knew all her favourite albums were on cassette in her glove box. She walked out of the large front doors of Farley Hall, unlocked her car, and sat in the driver's seat. She knew on the one side of a 90-minute tape she'd recorded *Nowhere,* the first album by a guitar group from Oxford called *Ride.* Both she and Jimmy loved them, and there was one song, in particular, she needed to hear right now. *Paralysed* track number seven. She found the tape in the glove box, noticing it had been rewound to the beginning; she slotted it into her tape player and hit fast forward. The sound of the tape whirring forwards gave her time to light a cigarette. She pulled one from her packet of twenty, put it to her lips and lit it with a disposable plastic lighter she'd left on the dash. She hit the play button and was impressed it had stopped on the song before the one she wanted; she listened to the sixth song, *Decay* fade away. The next song began playing, a couple of solitary guitars filling her car with sound.

Paralysed.

The title of the song she was now listening to.

The way Jimmy would be forever.

What the fuck am I going to do? She thought.

As she sat in her car smoking, tears streaming down her face. She turned the stereo down a little; she didn't want to be noticed by anyone arriving or leaving. She didn't want anyone to see her like this; she was a mess. As the song continued to play, she slowly began to try and compose herself, pushing the butt of her cigarette into the ashtray and wiping her tears with some tissues she had with her. She was in no hurry to go indoors and tell Jimmy he was paralysed from the waist down. He'd never mentioned his legs to her as he'd lay in that hospital bed, and he obviously didn't feel anything when she'd dropped her bag on his legs the last time she was here. Perhaps he already knew, feelings returning in every part of his body except his legs. She wasn't looking forward to it.

A short time later, Alison decided to face into it, lock her car and make her way indoors. Talking with Mr Davies, they walked along the white-walled corridor towards Jimmy's room. A woman who had spent almost two decades by his side and the senior consultant in charge of his rehabilitation. When Jimmy would eventually be discharged from the hospital, Alison was beginning to come to terms with the fact she'd be looking after him. Her husband, Simon, being happy with this, was a different matter entirely that she would address when she got back home. Once they'd both greeted the patient, Mr Davies checked the chart at the end of the bed before leaving Jimmy alone with Alison. He closed the door to the room when he left, turning the do not disturb sign over. Under the circumstances, he felt it necessary to give them some privacy.

"How are you feeling, Jimmy?" she asked tentatively.

"OK. Bit tired. Confused."

"It's OK, you know. Mr Davies tells me it's normal for someone who's been through what you have," Alison reassured him.

"Is it?"

"Of course. You've been through so much."

"It feels like ages since I last felt fresh air on my face, Ali. How long have I been here?"

"Well, you were admitted here at the beginning of September, so you've been here about five or six weeks, I think."

"It feels a lot longer than that."

"I'm sure it does."

"Do you know why you haven't been outside? Why you're confined to this room?"

"No. Why?"

"There's no easy way to say this, Jimmy, but you're paralysed from the waist down."

Silence and nothing to say. From Jimmy, no tears, though she'd expected them. They broke eye contact, and he looked away from her through the large window into the gardens at the back of Farley Hall. Neither of them said anything. Alison firmly gripped one of Jimmy's hands in both of hers. A moment passed, and Jimmy, still staring out the window, started to sing the word to the tune of the song by *Ride*.

"Paralysed, paralysed, paralysed."

"Oh, Jimmy, I've just been listening to that song in the car. Do you remember that album? The crest of a huge wave in the ocean on the cover."

Something she'd said had affected him; he turned to her, tears streaming down his cheeks.

"Ride?" He asked.

That really shocked her. She'd always had to prompt him in the past. He'd never said the name of a group to her like that before.

"Oh, Jimmy, you remember them. Come here."

She leaned up off her chair and into his arms, holding him as close as she could. He cried even more in the safety of her embrace. It made Alison begin crying again; she couldn't help herself. They remained locked in a tearful embrace for a couple of minutes until Alison pulled away from him and sat back down. They locked eye contact, and her heart began thumping in her chest.

"I'm so sorry, Jimmy," she offered apologetically.

"It's not your fuckin' fault, is it?"

"No, I know, but I am going to help you."

"Why?"

"Do you not remember what you used to say because our birthdays are on the same day?"

"No."

"You always said we're part of the same soul."

"That's because we are."

"Do you think so?"

"Yes, I do."

His smile toward her warmed her inside. She was in danger of falling for him again.

"Well, I spoke to Mr Davies earlier. They have an electric wheelchair for you. I thought we could go into the gardens together this afternoon. What do you think?"

"Wow, really? That would be amazing," he answered excitedly.

"OK then. I will go and speak to the consultant, see if I can arrange it."

"Brilliant."

"OK, won't be long," Alison promised him.

"OK," he mumbled.

He turned toward the window again, not wanting to watch her leave. He continued to stare out into the gardens as his damaged brain tried to make sense of the fact he'd never walk again.

#

After Alison had eaten lunch in the cafeteria, when she reached his room, they'd successfully hoisted Jimmy into what looked like an expensive-looking electric wheelchair. He was alone in the room with the nurse as she explained how to operate the chair. He could control a chair with his left hand, using a joystick at the end of the armrest.

Alison eyed the complexity of the thing before greeting Jimmy and the nurse, who said the hospital had a contract with a German company that provided all their electric wheelchairs.

"Hiya darling. Do you like my chair? This is my Panzer," Jimmy stated proudly.

"Panzer? What are you like? You've not lost your sense of humour, have you?"

"Aye, German engineering this. Can't wait to drive out in the gardens."

"Well, we don't want you tearing up the corridor, do we? They can go quite fast these things. You could injure yourself or, even worse, someone else," the nurse explained.

"Of course. Make sure you listen to Sarah. Jimmy, are you listening?" Alison said sternly.

"It's OK, Alison, we're done now. He's ready to go. Just take your time, Jimmy, OK?"

"Yeah, sure."

With his left hand, he clicked the joystick forwards, and the chair did the same, shooting towards the door of his room. He raised his right arm punching the air as he shot into the corridor.

"Yay!" He shouted as he shot out of sight.

"Jimmy, will you wait for me?" Alison said, racing after him.

She smiled as she walked down the corridor and out into the gardens. God, she was glad this chair was ironically focusing his attention away from the paralysis of his legs. She knew it was simply the novelty of the thing and being able to get outside. She knew the sadness for him, and the hard work for her was into the coming months.

#

He'd spent ten minutes cruising around in his chair as Alison sat in her usual garden spot. At last, a taste of freedom for Jimmy. That thought made her feel fantastic. It convinced her she'd decided to commit to his rehabilitation. She felt bound to help Jimmy, even though she'd remarried. She watched him glide to a stop at the bench she was sitting on.

"Having fun?" she asked him.

"Oh aye, I'm getting tired, Ali. I want to stay out here, though; it's nice init."

"Yeah, it's lovely out here. That chair looks comfy; you can sleep in it out here."

"Ali, can I have a cigarette?"

She knew he'd been a smoker when they'd been together in the past. She was surprised it had taken him this long to ask. Obviously, it was the first time he'd been out in the fresh air and seen her smoking.

"Sure," she said, passing him a cigarette which he put to his lips.

She lit it with the lighter she had with her and smiled at him. He took his first drag, exhaled, and asked her a question.

"Alison? What does it feel like when you smoke a joint?"

"Ah. Is this because you remembered buying joints off Reni's brothers?"

"Yes. Did I smoke it a lot?"

"Well, you introduced me to it, didn't you? Later, when we moved in together, we used to smoke it most evenings. We preferred it to wine or beer."

"Did we? Did we live together in India?"

"What? Of course not. What makes you say that?"

"I had this thing pop into my head when I woke up this morning. A posh gold sign where we lived together, India House in black lettering.

"Ha, ha, ha, ha," Alison laughed.

"Why are you laughing?" Jimmy asked, looking quite upset and saddened by her reaction.

"Oh, sorry, love, no. You remember I told you about us seeing each other again in eighty-three when The Smiths headlined at The Hacienda?"

"Yeah."

"Well, the following March, you found a flat had come up for rent on Whitworth Street in the centre of Manchester. It was in a building called India House. The gold sign with black lettering is on the front entrance to the building near the door," Alison explained patiently.

"Oh, right. What was it like, Ali?"

"Oh, it was a lovely flat, Jimmy. Great for you because you worked in town, and great for me because I only had a short walk to university." Alison noticed his eyes shutting.

She knew he wasn't sleeping, just resting his eyes. She continued to tell him what had happened; when Jimmy Smith, aged twenty, had moved away from his mother on King's Road, Stretford, and began sharing a flat with Alison Wells, aged nineteen, from Meadow Bank in Timperley, Altrincham.

#

Chapter 14

March 1984

Jimmy lay on his bed, everything packed and ready for the move. He'd spent a large portion of his teenage years in this bedroom. Learning to play his acoustic guitar or listening to records with Simon and Alison once he got to know her. As he lay there, a thousand memories raced across his mind. He'd celebrated his twentieth birthday last year and finally said farewell to his teenage years. Now, only six months later, he was leaving home. He thought about his thirteenth birthday in September 1976, when his mother had bought him his first full-size acoustic guitar. It was still there, leaning against a corner of his room. He smiled, remembering the month after that when he was bouncing around in here with Simon, listening to *New Rose* by *The Damned*, the first punk rock seven-inch single they'd bought. They listened to it repeatedly as loudly as they could get away with until his mother began screaming from downstairs, fearing the pair would fall through the ceiling at any minute. He'd lived in this house, in this bedroom, all his life. It would be strange tomorrow morning, waking up and looking at four different walls. He was the only child his mother had left, and it was hurting him to move away from her. Not long after he was born, Anthony Smith, Jimmy's father, died of a heart attack.

Consequently, there was no alpha male in the household. There rarely was after his father had died. It certainly explained Jimmy's slightly effeminate manner and non-macho behaviour.

Isobel Smith, Jimmy's mother, was comfortable in her own company. When she wasn't working at the library, tidying the house or looking after the children, she would read or listen to her records, mainly girl groups from the sixties. She'd shared her love of reading and pop music with him all his life. Along with raising Jimmy herself, it was the reason she was so close to him.

He turned to face his bedside table, and looking directly at the small framed picture of Alison, he smiled. She was the reason he was moving away from home. He knew that if he hadn't met her and fallen in love, he wouldn't be leaving his mother alone.

The plan for moving day was for Simon and Jimmy to load up the van they'd hired and drop his stuff at the flat. There wasn't much to take.

Then Simon would drop him at Piccadilly station to meet Alison off the
train from London and drive back to Stretford to get Jimmy's mother.
Alison's parents didn't want her to transfer her degree to Manchester
University and move in with Jimmy. They wanted her to finish her degree
in London. They wanted their daughter to find a boyfriend in London.
Jimmy wasn't good enough for Alison. They'd made that perfectly clear.
They refused to drive her north in their car, which escalated into an
argument. She'd had no choice but to get on the train, dragging along as
much of her belongings as she could.

Jimmy's mother was absolutely insistent she sees the flat for herself. She
wanted to see where her son would now be living. The flat they were
moving into was furnished, so he'd spent the last few weeks buying plates,
pots, pans, and cutlery and packed them in boxes stacked in the hallway,
ready to load into the van. He wanted everything to be perfect in the home
he would share with Alison.

He was looking forward to a city centre living as a couple. His mother
couldn't understand why he wanted to work *and* live in the city centre.
When she arrived, she was pleasantly surprised to see the apartment was
in an elegant Edwardian building. Although Jimmy was sure his mother
didn't approve of them living in sin, she never said as much and was
welcoming of Alison. She knew how much her son loved this young
woman.

#

When his mother and Simon left for Stretford, the cohabitating couple
could finally relax alone in their new home. While eating their first meal
in the flat, they listened to music. They listened to *The Smiths*. Their love
for that group was why they saw each other again. After almost four years
apart, they'd been reunited.

Most of Jimmy's stuff was still in boxes, and everything Alison owned was
in two large suitcases she'd struggled with getting on and off the train.
Jimmy had set up his stereo in the lounge and unpacked his vinyl, stacking
it along the wall next to his music centre. Alison went into the kitchen
with the takeaway rubbish once they'd finished eating and put the kettle
on to brew up. She was grateful Jimmy had remembered to buy milk,
unpack the kettle, tea bags and sugar.

The Smiths' debut album had only been released three weeks ago, and
they hadn't stopped listening to it since they'd bought it. Jimmy put his
copy on the turntable and took the sleeve to Alison. As he settled with
her on the sofa, the record began playing.

They had two tickets to see *The Smiths* play at the Free Trade Hall next week. The tickets were for seats near the front, three rows back from the stage. He'd telephoned Alison in London immediately to give her the good news. Both tickets were now on the coffee table so they wouldn't lose them. The concert was the day after tomorrow, on Tuesday evening. A fantastic moving-in present for them both to enjoy.

"I don't understand why Si didn't want to get a ticket for Tuesday?" Alison said.

"I know, he's mental. He says he's skint, but I reckon it's 'coz he doesn't like Morrissey," Jimmy replied, putting forward his own theory.

"Do you think so?"

"Yeah, Simon thinks he's weird, always has. He was moaning the other week because Morrissey's in all the music papers, and they were on Top of the Pops twice, weren't they, for What Difference Does It Make? It's doing his head right in."

"Oh, I saw both those. Brilliant, weren't they?"

"Oh yeah. I love that song. That guitar riff is amazin' init. That's why Si annoys me, Ali. You can't just go on about Morrissey if you're talkin' about The Smiths, can ya? What about Johnny? What about Mike and Andy?"

"Well, not everybody loves them as much as we do, darling. Leave him to his New Order, Happy Mondays and Factory Records."

#

The Free Trade Hall was packed full of people. When Love of the Loved by Cilla Black finally faded, the place was plunged into darkness, and *The Smiths* walked out onto the stage. The crowd erupted into absolute pandemonium. Everyone at the front began screaming. It felt like you were involved in a religious experience. The group began playing the song; *Hand in Glove* and everyone downstairs rushed for the front of the stage. People were standing on the seats to get a better view, and under the weight of all those people, the seating gave way. A pompous concert hall more akin to orchestras and seated affairs couldn't cope with *The Smiths* and their fans.

During this opening song, there were more screams as people trapped limbs between seats. Jimmy had hold of Alison's hand firmly; there was no way he was letting go of her. Everyone at the front stood on top of the collapsed seating, reassembling themselves quickly as a pushing throng, standing and swaying. When the first song finished, everyone in the building was either cheering, clapping, or screaming.

"Jimmy, this is crazy," Alison shouted.

"I know. You, OK?"

"Yes, I'm OK. My foot nearly got caught under my seat when it gave way."

"My seat was goin' anyway, so I stamped on the fucker and jumped off it. Watch where you're stepping; there's wooden spikes sticking up where the seats have broken off," Jimmy shouted back.

He managed to turn his head and glance around the hall. Everybody was going crazy. He felt really glad he'd managed to get tickets. The place looked full to the rafters.

As the cheering and clapping for *Hand in Glove* faded, *Morrissey* shouted at the crowd:

Hello!

The crowd said hello, and the group started playing *Heaven Knows I'm Miserable Now.*

The Smiths played for just over an hour, and then it was over.

Jimmy and Alison felt elated and glad to push out into the cool air outside the Free Trade Hall. Their clothing was soaked with sweat and stuck to their skin. It felt refreshing to be in the open air, and they walked up the road past the Midland Hotel and Central Library. It would only take them ten minutes at most to reach their flat.

They enthused all the way home about what they'd just seen and heard, concluding that *The Smiths* would always be their favourite group. Jimmy, having lived next door to *Morrissey* for several years, seemed irrelevant now that the group were beginning to enjoy real success. Their album had reached number two on the national charts, so *Morrissey* and *Johnny Marr* moved down to London. Jimmy's mother and *Morrissey's* mother were next-door neighbours, now both alone at home. At least they had each other for company.

#

Chapter 15

September 1999

It was mid-afternoon, with the sun still shining when Alison finished reminiscing. Sitting in the gardens, she looked at Jimmy in his wheelchair. His head tilted to the side as he drifted off to sleep. She'd watched him in an obvious deep sleep as his eyeballs seemed to move frantically underneath his firmly shut eyelids. She'd enjoyed spending time with him in the gardens instead of that sterile hospital room.

For the remainder of her week with him, he was always sitting in his chair when she arrived. The time they spent together exploring the grounds of this 18th Century hall brought them dangerously close. Away from the sights, sounds and smells of clinically clean hospital rooms and corridors. Together alone. Together again. Talking of the times, they'd spent together. Both were happy; Jimmy was slowly beginning to remember. To link the synapses. To make connections.

It felt good to be alone on the hospital grounds with Jimmy by her side in his electric wheelchair. Still, to Alison, it felt like freedom tinged with frustration because she couldn't really take him anywhere. There was no familiarity in these hospital grounds for Jimmy. She knew that taking him to King's Road in Stretford and other areas of Manchester he'd once known would stir his memories and help him remember. Though she had no way of making it happen.

The day before Alison was due to return to Highgate, Mr Davies asked her to come to his office. He wanted to talk seriously about Jimmy's care after his stay in the hospital. It didn't surprise her; she expected him to request a meeting before she left for London again. She was an intelligent woman. She knew that with his wheelchair and the right support, Jimmy could manage at home. But where was home for Jimmy? He had no family; he had no home anymore

In the meeting, Mr Davies suggested they could discharge Jimmy before Christmas. Against her better judgement, Alison agreed. His dramatic improvements had convinced her it was the right thing to do.

"When I speak to the families of paraplegic patients, I will always ask them about their provision for a vehicle. Some way of transporting the patient in their wheelchair."

"Ah, I see. Well, obviously, this is something I should discuss with my husband, isn't it?"

"Of course. Have you spoken to him in respect of Jimmy moving in with you?"

"No. I'm going to speak to him about it when I get back home tomorrow."

"OK. For your reference, there's a car dealer about half a mile from here. They have a contract with us to provide wheelchair-access vehicles. They offer discount for patients' families."

"Oh, that's really helpful, thank you. I'll go and speak to them when I'm next up here."

"Right, OK. Unless there's anything else? I'm about done for the day."

"No, that's fine. I'll go and see Jimmy. Spend some more time with him before I leave."

"OK, I look forward to seeing you next time you're here. I'm taking the day off tomorrow, so I won't see you. Have a safe journey home. Don't forget you can ring me with any concerns."

"Thank you."

Alison stood and shook the consultant's hand before leaving his office and going downstairs to see Jimmy.

#

They were in the gardens again the following morning. She'd not spoken to Simon on the telephone since she'd been in the north. Nine days without contacting her husband. He'd upset her, and she had no intention of making the first move. He knew where she was, yet he hadn't telephoned the hospital or the Midland Hotel once. This morning she wanted to see how Jimmy would react to her suggestion. Gauge his feelings about moving to London and living with them.

"Jimmy, have you thought about how long you might have to stay in this hospital?"

"Forever. They look after me here. Anyway, I don't know where I live."

"That's what I wanted to discuss with you this morning. How would you feel about moving in with Simon and me in London?"

"Really? That's weird."

"What do you mean 'weird'?"

"Simon is your husband. I thought I would be with you forever, Ali. We share birthdays. We're part of the same soul."

"Oh, Jimmy. Don't say that."

"Why not? It's true."

He pressed his left hand firmly on the joystick of his chair, the tyres flicking the gravel behind him as he sped away. He was looking directly ahead, intentionally avoiding eye contact.

"Jimmy. Wait. Let me explain."

Thankful she was dressed casually in jeans and trainers, she gave chase and caught up with him. Her continued pleas for him to stop as she ran alongside him convinced him to ease up, and he slowed and then stopped.

"Jimmy. Who else can look after you? We spent almost two decades together. It's my duty to help you get back on y.... help you get stronger, help you to remember."

She looked down at him, and he looked up, and they made eye contact. He sat with his arms folded, holding himself tightly, hugging himself in sympathy.

"You don't have to," he whined.

"I know, but I want to, Jimmy. Only I can recall the things we shared in the past."

"Is Simon OK with me moving into your house?"

"He doesn't know yet. I'm going to have a chat with him about it tonight when I get home."

"Oh, right. When would I be moving?"

"Hopefully before Christmas."

"What month is it now?"

"It's Sunday the 10th of October today, Jimmy."

"Is it?"

"Yes. So, in about four or five weeks, you could be saying goodbye to this place forever."

He smiled up at her; he wanted to kiss her. She *knew* he did. She turned away. It was a bad idea. She was adamant she wouldn't be leading him down whichever path he was hoping their relationship would go down. Not now, and not when they will be living together in Highgate.

"How am I going to get to London?" He asked her.

"Don't worry about it. I'll sort it."

"How d'ya mean?"

"Listen, we should go back to your room now. I need to leave. I have a long drive back."

"You're leaving again?" he asked, sulking.

"Yes, I have to. I'll be back soon, though," she said, smiling at him.

He seemed to accept it from her this time and smiled back at her.

"Come on, Jimmy, let's go inside."

As she walked alongside him toward the hospital entrance ramp, she wrestled with the thought of how she would break all this to Simon. Her husband, who allegedly cares, hadn't contacted her since she'd been up here. He'd obviously spat his dummy out that was obvious. Men. As she walked up the ramp toward the hospital door, she looked down at her ex-husband, trundling alongside her. Thirteen years together, and look at what's happened to him, and I have to deal with that. Five years with Simon and his ever-increasing cocaine habit with a propensity for spitting his dummy out probably down to the drug, I don't want to deal with that. It's too much, she worried. Wherever her mind was wandering, she knew she shouldn't really go there. Jimmy *was now* a different person to Jimmy *then*; she understood that completely. The hardest part of having Jimmy live with them for her wouldn't be the work involved in caring for somebody paralysed; it would be trying to hold feelings at bay she knew she'd always had for Jimmy and always would. Could she cope with an old friend, her ex-husband, Simon's best friend from a long time ago, living with them, sharing their home? The prospect of discussing this with Simon and making practical arrangements, such as trading her car for a wheelchair-access vehicle, worried her. She had a nagging doubt that her husband wouldn't be as forthcoming as she was in offering Jimmy the support he needed.

#

Chapter 16

The sweep of her headlights across the front of their home lit up the house in Highgate. She pulled her car onto the driveway just after six in the evening, darkness outside as she stepped through the front door. She was hungry, she was angry, but she was tired. Lunch at Farley Hall earlier felt like a distant memory.

Simon was sitting in the lounge watching television, obviously having enjoyed a lazy Sunday afternoon. He didn't move from his slouched position across the sofa. She dropped her handbag on the kitchen island, and when she stepped into the living room, he didn't avert his gaze from their large television set.

"Hello?" Alison said sarcastically.

"Alright? How's Jimmy?" Simon responded.

"Oh, so you do care?"

"How d'ya mean?"

"Nine days I was away, and you didn't ring me."

"You didn't ring me."

"Oh, so we're playing it like that, are we?"

"What?"

"Brilliant. I've been busy with Jimmy. Why should I have to find the time to ring you?"

"Yeah, well, I was pissed off with you. Fuckin' leaving Friday morning before I got up."

"What do you expect? At least Jimmy was appreciative that I'd gone to visit him."

"Whoopee fuckin' doo. I appreciate you."

"What've you been doing all week?"

"Working."

"Oh yeah, and the rest."

"How d'ya mean?"

"You've been out chasing white lines with those two from work, haven't you?"

"So, what if I have?"

"If you think we can afford it, and I'll put up with it. Fine," she seethed. Alison stood firm, both arms folded across her chest.

Simon bolted upright from his slouched position, standing aggressively in front of her. He seemed infuriated that she'd disturbed his peace.

"Put up with it? Ha, you do what you want, love."

He walked away from her through the lounge; she ignored him and sat on the sofa.

"I'm going the shop; we've no beer left," he shouted from the hallway just before he angrily slammed the front door shut.

She stepped over to their music system and record collection. While she rolled and smoked a joint, she wanted to escape into the music she loved.

She slipped the vinyl record from the sleeve of *A Storm in Heaven,* the first *Verve* album and placed it onto the turntable. The song *Star Sail* began playing as she settled on the sofa before pulling open the coffee table drawer and retrieving her cannabis, tobacco, and cigarette papers.

As she began smoking the first joint she rolled, Alison resigned herself to making more effort with Simon. The effects of smoking cannabis for the first time in over a week mellowed her anger with her husband. Things aren't that bad, are they? She thought it would be great if she could accept Jimmy moving in with us as she exhaled thick smoke across the living room.

She turned the record over to play side two and then lay back down. She knew she would try with her husband, but it was so exhausting at times. She felt sure she could talk Simon around to the idea of Jimmy living with them. The house was big enough. It was a huge place for two, anyway. What she wasn't convinced of was being just a friend to Jimmy. Since the day they'd first met in 1978, she'd felt it. She couldn't stop herself from thinking about him. About the times they spent together in the past. About how much she loved him. She'd listened to music they both adored all the way home from the hospital down to Highgate. Now she was exhausted. She was asleep before side two of the record finished playing.

#

The following day, Simon telephoned home from work during his lunch break. She was glad he'd started the conversation with an apology. They'd repaired any wrongdoing by the end of a call that lasted almost an hour. She'd carefully managed to avoid any discussion of Jimmy being discharged. She promised dinner ready for six thirty and would bring up the subject then.

She made herself a cup of tea and telephoned the car dealer near the hospital. She was pleasantly surprised when she described her current car to the salesman, and he offered her a part exchange for a brand-new wheelchair-access vehicle with affordable monthly repayments. She made a promise to the salesman that she would visit the showroom in person and soon.

Alison laid the table, served the dinner on two plates, and opened a bottle of wine. Her husband was in the shower, having just arrived home from work. He joined her in the dining area, both sitting at the table to eat. Simon poured each a glass of red wine to go with their meal. As they ate dinner, Alison felt the moment was right to talk about Jimmy.

"I had a meeting with the consultant and the other people looking after Jimmy."

"Oh yeah. What about?" Simon sighed.

"All around Jimmy's rehabilitation, really. There was a psychiatrist there, a dietician, a speech therapist and a physio. Oh, and Mr Davies, obviously."

"Did you get much out of 'em? What was said?"

"The psychiatrist was helpful, describing Jimmy's brain injury in ways I could understand."

"Why? Has it changed him much?"

"Oh yes. Apparently, people with brain injuries can say things without thinking or sometimes do things without contemplating their actions."

"Really?"

"Yes. She told me they can be impatient and opinionated. They get frustrated and angry if things aren't 'just so'. If you know what I mean?"

"Yeah, I get it."

"That's why Jimmy needs our support so much. Out in public, he could offend people without intending to."

"Right."

"That psychiatrist says they call brain injury the 'hidden' disability."

"Right, because he doesn't look disabled."

Alison's heart sank when her husband said that, thrusting Jimmy's paralysis into her mind.

"Jimmy will look disabled, babe."

"Why? What else is up with him?"

Simon looked genuinely concerned now. He'd certainly stopped smiling. It convinced Alison to just come out with it.

"He's paralysed."

"He's what!?"

"He's lost the use of his legs. He's going to need a wheelchair for the rest of his life."

The news hit Simon hard. So hard he dropped the fork he was holding. He reached for his wine glass and took a huge gulp, slowly shaking his head.

"Fuckin' hell. What a bastard. He's not having much luck, is he? That's shit that. I feel *really* bad for him now."

"I know. It's horrible."

Simon looked through those large, floor-to-ceiling windows into darkness at nothing in particular. She knew he was thinking of Jimmy and some of the times they'd spent together. She reached across the table with an upturned palm, beckoning him to drop his hand into hers. He did so, and she gripped it firmly, smiling at him as he turned to face her.

"You remember when the three of us used to go to The Hacienda on Thursday nights?"

"Oh yes. Jimmy loved it there, especially if we were all on E."

"I was just thinking then; he used to dance for hours in that place."

"Yes, I know."

Neither of them attempted eye contact; they just gazed through those huge windows, deep in thought about Jimmy. Alison remembered what the psychiatrist said about focusing on the positives.

"Hey, at least he survived the accident and coma. He's doing really well."

"What? Yeah, I know, you're right. What else did they say?"

They both began chewing their way through their meals as the conversation continued.

"Well, he's got an electric wheelchair, so we spent a fair bit of time in the gardens at the hospital. He loved it."

"Yeah, it's good that he can get about, I suppose."

"It is. I wanted to take him to King's Road, see if it helps him remember. Obviously, I couldn't take him in my car."

"Why not?"

"It's not like one of those foldaway wheelchairs, Jimmy's chair. It's fully electric, it's quite a big thing. It doesn't collapse down; it has to go in a vehicle with him sitting in it."

"Oh, right. Has Jimmy got it sussed? Driving it about an' that?"

"Oh yes. It's German-made. He calls it his Panzer."

"Ha, what's he like?"

There was no better chance than this to bring it up. Simon was laughing. It's now or never.

"Mr Davies thinks Jimmy could be discharged before Christmas."

"What, this Christmas?"

"Yes. He's made huge improvements since the first time I saw him."

"Right. Where is he gonna live? Has he got any money?"

"I've no idea about his financial situation; I've not asked. It never seemed important. As far as where he's going to live, I don't know. He has no one else. You know that. There was only his mother left when we split up, and she died of a heart attack not long after."

"Probably why he fucked off abroad."

"Exactly. So, what can he do now?"

"Well, it's not our problem is it, love."

"Not our problem? Well, haven't you changed?"

"What?"

"You two grew up together. You were together the first time I met you. I was in love with Jimmy for the best part of two decades. I can't ignore his predicament, and nor should you."

"What d'ya mean, ignore it?"

"Well, it's obvious. We've got the room; Jimmy should move in with us down here."

Simon stopped everything and looked up from his meal in disbelief, shaking his head.

"No way. We'd have to spend a fuckin' fortune widening doors and putting ramps in."

"No, we wouldn't. It wouldn't cost that much. I'll speak to mum and dad."

"No, you won't. I don't want him here."

"Why not?"

"I just don't."

"That's not fair honey, why not? You don't think I wanna get back with him, do you?"

"You might."

"I won't; I'm happily married to you. Jimmy's different now."

She gave him her best sultry and sexually suggestive look. Straight into his eyes, noticing he was going through the idea in his mind.

"I'll think about it, love."

"OK, it's a start, I suppose."

"Anyway, how would we get him down here?"

"I spoke to the consultant about that as well."

"Oh, so you've been doin' all the organising then?"

"Not really, no. Mr Davies said there is a car dealer not far from the hospital. They have a contract with the hospital to provide them with wheelchair-access vehicles."

"Are they gonna transport Jimmy down here?"

"No, they won't do that. The car dealer offered me a discount. I could trade in my car?"

"Oh no. That's not happenin'. We can't afford a new car."

"Listen, my business is doing well. I'm getting a lot of high-profile work at the moment."

"Yeah, and tending to the patient's needs. What about my fuckin' needs?"

"Oh, right. I get it. So, if I give you a blow job, Jimmy can stay."

"No, but it's a start init."

She hated the crudeness of his last statement, but she was confident her technique in that area would win him around to her way of thinking. Perhaps over the next few days.

#

Chapter 17

It was yesterday when Simon broke the news; he had to be at work. Not only Thursday and Friday but the whole weekend as well. They had a major project deadline to meet, and many staff worked the weekend with him, hoping to land the finished project in time. The news left her feeling pretty angry; no, infuriated. She felt her husband had changed since they'd married, since his major promotion at work. Sometimes it would seep into their home life if he'd had a stressful day working in advertising. Though a verbally aggressive outburst was given little credence, as you would expect from a woman like Alison. He had no response to her usual self-assured, intelligent answers, which frustrated him. It always forced him to go and sit in the study and sulk. The study had become Simon's man cave. He had a music system and a television in there and usually a stash of cocaine which Alison knew nothing about. If she wouldn't 'bite' and argue with him, he would grab some beer from the fridge and run away to his man cave. Which suited her perfectly because she could sit alone in the lounge and listen to the music she loved. She drove away from their home at six thirty on Thursday morning, following her husband out of the house. Simon was in his car spinning his wheels, skidding out of sight before she'd even locked the front door. She was still furious after their last confrontation, which had happened in the kitchen just before they'd left.

After many delays on the motorway, checking in and freshening up at the hotel, Alison didn't arrive at Farley Hall until just after four o'clock that afternoon. When she drove onto the forecourt to park her car in front of the hospital, Mr Davies was just about to get into his car. She pulled up and parked alongside him before switching her ignition off and getting out.

"Alison, hi, you've just caught me."

"Hi, Mr Davies. I'm glad I did; I need you to arrange a meeting with me, you and Jimmy if possible? If you're free, obviously."

"Sure. One second."

He lifted his briefcase from the passenger seat of his car, opened it on the bonnet and retrieved his diary.

"How long are you staying up here?" he queried, scrutinising the pages of his diary.

"Until Tuesday at least. Maybe longer."

"OK, good. We can have a meeting with Jimmy in his room on Monday at two o'clock. I'll make sure we're not disturbed."

"Great. How is he?"

"Getting better every day. His speech is continuing to improve. He seems to have accepted the loss of the use of his legs, with only the occasional emotional outburst, according to the nurses."

"Oh, that's fantastic," Alison enthused.

"Did Simon not travel up with you?"

"No. He let me down. He's needed in work all weekend for a big project."

"I see. Well, I must go. Are you here tomorrow?"

"Of course."

"OK, I'll see you tomorrow."

"Thanks, Mr Davies. See you tomorrow."

Once inside the hospital, she walked through reception smiling and saying 'hi' to a patient's family she recognised before confirming with the receptionist that she could go through and see Jimmy. As she walked along the corridor, the nurse outside his room told her that Jimmy was asleep. She'd expected him to be sleeping at this time of day, and in a way, she was grateful he was. She hadn't stopped since six this morning and needed to eat. Her anger with her husband had slowly subsided on her journey up the motorway; she felt calm and relaxed in the cafeteria as she ordered some food. Before seeing Jimmy, she decided she would visit the car showroom tomorrow and ask about trading in her car for a wheelchair-access vehicle.

When she walked into Jimmy's room, he was just finishing the meal the hospital had prepared for him. The table on wheels was across his legs. His plate was on it, which was now empty, but for the knife and fork, he'd just used. Next to his plate was a little bottle of nutritional supplement milkshake the dietician had prescribed. They'd been mentioned to Alison in the meeting with Jimmy's care team. He'd been prescribed four of these drinks daily to build his body's protein levels. She knew she would have to stock up on them when the day finally came to take Jimmy with her down to Highgate. He looked toward the door when he heard her enter the room.

"Ali. When did you get here?"

"Just after four, you were asleep," she responded as she approached him. They smiled, and she hugged him before pulling a chair next to his bed and sitting down.

"How've you been since we last spoke?"

"Getting better. I feel a lot stronger now."

"Great. I saw Mr Davies when I arrived; he says you're remembering more now."

"Yeah. Loads of little bits. Walking across the bridge to school with Simon."

"Ah, the monkey bridge," she exclaimed

"Of course! That's what we used to call it! I couldn't remember."

"Yes, you did. That bridge is on King's Road, where you used to live, Jimmy."

"I remember. Under that bridge was where we first smoked weed."

"Did you? I didn't know that."

She thought about probing him for anything else he'd remembered.

"What else have you been able to remember?"

"I keep looking at the pictures in that book about The Smiths. Johnny Marr looks so cool; he looks familiar to me. Were we friends?"

"Oh yes. When I saw you again in eighty-three, you told me all about it. How he gave you some help learning to play your guitar. You introduced me to him once; he's a lovely guy."

"Is he?"

"Yes, but we lost touch with him and Morrissey when they both moved down to London."

"Right."

"How do you fancy a ride out to the monkey bridge one day?"

He didn't really need to verbally answer; the child-like enthusiastic smile was enough.

"Oh yes. When?"

"Soon. Once I get my new car, then we can get you out and about in your Panzer."

"You'd do that for me?"

"Yes, of course. It makes me sad you can't remember what we had, Jimmy."

"Well, I know that I've always loved you. I just can't remember why I stopped."

"Oh, Jimmy." Alison fawned toward him, and they kissed.

Their first full-on, romantic, sustained kiss since that day they'd met in this room two months ago. Open-mouthed and tongues exploring became too much for Alison, and she pulled away. They looked into each other's eyes, and she ran.

"I need a cigarette," she said, running out the door.

"Alison. Wait. I'll get the nurse to get my chair," he shouted in vain at a vacant doorway.

#

The journey from the car showroom back to Farley Hall took her ten minutes. She spent the whole of it deep in thought. Thinking about yesterday when they'd kissed. Thinking about what she'd just done, the emotional turmoil she'd stirred up with that kiss, then trading in her saloon car for a larger car you could almost describe as a van. Something to transport Jimmy around in. She was wrestling with an obvious juxtaposition. Although she couldn't care less about her husband right now, she still feared his reaction to what she'd done. This directly opposed her absolute joy, knowing she could drive Jimmy anywhere. They could be together, alone again. To all intents and purposes, as they used to be but with one obvious difference between them, not his ill health and disabilities. She knew why they'd split up. He just couldn't remember. I should tell him one day, she promised herself. Perhaps he would remember it for himself, she feared. I can't tell him; I don't want to upset the apple cart. Jimmy's doing so well; it would be a huge step backwards for him to put him through all that again. Alison mulled over the situation. When she parked her brand-new vehicle in front of the hospital, she didn't immediately move from sitting in the driver's seat; she just looked through the windscreen at Farley Hall, thinking about Jimmy and their life together in the past. Staring at a building that had become so familiar to her during those two lengthy visits here over the last two months. The past was the past, and this was happening right now.

#

Chapter 18

Getting Jimmy into her new vehicle proved straightforward, so they were on the motorway heading towards Manchester by two o'clock that afternoon. A little later, in a queue of six or seven cars, Alison slowed her new vehicle to a stop as the lights changed to red on the A56.

"You OK, Jimmy?"

"Yeah."

"See that big place on the left? That's Stretford Arndale. Do you remember?"

"When you said the name, it sounded familiar. I just don't recognise that building."

"Don't worry; we're only around the corner from your old house now. We'll be there in a couple of minutes."

"Brilliant," Jimmy responded enthusiastically.

The traffic lights changed to green, and Alison edged her vehicle forward, waiting patiently behind a car also turning right. When it moved, she turned and accelerated up the gradient as the road crossed the bridge over the railway line before slowing her new vehicle gently down the slope, indicating left and turning.

"This is the street where you grew up, Jimmy. King's Road."

"Right. These houses are posh Ali."

"I think they're just bigger houses up this end. It's quite a long road."

She spotted the bridge next to the shop on the left, indicating to pull over; she slowed her vehicle to a stop at the side of the road. She was glad it was so quiet, and there were no people on the street. Alison was nervous Jimmy could get into a confrontation with someone if they were in his way, losing his temper with someone they both didn't know.

"There's the bridge you remembered walking across to school with Simon. Let's get out and have a look, shall we?"

"Oh yeah, this looks so familiar to me, Ali," he was smiling at her.

"Good. I'm glad," she said, turning to face him.

She stepped out of her vehicle to open the back doors and lower the ramp for him. He slowly reversed his electric chair out; she stowed the ramp away and locked her car, walking alongside him as he gently accelerated towards the bridge. It was a cold, bracing day. Alison was wrapped in her winter coat and scarf. Jimmy had his coat on with a thick blanket covering his legs.

When they arrived at the bridge, he stopped at three large concrete steps that led up to it.

"Well, I guess I can't go on the bridge anymore."

"No, but does it help you to remember?"

"That fence has been fixed."

"What do you mean?" she questioned him.

"We used to sneak through a gap where the fence was broken and go under the bridge for a smoke. It kept you dry under there if it was raining."

"Well done. Something more that you've remembered. Do you want to see your old house?"

"Oh yeah."

"OK, we'll leave the car here, and we'll walk up. It's only a little bit further."

Oh, Christ, I said *walk*; thank God he didn't seem to notice, she thought. She walked alongside him, keeping to the edge of the pavement, protecting him from swerving into the road. She was holding his right hand in her left as he operated the chair's joystick with his left hand. As soon as they moved away from the bridge, he held his right hand up palm out, demanding she holds onto it. Walking along a pavement, she'd stepped on so many times in the past with him felt strange. She'd never expected to see Jimmy again and certainly not paralysed and in a wheelchair for the rest of his life.

As they approached the house where Jimmy grew up, he accelerated. He was getting the hang of controlling his chair and span around to a stop at the place he'd called home for so long.

"This is my house," he shouted at her happily.

"Jimmy, don't shout. Someone might come out."

"Who?"

"The people who live in the house."

"Oh."

"Yes, it is your house, Jimmy. Number 386. It's great that you remember, isn't it?"

"Yes, it is. I do remember being here, Ali. Lots of little things."

"Terrific. That's brilliant. Well done."

"That's my bedroom above the door, isn't it?"

"It sure is. We spent a lot of time in there when we first got together. Listening to records. Talking and getting to know each other. Just being alone together."

"Yeah."

After that tired response from him, she could sense the day was taking its toll. They hadn't been out long, but she remembered the consultant's words about how tired Jimmy could get.

"You OK?"

"Yeah, just a bit tired."

"Why don't we go and sit in the park?"

"The park? Of course. I remember. Me and Si used to sneak through the back gardens of those houses opposite to get in the park. It used to feel like ages walk…."

His words were stunted by emotion.

She knew he'd wanted to say, 'walking round,' but he couldn't.

Alison saw how much it hurt him, remembering running around these streets herself as a teenager two decades ago. Through no fault of his own, he was now paralysed from the waist down. She stooped down and hugged him, speaking gently into his ear.

"I know, darling. Look how far you've come. You couldn't speak when I first saw you."

She pulled away from him, and he smiled.

"Yeah, you're right."

"Come on then. Tell me what you used to get up to in the park."

"Football with Simon loads. We used to bunk off school and smoke joints there when we were older, when we were in our last year at school, I think?"

"Yes, it was. You and I shared a joint in the park. Once your mother was fine with me sleeping over at your house."

"Yeah, we did. I remember. In a bunch of trees near a slide, I think?"

"Yes. You're right, Jimmy. Well done. Hey, shall we revisit our old haunt then?"

"Can we?"

"Yes, why not. We need to go up to the Quadrant to get in the park."

"Oh, the roundabout. The pub. I remember."

"Brilliant, well done. OK, let's go then. Careful crossing this road, OK?"

"Yeah, don't worry," he shot across the quiet, empty road, and she followed him.

When they entered the park, Jimmy confidently took control of the situation. It made Alison smile; she knew he remembered these things for himself instead of agreeing with her recollections. She was glad the park was empty. No chance encounter with a member of the public. She was worried Jimmy could say something, his first time in public with an acquired brain injury.

"Follow me. I know where it is," he said as he clicked the stick on his chair forward and headed for the trees between the play area and the houses on King's Road.

"OK, wait for me," she pleaded, hurrying to catch up with him.

He stopped his chair and turned to face her next to an old, established oak tree with a worn horizontal branch two feet from the floor. Alison sat on the branch, Jimmy facing her.

"I remember us coming here, Ali, after seeing The Smiths at The Hacienda. We sat on that branch. We smoked a joint and snogged for ages," he was smiling.

"Yes, we did. I can't believe you're actually remembering it yourself. Well done. It was the next time I saw you and the first time we went to see The Smiths *together*. November eighty-three. Sixteen years ago, Jimmy, can you believe that? You phoned me at my parents' house in London, telling me you had two tickets Johnny had given you. Your mum said it was OK for me to sleep at your house that night."

"Oh yeah, of course. It was incredible that gig; I think I can remember it?"

"Yes, they were incredible that night. One of the best times we've seen them, I think."

"Really?"

"Oh yes, we spent a couple of hours here talking about that gig. We didn't get back to your house until two in the morning, as I recall."

"Right," he responded slowly.

"What's wrong, darling? You OK?"

"Yeah, I'm just tired."

"Is all this too much for you?"

"Yes, but I'm glad we came here. Thanks. I just feel drained now. Tell me about the night we went to our first Smiths gig together. How old was I?"

"You were twenty, and I was nineteen. OK honey, you close your eyes and rest, and I'll tell you what happened."

It was cathartic for her to speak out loud about their past experience. She watched him in his chair as she spoke, his eyeballs moving frantically underneath his closed and sleeping eyelids. He'd obviously fallen asleep and was dreaming.

#

Chapter 19

November 1983

Jimmy was standing on the platform when the intercity train slowed to a stop in front of him. It was dark outside, but the station was brightly illuminated by huge lamps suspended from the ceiling. He immediately saw Alison with one large suitcase on wheels stepping from a carriage three away from the one in front of him. She looked over and saw Jimmy and began running toward him, pulling her suitcase on wheels behind her.

"Jimmy."

"Hiya Ali, you OK?"

"I am now."

"Me too."

They embraced and began kissing passionately as multitudes of people spewed from the train, rushing past the couple who only had eyes for each other. He was cold from standing around and appreciated the warmth she offered as he held her close. They couldn't afford to hang around, and time was against them, so they ran out of the station to get the bus to Stretford. They only stayed at Jimmy's long enough to eat the meal his mother had prepared, and they were back on the bus into Manchester by half past seven.

They didn't expect to see what greeted them as they walked down Whitworth Street towards the Hacienda. Hundreds of people were on the street outside the venue, much more than the place could hold. They were thankful that Johnny had given them two tickets; it was sold out.

Once they got inside, they could relax until The Smiths came onto the stage. When they did, the place was full, and there were cheering Mancunians everywhere. Johnny had told them they'd just got back from London after recording their first ever *Top of the Pops* appearance today. Jimmy said it was like your football team coming home after winning the cup.

The Smiths started the concert by playing *Handsome Devil*. Jimmy and Alison spent most of it locked in a passionate embrace, only coming up for air to cheer as the group finished playing that first song. When the second song, *Still Ill* started, they began bouncing up and down with the rest of the crowd packed into this quite small venue. Everybody was singing the words they'd learned from listening to the radio sessions the group had recorded in London and buying the two singles they'd released.

When Alison looked around the crowd, she noticed how many people were singing or smiling, exuding love for a group from their city. A group that was so original and so unique. Born from the immigration of the Irish to the city in the 1950s.

The jumping up and down continued when *This Charming Man* followed next. Jimmy and Alison held hands or held each other as they bounced around, watching and hearing a group; they both loved to play a song they both loved, with a singer Jimmy had grown up living next door to. They'd both been to the Hacienda to see groups play before, usually together. She'd never seen this place so packed before. It was incredible.

For the rest of the concert, neither of them really stopped smiling. Alison attentively studied *Morrissey's* every move, impressed by his command of the stage and the audience. Jimmy spent a good portion of the concert on his tiptoes, watching *Johnny Marr*, trying to work out how he was making those sounds.

The concert was everything Jimmy and Alison hoped it would be and more. The group were on stage for an hour, yet it passed them by in a flash. At the end, they played Jimmy's favourite song, Accept Yourself, before playing their debut single, *Hand in Glove*, for a second time. When that song finished, they were gone. Throughout those last two songs, Jimmy and Alison had watched *Morrissey* at the edge of the stage, leaning over into the crowd and singing to them as though his life depended on it. In all honesty, it probably did. It was *the* love song for him. It was *the* love song for Jimmy and Alison.

And I'll probably never see you again.

As they looked lovingly into each other's eyes, they both knew at that moment had she not travelled up to Manchester to see The Smiths play here four months ago, then they, too, would have probably never seen each other again.

The Smiths left the stage triumphant and to rapturous applause and cheering. Jimmy and Alison saw it as a good opportunity to get outside before the rest of the crowd. There seemed no point in hanging around anyway. There would be a cavalcade of hangers-on around the group backstage, so they wouldn't get a chance to speak to Morrissey or Johnny anyway. They were in the open air of Whitworth Street in less than a minute, both elated and smiling.

When the pair arrived back at King's Road, it was almost midnight, and Jimmy's mother went straight to bed, knowing they were home safe. Jimmy gave it ten minutes before opening and closing the front door behind them as gently and as quietly as he could. If his mother woke up and caught them sneaking out, they'd be trouble.

He had his weed, cigarettes and a lighter in his pocket. He'd just seen *The Smiths* play a triumphant homecoming concert at the Hacienda; with a girl he loved. Life couldn't get any better.

In the park wearing thick winter coats, scarves and woolly hats, they lay next to each other on the hard ground by the tree with the low horizontal branch. Jimmy had taken his time to roll a long joint for them to share. He offered it to Alison.

"No, you start it, darling," she said.

She cuddled her head into his chest as he lay on his back. He put the joint to his lips, lit it with the lighter he had with him, and sucked in smoke as the end of the joint glowed brightly like a solitary firefly in the park at night. He relaxed his head back onto the firm ground, slowly exhaling all that smoke up to the heavens, before stating:

"Fuckin' hell, did you see Johnny? The lad's a genius. I struggle to work out what he plays, sitting in my bedroom concentrating. He was dancin' about tonight. Still sounded amazin'."

"Yes, he looked like he was really enjoying himself. They all did. Even Steven, though we're supposed to call him Morrissey now, aren't we?"

"Yeah, it's what he wants init. Are your ears ringing?"

"Yes, they are. Do you think that concert was better than the July one?"

"Oh yeah. More songs and they seem more confident now. They were amazin' tonight. Easily the best concert I've been to."

"Oh yes, me too."

Neither of them knew what time it was. Neither of them cared what time it was. They lay next to each other in a stoned state, symbiotically sharing body heat. Both basking in very recent memories of Jimmy's next-door neighbour and his group playing a concert at the Hacienda. A concert that neither of them would ever forget.

#

September 1999

Alison had spent the latter part of the afternoon subconsciously helping Jimmy to remember, occasionally slipping into a nostalgia fuelled daydream herself. As he'd slept, she'd continued to verbalise her memories of a night sixteen years ago when they were so close and so much in love. She felt completely in love with him now, as a thirty-five-year-old. It was impossible for her not to be affected by this. Recollecting their relationship in the hope Jimmy can remember one day was dangerously close to imparting a Florence Nightingale effect on her. Still, she knew it was much deeper than that with Jimmy. She had no intention of leaving Simon; they'd been through so much sorrow together. You can't walk out on your husband. Behave yourself. Jimmy's disabled; what sort of relationship would that be? Could that be? Her thoughts clouded with worries, fears and indecision as she checked her wristwatch. It was almost six o'clock in the evening, and her heart began to beat fast, worrying about getting Jimmy back to the hospital.

"Jimmy. We need to go," she said intentionally loudly, waking him from his sleep.

His eyes flickered open, and he rubbed them with both hands.

"I was dreaming about being at a Smith's concert with you."

"Really? You sure you're not just saying that because of what I've been telling you."

"No, I was asleep."

"OK, OK. I believe you. I guess Mr Davies was right; I *am* helping you to remember. Bringing you here has really helped, hasn't it?" she questioned. She reassured herself, as much as Jimmy, that everything she'd done since he'd come back into her life had been the right thing to do.

"Oh aye," he said, smiling.

Alison leaned over and gave him a hug.

She worried the love they once had was informing her current feelings toward him, and she was in danger of getting lost in it. When the organised and proactive element of her personality got a grip on the situation, she pulled away. She stood straight with the need to get Jimmy back to the hospital nagging at her.

"Come on. We should get going."

"Oh, OK then."

"We've got to get back to Farley Hall. They'll be wondering where we are. It's gone six."

It was almost six thirty when she'd gotten him into the vehicle and driven along the A-road to the motorway. When they arrived back, it was just after seven in the evening. She followed Jimmy up the ramp through the hospital's front entrance and into the reception area. The receptionist who greeted them on their return was the first to speak.

"Hi, Jimmy. Hi, Alison. We weren't expecting you to be this late back."

"I know. My fault. We got a bit lost in our memories at the park near Jimmy's old house in Stretford," Alison explained to the receptionist.

"It's fine. I'll buzz the nurses on the ward to come and get Jimmy and get him into bed. Oh, Alison, your husband rang three times while you were out."

"My phone's battery died while we were out. Can I use your phone to ring him?"

"Sure. I'll help the nurses with Jimmy. Give you some privacy."

"Thanks."

She waited briefly until the receptionist, and the nurses took Jimmy away to his room. Sitting alone on the chair behind the desk in reception, she dialled the number of their home in Highgate.

"Hello?"

"It's me."

"Where've you been 'til this time?"

"Over to King's Road with Jimmy."

"You've traded in your car, haven't you? The girl on reception told me."

"Yes, I have. I told you. It's my car, Simon."

"So why didn't we talk about it first?"

She could sense the anger in his voice, but she was tired; the day had drained her.

"Look, we'll talk about it tomorrow night, OK. I'm going to go and see Jimmy. I need to get back to The Midland for an evening meal and a soak in the bath. I'm exhausted."

"Right. So, you're coming home tomorrow, then?"

"Yes. I'll set off from the hotel in the morning."

"Right. I'll be home usual time."

The line went dead before she had a chance to respond. She slammed the receiver down.

"Imbecile" she muttered.

She was thankful nobody was in reception to witness her frustration with her husband.

#

Chapter 20

When Alison arrived home in Highgate, she parked her new vehicle on the driveway. She stepped inside their home, walked through to the kitchen, and flicked the kettle on. She was expecting her husband home from work in a couple of hours. After she'd prepared the evening meal and put it in the oven, she sat on an armchair in the lounge, facing the large bi-folding glass doors that gave an uninterrupted view of their large, lush back garden. She heard his car pull onto the driveway. She knew he was still angry from the ferocity with which he slammed their front door shut.

"All right," he bellowed from the hallway before stepping into the kitchen.

"You're in a cheery mood, love" she smiled, intentionally mocking him as she stood up and walked over to the kitchen island.

There was no way she would allow her husband's aggressive attitude to spoil her elated mood. She'd spent the journey home mentally preparing herself for Jimmy's move from the hospital to come and live here.

Simon dropped his briefcase down aggressively and with such force that it slid across the kitchen island before dropping onto the kitchen floor with a loud leathery slap. He pulled his cigarette packet and lighter from his trouser pocket, put a cigarette to his lips and lit it before throwing his lighter onto the island.

"So that's what you've traded your car in for, is it?" he asked, facing her, thumbing behind himself toward the driveway at the front of their home.

"Yes," she responded icily.

"Well, you can take it back to the dealer when you're next up there and get your car back."

"I will not," Alison retaliated.

Infuriated with his attitude, she walked away from him in silence across the open plan layout of their home, standing facing the glass doors at the back of the house. She picked up her cigarette from the ashtray and her lighter from the coffee table. She took a much-needed drag to quell her anger toward her husband.

"I haven't finished with you," he threatened, approaching her angrily from behind.

She turned to face him but wasn't expecting so much aggression. Standing in front of her, he swept the back of his right hand across her face. He caught her jaw firmly, knocking the cigarette between her lips to the floor. Grabbing her by the throat, a loud bang and rattle were made as he pushed her back against the large windows. Had she been a bigger woman, the window would have shattered with the force he used to push her.

The choking sensation she felt didn't last. She was shocked and reacted quickly, using the palms of both her hands to push him hard in the chest. He stumbled backwards and fell, a loud crack as the back of his head forcefully hit the solid oak floor. She stepped quickly past him as he lay dazed on the floor, holding the back of his head, shouting at him as she hurried past.

"Sort your own tea out! Arsehole!"

She raced upstairs, quickly packed a bag and ran back down, slamming the front door shut loudly before he could compose himself. She knew he wouldn't chase after her. She reversed off their driveway before slamming the vehicle into first gear and revving the engine loudly. She drove away from their home infuriated, shocked, and upset by her husband's behaviour.

She went straight to her best friend Tracy's house in Crouch End. When she opened the front door, Tracy was surprised to see Alison standing in front of her, visibly upset.

"Hi, Ali, what's up?"

"My fucking husband."

"Oh, right. Come in; it's cold out." Tracy smiled warmly, inviting her friend inside.

Alison followed Tracy along the hallway towards the kitchen before continuing.

"I traded my car in yesterday, Trace."

"Right, and Simon's blown his top?"

"Worse than that."

"What? Go through."

Alison walked into the lounge with her best friend behind her. Tracy sat on the armchair facing Alison, who sat down on the sofa. She lit a cigarette, passing one to her friend.

"Thanks, Ali. What's he done?" She asked.

"He cracked me across the jaw with the back of his hand, grabbed me by the throat and pushed me into the windows at the back of our house," Alison stated angrily.

"He what?! Shit. You, OK? Did he hurt you?"

"My face stings a bit; I'm OK, though. I was just shocked, to be honest. Telling me, I had to take it back and get my old car."

"What? He needs to get out of the fifties he does if he thinks you're gonna put up with a husband with that attitude towards his wife."

"I know. His career is changing him, Trace. The amount of coke he's shoving up his nose is changing him too."

"Really?"

"Yes. It's turning him into an arrogant arsehole. That's not the guy I married, Trace."

"What are you going to do?"

"I don't know. He's got worse since Jimmy came back into our lives."

"He's jealous. Probably worried you're gonna get back with Jimmy."

"Maybe?"

"I don't think you've ever stopped loving Jimmy, have you?"

"No, and Jimmy's never hit me either. I can't remember if we ever argued, to be honest, Trace. Maybe it's just nostalgia, but since Jimmy came back into my life, I've been thinking a lot about my wedding day with him."

"Have you?"

"Oh yeah."

"When did you get married?"

"20th of September eighty-six. Two days after our birthday. Jimmy was twenty-three. I was twenty-two."

"Aw. I'm guessing it was a good day?"

"Yeah. We were lucky with the weather. Jimmy's mother was insistent we get married at her church. We've only small families, Jimmy and I, so we didn't have many attending at the church. We had the evening do at the social club where Jimmy's mum goes; it's only around the corner from her house."

"Were there more people at the evening do?"

"Oh yeah. Reni came, obviously, his two brothers. Even Reni's mother turned up with them. Well, she was bound to. She likes a drink, that woman."

"Really?"

"Oh yeah. She brought those three up herself. It's no wonder she turned to drink."

"Ha, ha. Was it a good night?"

"Oh, it was brilliant, Trace. Jimmy made a speech; he was so happy. I was so happy."

"Aw, that's so sweet."

"Even Johnny and Angie turned up. That really made the night special for Jimmy and I."

"Really? Wow! I know how you both feel about that group."

"Yeah. It was all Johnny's doing, really, but we were quite lucky in that respect."

"How d'ya mean?"

"Well, they'd been touring America that summer. The last gig of the tour was on the tenth of September, so they'd only flown back to England the weekend before our wedding."

"That was fortunate."

"Yeah. I'd rang Angie and given her the date of our wedding, but Jimmy and I didn't think they would actually show up."

"I guess you and Jimmy got on well with Angie and Johnny?"

"Oh yeah. It was lovely to see them there. Even Morrissey showed up later on."

"Really? He's not one for goin' out socialising, is he?"

"Ha, ha. No, he isn't."

"Did your parents go?"

"Oh yeah. Didn't stay long at the social club in Stretford, though."

"Really?"

"Oh yeah. Especially when they met Reni and his older brothers. They're football hooligans who follow United. My parents didn't pay a penny towards the wedding either. If the split hadn't happened and Jimmy and I were together, they still wouldn't be talking to me."

"No way? They disliked Jimmy that much?"

"Yeah. Simon's obviously a different person. When my father got to know him and see how he was progressing confidently through promotions at work and earning big money, it convinced my parents to try and re-establish a relationship with me."

"Your parents like Simon, then?"

"Oh yeah. They bought the house for us, didn't they."

"Simon was there for you, wasn't he, when Jimmy left the country after what happened."

"Yes, I know."

"Has Jimmy remembered why you split up?"

"No, but I'm going to tell him at some point?"

"Are you?"

"Yes. I'd rather tell him, Trace. If he remembers what happened of his own accord, he could hate me as much as he did when it happened."

"Oh, I doubt that."

"I'd rather tell him myself anyway. The brain injury has changed his personality. He can get angry quite easily. It'll be easier if I tell him on my own terms."

"I'm surprised about Simon's reaction to you helping Jimmy so much. They grew up together, didn't they?"

"Yeah. They've known each other since infant's school. I honestly thought Simon would be as keen as me to help Jimmy."

"Didn't they have a big fight, though, when Jimmy found out what had happened?"

"Yes. Worst mistake I ever made."

"You can't blame yourself, Ali; you were both off your heads on E. Simon's more at fault than you are. He knew exactly what he was doing."

"Do you think so? Well, it's all in the past now, isn't it? I still wish it had never happened."

"It's pretty unbelievable. Jimmy doesn't remember any of it happening. Must have been a horrible accident he was involved in. To wipe out all of his memories like that."

"Yeah, must have been horrific."

"I guess it's a complicated thing, the human brain. It's incredible he's doing so well when you consider what he's been through."

"It's his legs and being in a wheelchair. It's so hard to get my head around Trace."

"Yeah. Well, I didn't wanna bring it up. It must be horrible for you. It's you that spent all those years with him. Ya know, when he was able-bodied. Sorry, Ali."

"Ah, it's OK. I know what I'm getting into with Jimmy. I have to do it. He has no one else."

"He's no idea how lucky he is having you on his side."

"Aw, thanks, Trace. Means a lot, you saying that. Jimmy has no one else to turn to."

"No family?"

"All he had left was his mother as far as I knew when we divorced. When I got that call out of the blue in September from a nurse at the hospital where Jimmy is, she told me his mother had died of a heart attack near Christmas ninety-four."

"Oh, right. You really are all he's got. What are you gonna do about Simon, though?"

"God, I don't know. Stick kettle on Trace. I've a lot of thinking to do."

"Have you convinced Simon to let Jimmy live down here with you?" Tracy shouted from the kitchen.

"No, not yet. The consultant up at the hospital said Jimmy can be discharged before Christmas if there's a home care package in place for him," Alison shouted back as Tracy came in.

"That'd be great, wouldn't it, Ali? Big New Year's Eve this year. A new century begins."

Alison smiled at her friend, taking a much-needed drag on her cigarette.

Tracy's home telephone didn't ring once. If Alison was expecting her husband to ring, he'd decided against it. Though she was sure, he would come grovelling back to her tomorrow. He would know where she was. There was no way that she would make the first move after her husband had attacked her with such forceful aggression in their own home. Bastard.

#

Chapter 21

Saturday 12ᵗʰ July 1986

Everyone important in Alison's life made it to her graduation. She'd studied for the first year of her photography degree in London before transferring her studies north to complete her second and third years at the highly acclaimed Manchester University. Jimmy attended the graduation with his mother, and his best friend Simon sat to his right. Alison's parents boarded an early flight from London to Manchester on the morning of the celebrations. They just made it for the start of the ceremony at Whitworth Hall, on the campus of the University, at precisely one o'clock. Jimmy's mother sat between her son and Alison's parents, who had the two seats at the end of the row. It was advisable Jimmy didn't sit next to Alison's parents, preventing any potential arguments from spoiling her precious day. All the graduating students sat on the other side of the hall, and Alison smiled nervously, looking across at her family, particularly at her one true love, Jimmy.

The University Chancellor stepped up to the lectern and microphone, a lone voice inside the huge historic hall. You could hear a pin drop. An expected silence from an audience of graduating students and their proud parents. Following the speech, as each student's name was called, they made their way to the stage to rapturous applause and cheering.

When a man took to the lectern and began speaking into the microphone, Jimmy recognised him as Alison's lecturer, whom he'd met once or twice.

"It must be Ali's turn. That's her lecturer," Jimmy announced.

"Is it?" Simon asked for clarification.

"Yeah," Jimmy replied quietly, and the man began speaking into the microphone.

I am delighted to announce a number of prizes. Firstly, in Photography, the departmental award for highest achievement goes to Alison Wells.

Applause. Cheering. As Alison walked up to the stage to receive her award, Anthony and Joan began applauding their daughter's achievement. To the right of them, the Smiths from Stretford. Isobel Smith proudly clapped and smiled, her son and his best friend with arms aloft cheering loudly. Jimmy's heart was bursting with pride as he watched her receive the award she so richly deserved. This recognition offered Alison a life full of promise.

The empty front three rows of seats across the width of the hall were reserved for students who'd just received their awards. The families had to sit through the entire graduation ceremony before they could meet up with their son or daughter to congratulate them. Alison sat elated, a huge weight of responsibility lifted from her shoulders. Three years of hard work and application had paid off. As she sat down, she turned around to make eye contact with Jimmy halfway up the hall in his seat on the fourteenth row.

She mouthed the words; *I love you.*

Jimmy responded; she knew exactly what he'd say.

Part of the same soul, babe.

She smiled back at him and said the same, knowing he always wanted the best for her.

Part of the same soul.

She blew him a kiss, and he caught it, pressing it close to his heart, smiling back at her.

The ceremony eventually drew close, and parents and families were directed from the building into the blazing sunshine on Oxford Road. Many families had met up with their graduating sons and daughters, congregating on the open grass across the road.

As Alison walked from the main entrance onto Oxford Road, she noticed her parents standing with Jimmy's mother on the pavement across the road. Jimmy and Simon had chosen to sit on the grass away from them, smoking cigarettes as they waited for Alison to emerge. Rented mortar board and gown returned, she looked smart in her own clothes she'd bought especially for the day. She walked across the road, her parents embracing her immediately. Jimmy stood up to speak to her.

"Did you get some photographs done?" he inquired.

She parted her embrace with her mother, turning to face Jimmy. She held him close. As tightly as she had ever held him.

"Oh yes. They post them out to your home address," Alison replied.

"Where we goin' to celebrate?" Simon asked, standing up and stamping on the butt of his cigarette. He really wanted a pint.

"I don't know. A load of 'em are going into town. Where should we go? Mum? Dad?"

"We can't stay, Alison. We have a flight to catch. We wanted to see you graduate. We've done that," her father sternly announced.

Jimmy didn't hide his annoyance at the statement, turned to face Simon and rolled his eyes. He was furious with them. He knew Alison would be hurt by their selfish actions.

"Are you not coming for a drink to celebrate Joan?" Isobel asked Alison's mother.

"We have to get back, Isobel. Sorry." Joan Wells replied sharply.

"Oh, OK. Your loss, I suppose," Isobel said sarcastically.

As proud as Anthony Wells was of his daughter, he didn't want to be there celebrating his daughter's success. Sharing her with a family, he looked down upon. Despite being from Altrincham, the Mancunian sarcasm was lost on him. He felt he was living in a different world from Jimmy and his mother, who were proudly and resolutely working class.

"I'm going to ring a taxi to take us to the airport," Anthony Wells said aloud to no one in particular after spotting a telephone box a few yards up the road.

He walked away from everyone, his wife tottering behind him in her heels.

"Dad. Wait," Alison said, chasing after her parents up Oxford Road.

Jimmy stood on the pavement with his mother and best friend, Simon. He wanted to punch Alison's father for hurting her. Nobody was smiling until Simon spoke aloud.

"What a pair o' wankers." Simon said, laughing.

"They don't like us, do they? They don't like me; I know that much."

"They do, Jimmy; they just don't like mixing with the ordinary folk. They think they're something special, and they're not," Isobel suggested, but Jimmy knew better.

"They've got an over-inflated sense of their own self-importance, them two," Simon said.

"Ha, ha. Brilliant. Nice one Si," Jimmy agreed.

"Well, it's true init. Fuck 'em."

"Simon! Language." Isobel rebuked.

"Sorry, Mrs Smith."

"You'll be seeing more of them if you and Alison get married," Isobel suggested.

"I won't."

"You will; yer mam's right," Simon agreed, winking at his best friend.

As her parent's taxi pulled away from the curbside, everyone waved as they drove away towards the airport. Jimmy, his mother, Alison and Simon began walking down Oxford Road towards Manchester city centre. They stopped outside a pub halfway down the road, all its doors and windows open with loud music coming from inside, clearly audible over the traffic noise.

"They're playin' Rise by P.I.L. Top tune. We should go here," Jimmy suggested.

Simon noticed the writing above the entrance.

Beer Garden at rear.

"Yeah, defo Jim. They've got a beer garden at the back."

"OK, let's go and get a drink," Alison agreed.

"Yes. A drink to celebrate your achievements, Alison. Well done," Isobel said proudly.

"Oh, thanks, Mrs Smith," Alison replied and hugged her.

"Isobel please, Alison," Jimmy's mother suggested.

"Sorry. Isobel," smiled Alison looking fondly at Jimmy's mother. Recognising the decent, honest, uncomplicated, and hard-working woman she was.

"Come on, darling," Jimmy said, holding open his palm so they could hold hands as they entered the pub.

Simon said he would organise the drinks from what looked like a very busy bar area so that Jimmy, his mother and Alison could find a vacant table in the beer garden.

"I'll go and help Si," Jimmy suggested once they'd found a free table with seats.

Inside the pub, the two lads chatted while waiting to be served.

"You got that ring, Jim?" Simon asked.

"Oh, aye. As soon as we get these drinks to 'em, mate, I'm going to ask her."

"Nice one."

They sat at a table in the beer garden with their drinks, celebrating Alison's achievement.

"Well done, Ali. You worked really hard. You deserve it, love," Simon said sincerely.

"Yes, well done, Alison. I'm sure Jimmy is as proud of you as I am. As your parents are."

"Thanks, Isobel. Thanks, Si. Jimmy?" Alison queried.

He wasn't looking in their direction or facing the table where they were sitting. Instead, fiddling with something in his pocket. He turned to face everyone at the table. Then, looking directly at Alison, he held her left hand in his and dropped down onto one knee. She pulled her hand away from his, placing both hands up to her face in shock and embarrassment.

She knew what was coming, even though she'd had no inclination that this would be happening today. Everyone in the beer garden stopped what they were doing when Jimmy got down on one knee. He looked up at her face as he began speaking gently and wholeheartedly.

"I'm so proud of you, darling. Well done. Alison Wells...will you marry me?"

Jimmy had only told Simon and kept this news from everyone else. Isobel Smith was as shocked as Alison when she heard her son say that. She began to cry. Alison began crying, but not before she'd responded.

"Of course, yes, Jimmy! I love you."

He placed the ring on her finger and stood up, Alison standing with him, tears streaming down her face. Everyone in the beer garden cheered, whooped, and began clapping, congratulating the pair.

"I love you so much, Alison," Jimmy said, smiling proudly.

They parted their embrace so his best friend could shake hands with Jimmy and hug Alison.

"Congratulations, mate. Nice one," Simon said.

"Oh, Jimmy, Alison. Congratulations. When did you decide this, son? When are you thinking of getting married?" Isobel asked.

"I've not thought about it, mam. I wasn't sure if Ali would say yes."

"You weren't sure? Really?" Alison asked, perplexed.

"Well, I don't know, do I?" Jimmy said, embarrassed.

"Jimmy, I've always loved you. We could have a triple celebration in September. Get married near our birthday. What do you think?"

"September? That's a bit soon, isn't it?" Isobel asked concernedly, wondering how such an event could be organised in so little time.

"That's a top idea, Ali; let's plan it for September," Jimmy agreed, delighted with the idea.

He started bouncing on his toes, full of excitement. It was poetically flawless when they instantly recognised Johnny Marr's guitar playing coming from the speakers in the beer garden.

"Perfect! The new Smith's single! Now that's timing, that is," Jimmy announced delightedly.

Laughter, smiles and happiness at their table in the beer garden as *Bigmouth Strikes Again*, the newly released *Smith's* single, provided the soundtrack to their celebrations.

#

Chapter 22

Saturday 20ᵗʰ September 1986

When Jimmy and Alison looked into each other's eyes as they pronounced man and wife inside the church, they smiled and began kissing passionately.

Marriage. Unity. Together forever. Two parts of the same soul united. Things they both knew anyway; it just meant that it was official in the eyes of the Lord.

As they entered the Stretford social club in the evening, the uneasy looks from Alison's parents made Jimmy and Simon laugh out loud. They both knew her parents would make up some excuse and leave early. They didn't leave immediately, but when Reni turned up with his brothers and their passive, aggressive demeanour, talking of travelling to Goodison Park tomorrow with the rest of the United hooligans, Anthony and Joan Wells had seen enough. It was entirely a working-class celebration, which Jimmy's mother was very proud of.

When Johnny and Angie Marr came into the room later, they immediately approached Jimmy and Alison.

"Congratulations, you two and well done with your degree Ali. Oh, and happy birthday to you both as well," Angie said, smiling, gently hugging each of them.

"Oh wow! Thanks for coming, you two. Means a lot," Alison replied.

Everybody hugged each other, and everyone was smiling. Alison and Angie had always got on well; they found it hilarious that they shared their birthday with their spouse. Alison and Jimmy were saddened they couldn't attend Johnny and Angie's wedding last year, as they had tied the knot whilst on tour in America in June.

"Thank you. I guess we timed it right for you, Johnny. We only said September because we wanted to get married close to our birthday," Alison stated.

"Yeah, you did. We only flew back to England last weekend. We've a few weeks off before we start the British tour," Johnny explained.

"When does that start?" Jimmy asked.

"First date's in October, Monday the 13ᵗʰ. Carlisle, I think?"

"Right. Does that mean you'll be on tour when it's your and Angie's birthday?"

"Nah, no way. The last gigs at the Free Trade Hall, on the 30th."

"Buzzin. The day before," Jimmy said, smiling.

"Exactly. I'll get you and Ali on the guest list for the tour."

"Thanks, Johnny," Alison interrupted.

"Hey, no worries, guys."

Simon approached from the bar carrying a pint. He'd caught the back end of the conversation. Everyone knew he didn't share Jimmy and Alison's obsession with The Smiths. He'd certainly never understood what Morrissey was all about.

"Is Morrissey coming down? I've heard he doesn't go out?" Simon questioned, smirking.

He knew Morrissey's propensity to stay indoors and never go out was well documented.

"I spoke to him on the phone this morning, said he'd try and come down," Johnny informed the three of them.

"Oh really? I hope he does. Jimmy and I haven't spoken to him in ages," Alison replied.

Isobel Smith sat with her friends from Stretford on the other side of the room, proud of whom her son had chosen to marry. Everyone heard her shout under the influence of alcohol as Morrissey's mother entered the room.

"Liz!"

"Isobel, hi. How was it?" Elizabeth Dwyer asked.

"Oh, terrific. I couldn't stop crying, love."

"No, I understand. You've had such loss in your life. It's a great day for you and your son."

"It is. Thanks, Liz. I knew you'd understand."

"Steven. Come and say hello to Isobel."

Morrissey appeared from the comfort blanket of standing behind his mother. He held out his hand as he spoke to Isobel.

"Congratulations, Mrs Smith," he said coyly.

"Thank you, Steven. Jimmy and Alison are over there with Johnny and Angie. You should go and congratulate them."

"Yes, of course. Mother, are you OK here with Isobel?"

"Yes, son. Go and say hello to your friends."

Morrissey began walking across the room, all eyes upon him. As he walked across that open dancefloor, everyone stared. People elbowed each other, nodding toward him. The younger people in the room, mouths agape. The older generation of bitter-drinking males just confused by him.

Jimmy approached him alone before he reached the group of friends. They looked at each other. Morrissey, who was actually smiling, was the first to say something.

"Well, Jimmy, look at you. Did it go well?"

"Oh yes. We're Mr and Mrs Smith now."

"Yes. I hope it lasts." Morrissey said, laughing.

"Of course, it will. Congratulations on your continued success, by the way. Johnny has been telling us you've only just returned from America."

"Yes."

"How was that?"

"Odd. Very odd. Difficult to find food when you refuse to eat dead animals."

"I'm sure. Come and meet my wife."

Jimmy felt so proud, so happy tonight. Now that he was married to Alison, the two most important musicians in his life had just turned up to pass on their best wishes for the future. The conversation bored Simon, who was getting drunker with each passing minute. He wandered away to go and speak to Reni and his brothers about fighting.

The five friends continued to talk about life, marriage, music, Manchester and The Smiths. They'd always gotten on well before the group became successful. Jimmy said to Alison in front of those three friends.

"This is the happiest day of my life Ali."

"It's the happiest day of mine too, darling."

"Part of the same soul." The pair chorused together, so much in love with each other.

#

November 1999

The morning after Alison arrived at Tracy's house, they sat in the lounge, drinking tea and chatting about her dilemma. There was a loud knock at the front door; Alison suspected it might be Simon. When Tracy stood up, walked along the hallway, and answered the door, Alison heard the familiar voice of her husband.

"Is she here? That thing she's bought is parked outside your house."

"She's here; come in," Tracy said, doing her best to look disinterested.

He closed the front door and followed Tracy into the lounge. Alison was standing in the centre of the room, prepared for battle. She didn't say anything.

"I'm sorry, love." Simon pleaded from his position just inside the lounge doorway. He sensibly avoided moving closer to Alison.

"Are you?"

"Of course."

"You've never hit me before."

"I know, I know, and I'm sorry."

"We need to talk," she said, turning to her friend.

"Trace, I'm gonna go for a walk with him. Shouldn't be too long."

"OK, no worries. I'll see you in a bit."

Alison grabbed her coat and brushed past Simon.

"Come on, you, there's a park five minutes' walk from here." she commanded.

He followed her lead, walking the street away from Tracy's house.

They arrived at the Priory Road entrance to the park, her in absolute silence and Simon using the walk to continue his apology, his pleading.

"I should never have hit you, Ali. I'm so sorry," he appealed to her as they walked along the tree-lined pathway through the park.

She looked straight ahead. She continued to look straight ahead even when speaking to him.

"Well, you shouldn't have, but you did, didn't you?"

"I know. It should never have happened. I'm under pressure at work, love, and I felt like you were going against me. Against what I thought was right."

"Against you? It has nothing to do with you, does it? Ask yourself why I traded my car in? Why I've spent so much time with Jimmy up at the hospital? He has no one else. We're the only people he can turn to."

"Yeah, I know that."

"You say you know, but you're dead against me helping him. Dead against Jimmy coming to live with us."

"I'm not dead against it, love. I'm just worried because of how long you two were together. I saw it all, didn't I? I watched you and Jimmy fall in love."

"Yes, I know. Which is precisely why you should agree to let him move in."

"After what happened in ninety-four? He was a fuckin' maniac when he found out. He put me in hospital, for fuck's sake. He might have forgotten that, but I haven't and nor should you."

"No, I know, but you've not seen Jimmy since the accident. He's changed. He's different."

"Are you going to tell him why you two split up?"

"Yes, I am. Not just yet. It'll overwhelm him."

"You just don't want him to hate you all over again."

"No, I don't; you're right."

"Don't you think him moving in with us is a huge risk to our relationship?"

"No, I don't. I just don't get why you can't let him move in with us? He has no one else."

"I don't know."

He walked away from her, sitting on a nearby park bench and lighting a cigarette. He had his back to her and was staring out across the open expanse of grass in the centre of the park. She lit a cigarette, walking over to sit on the park bench next to him.

"When do you think you'll know?" She sarcastically asked.

"Stop trying to be funny. How many blokes do you know that would be happy for their wife's ex-husband to move in with them? I bet it isn't many."

"No, probably not, but I don't care about other men. I'm married to you, and I need your support with Jimmy's recovery."

"Well, I've got work, haven't I. As long as you sort it out and take care of him."

"Are you saying Jimmy can move in then?" She asked cautiously, making eye contact.

"Yes. Ring the hospital tomorrow morning and ask about a discharge date."

She was glad he'd realised it was the right thing to do to help Jimmy. Despite her husband's horrific behaviour toward her last night, she smiled.

"Thank you," she said, turning to face him.

They kissed and embraced as they sat on the park bench. He briefly pulled away from the kiss, only to say something to her.

"I love you so much."

She didn't respond, but the kiss continued.

A short time later, hand in hand, they made the short walk back to Tracy's. Alison was happy now things for Jimmy could really start to progress. When Tracy opened her front door, she knew Simon had made up with her friend. They were standing close together, holding hands and smiling. Simon jumped into his car to make the short drive home as Alison and Tracy parted with an embrace, promising to keep in touch. Alison's journey back home adopted a much more leisurely approach than yesterday. She was in no hurry. She wanted to think about the future, how

Jimmy would cope and how they would cope with the three of them living together.

#

Chapter 23

Alison stepped down the stairs with an obvious spring in her step, happy she'd be telephoning the hospital this morning. She went into the kitchen to make a cup of tea and then sat at the dining table, where she lit her first cigarette of the day. It was just after nine in the morning, and her husband had left for work over two hours ago. She was alone in their large house and appreciated the silence to allow herself time to think. The dining area of their open-plan living space was bathed in morning sunlight through the large glass doors. She looked over her work diary. She'd committed to two photography jobs for the rest of the year, one in the middle of next week and one in early December. She had money saved and intentionally kept work to a bare minimum; her priorities had changed considerably in the last couple of months. She looked up from her diary, across their open-plan living space into their large back garden and the blue sky. The sunshine inspired her soul as she took another long drag on her cigarette. She was really focusing on the meeting with Mr Davies at the hospital and moving Jimmy in before Christmas. For today though, she still had to chase up a couple of unpaid invoices and prepare an evening meal for when Simon arrived home from work.

When she did ring the hospital, Jimmy's consultant was out on his rounds and couldn't take the call. The telephone rang an hour later, and she suspected it was him.

"Hello?"

"Hi Alison, it's Mr Davies from Farley Hall. You telephoned earlier, I believe."

"Yes. Thanks for ringing me back. I was wondering if we could set up a meeting with Jimmy's care team. My husband and I would like Jimmy to come and live with us."

"That's wonderful news."

"Yes. Could we have the meeting on a Saturday, if possible? Simon can't attend a meeting during the week because of work."

"Sure, I'll have a look now. Just give me a moment to look over my diary."

"OK."

Alison waited patiently for the consultant to respond. She was happy now things were moving forward for Jimmy. Witnessing herself how much he was improving. Although paralysed and with a brain injury, he was now beginning to grasp who he once was. Though he was still struggling with more recent memories. He couldn't remember his thirtieth birthday or anything else that happened in the 1990s. Her only real nagging worry was that one day he would remember why they'd split up.

"We could have the meeting a week on Saturday at ten in the morning. That gives me enough time to speak to everyone from Jimmy's care team, make sure they can attend."

Alison wrote down in her diary:

Saturday the 27th 10am, Jimmy's meeting.

"That's the 27th, yes?"

"Yes, is that date good for you guys?"

"Perfect."

"Well, unless there's anything else, Alison, I will see you and your husband on the 27th."

"OK. See you a week on Saturday, Mr Davies."

"OK, Alison. Take care, bye."

"Bye."

She smiled when she put the receiver down, happy she had a date set for the meeting. Hopefully, Simon can take Friday off work, she thought as she stepped over to the kitchen to make another cup of tea. I'll ask him when he gets home later. She thought he'd better not let me down again as she flicked the kettle to boil.

#

On Saturday morning, seventy-five days had passed since Alison made her first visit to see Jimmy. When she'd first seen him, debilitated by the car accident, he couldn't speak and barely move. He'd improved considerably in the last two months. So much so Mr Davies was only one meeting away from discharging him.

The familiar sound of crunching gravel as she parked her vehicle, the cloudless blue sky and unexpected sunshine in November, and the thought that Jimmy could be moving in with them soon, all combined to make Alison feel uplifted and hopeful as she walked into the hospital with Simon. The girl on reception recognised her immediately when she walked in. Alison had spent so much time here; she was on first-name terms with the receptionist, quite a few of the nurses and most of the cafeteria staff.

"Alison, hi." the girl said.

"Hi Claire, you OK?"

"Yes, I'm fine."

"Claire, this is my husband, Simon."

"Hi. Nice to meet you," the receptionist said.

"Hiya, love," Simon replied, nodding and smiling as he did so.

"How was the journey north?" Claire asked.

"Fine. We travelled up yesterday. We stayed at the Midland in town last night," Alison said.

"Mr Davies is in his office. He said you can go right up. You know the way, don't you?"

"Thanks, Claire," Alison said, smiling and making her way up the stairs with her husband.

"Hope it goes well," Claire shouted up the staircase behind reception.

"Thanks," Alison shouted back as she reached the landing with her husband before walking to the Consultant's office.

She knocked firmly on the solid oak door, underneath a polished gold plate the size of a children's ruler, which read: Mr Davies - Lead Brain Injury Consultant.

"Posh," Simon whispered into Alison's ear, making her laugh.

"Yes?"

Alison was the first to step inside; she noticed how the room was laid out as it had been the last time she'd attended a meeting here. Jimmy's care team sat on the opposite side of the large oval table; they all stood to greet Alison and Simon. Mr Davies was at the head of the table; he was the first to speak.

"Alison, hi. This must be your husband?"

"Hi, Mr Davies. Yes, this is Simon."

The consultant offered his hand to Simon, who approached him smiling.

"Hi. Thanks for everything you've done for Jimmy," Simon said as he shook the consultant's hand.

"It's a pleasure, Simon. These are the people you should be thanking. Let me introduce you to his care team."

Simon sat down, and Alison sat next to him, watching and smiling as he was introduced to people she'd already met.

Alison and her husband listened attentively to everything each care team member said. How to support Jimmy, the change in his personality and how best to deal with any challenging behaviour. They were made aware that tolerance, understanding, and patience were needed to support somebody with an acquired brain injury. Buckets of patience. She looked at her husband, prodding him and repeating the most salient points made by the psychologist. She wanted Simon to understand how to support and nurture his childhood friend. She especially wanted him to understand that he needed to be tolerant of Jimmy. She knew, at times, it would be difficult having him live in their home. She knew that it would test her husband's resolve.

She wanted Simon to forget that horrible period in 1994. The violence. A close friend since childhood was crushed. Smashed to pieces. She didn't want her husband to hate Jimmy. Not now. Not after what he'd been through. The person he now was. Vulnerable. Weak. Childlike. Emotionally unstable. In need of friendship and support. Their friendship and support.

When the meeting came to a natural close, Mr Davies suggested they break for lunch before seeing Jimmy. Alison, Simon, and the consultant could then have a much more informal chat with Jimmy about the prospect of him being discharged into their care.

#

Chapter 24

In those last few steps down the corridor to his room, all Alison thought about was Jimmy's reaction to seeing Simon again. She was terrified. She was sure he would at least recognise his friend; they'd known each other since infant's school. In the time she'd spent with Jimmy, she noticed his memory recollections getting increasingly frequent. Sporadic memories of his life as a child and a teenager returning, but he couldn't remember anything about the decade they were in now. She'd asked him last time she was here if he remembered *Oasis,* and he'd replied what's that? It shocked her because she knew how much he loved that group. Although it saddened her then, she didn't think it wise to play him an *Oasis* song. Those songs and that time were intrinsically linked to the horrible circumstances of their divorce in ninety-four. However, it took the edge off her sadness with a twisted reassuring comfort, knowing he couldn't remember it without her help. She had time on her side, but fear he would hate her again was holding her back, making her keep things from him. Mr Davies had said Jimmy's more recent memories close to before the accident would be the most difficult for him to remember. She'd witnessed him over the last few weeks remember so much of his childhood, his teenage years and at fifteen when they met. Jimmy had no idea he was divorced from Alison or why he was divorced from her. It was impossible to predict what Jimmy may remember next. What if he took one look at Simon and remembered the conflict? She worried.

The consultant was paged, it focused Alison's mind back into the present, and he left them in the corridor, suggesting they go in without him. They both entered the room, and Alison laughed out of sheer relief when she saw how Jimmy reacted toward Simon.

"Soul Brother!" Jimmy shouted.

He instantly recognised his friend. As close to each other as brothers, they would always refer to each other in this way. It was their 'thing', and it got up people's noses, which they both found hilarious. When Alison heard him refer to Simon that way, her heart was warmed, and two decades of time dissolved as the childhood friends were together again.

"Great to see you, Brother Jimmy. How ya feelin'?" Simon happily responded, shaking hands with his friend.

"Good Brother Si. I'm getting there."

Alison was so happy Jimmy hadn't reacted as she'd feared, quite the opposite. The tension in her body completely dissipated, and her shoulders relaxed. She grabbed the chair and sat by his bed; Simon sat on the edge of the bed by Jimmy's feet. She smiled when everything Jimmy had told her about his relationship with Simon all came flooding back to her as she watched them laughing together:

They heard punk music for the first time together.

They got the leather strap for misbehaving at St. Mary's together.

They fell in love with *Joy Division* together.

They smoked a joint for the first time together.

They always went to The Hacienda together.

Both their fathers had died before they reached two years of age.

The two lads had grown up inseparable.

"Hey, I remembered that fight I had after school with Codge the other day. You were my trainer, ha, ha. Do you remember?" Jimmy asked.

"Yeah, I do. Ha, ha. He wasn't expecting you to come out fighting, was he? Two good punches from you, and it was all over," Simon responded, laughing with his friend.

"Yeah, well. He was a cocky bastard Codge. I don't like fighting. He pushed me too far."

"How've you been since I last saw you, Jimmy?" Alison asked, changing from the subject of fighting as nimbly as she could.

"More confident. Stronger," Jimmy happily announced from his position and sat in bed.

"That's fantastic. We had a meeting about you earlier, Simon and me. With your consultant and the other people helping you get better," she told him gently.

He looked at Alison, smiling intently at her.

"Oh yeah. Why?"

Before Alison could speak, Simon interrupted, and she was glad it came from him.

"You can escape, Jimmy. They say you can move in with us."

"Brilliant. When?" Jimmy asked.

"Soon. We just have to confirm a date with Mr Davies and the team," Alison said.

"Where is he?" Jimmy asked.

"Oh, he got paged in the corridor and dashed off. I'm sure he'll be back," Alison responded.

"Good. I'm sick of it here now. It's boring."

Just then, Mr Davies came into the room.

"Hi, Jimmy. Who's this guy in your room today?" the consultant asked the patient.

"It's Simon. My soul, brother. My best mate."

"Is it? I'm sure he'll be able to help with your memory like Alison. What do you think?"

"Oh yeah. Definitely," Jimmy said, turning to smile at a lad he'd been inseparable from for all the years growing up together in Stretford.

"That's terrific, Jimmy." Mr Davies said.

"Yeah. They say I'm moving into their house in London. When can I?"

"Soon, Jimmy. Alison and Simon will need to make adjustments to their home first."

The ball was obviously now in their court. Alison thought about taking Jimmy home with her. She didn't want to waste time travelling back to London, to then drive back up here to the hospital to collect him. She had the bit between her teeth and turned to face her husband.

"Honey, how quickly can we get a ramp put in and get the doors widened downstairs?"

"I could ring a builder. Might take a few weeks; he could be busy. It's short notice, love."

"I know, but we could get Jimmy into our home between us, couldn't we? We've enough room, and we have the bathroom downstairs, haven't we?"

"Oh yeah."

"I can manage," Jimmy interrupted.

"I know, Jimmy. Why don't you get a train home from Piccadilly tomorrow morning, babe? I can stay at the Midland again on Sunday night, then drive Jimmy home with me on Monday."

"Yeah, OK, why not. I'll ring the builder Monday morning," Simon said.

"Would that be OK, Mr Davies?" Alison asked.

"Yes, of course. I'll prepare Jimmy's discharge notes over the weekend, which you'll need to pass on to your GP in Highgate. We'll need the pharmacy to organise his medication and protein drinks. I'll speak to them on Monday morning. Once they're organised, you can leave."

"Great." The married couple chorused together.

"OK then, that's settled. Is that OK with you, Jimmy?" Alison asked.

"Brilliant," Jimmy exclaimed.

There were smiles all around Jimmy's room; he was on the verge of leaving the hospital, which had been his home for the last three months.

"Could we take Jimmy out into the gardens, Mr Davies?" Alison asked.

"I don't see why not. I'll go and ask the nurses to bring his chair in," the consultant said before disappearing from the room.

"You fancy a cup of tea and a cigarette Jimmy?" Alison asked him.

"Oh, aye. Defo."

"Right, I'll get the brews. How many sugars, Jim?" Simon asked him.

"One, please, Si," Jimmy said, smiling.

"Can you get me a chocolate bar?" Alison asked.

"Which one?"

"I don't know. Surprise me."

"OK, I'll see you out there," Simon said as he turned and left the room.

#

As Alison approached her husband sitting at the table and chairs outside, Jimmy was racing around on the other side of the gardens in his wheelchair. She sat down next to Simon.

"That was heavy, that babe," Simon said, his shoulders slouching as he sighed.

"It went well, though, didn't it?"

"Yeah, I know. It's just weird. After what happened and what he did."

"I know."

They both looked across the gardens watching Jimmy race his chair up and down.

"He's no fucking idea why you split up, has he?"

"No. I'll tell him when the time's right, though. When he's settled with us."

"Yer gonna tell him?"

"Yes. I'd rather that than he remembers it for himself, hating the pair of us all over again."

"Yeah, maybe you're right."

They stopped talking when Jimmy drove up and parked his chair next to the table. With the three of them outside in the gardens smoking cigarettes and drinking tea, it was as if the rift between them had never happened. Alison smiled when the lads laughed loudly as Simon described stories of bus journeys home from town and some of the scrapes they got into at St. Mary's across the railway bridge from their homes.

"Hey Jim, you remember when that lampshade fell from the ceiling in assembly?" Simon asked his friend, passing him a cigarette.

"Cheers, mate. No, what happened?" Jimmy asked.

"Fuckin' 'ell mate, it was hilarious. Here y'ar."

Jimmy settled back into his electric chair, taking the ashtray Simon passed him and resting it on his lap with his left hand, a lit cigarette in his right. "Ta mate."

"Have you remembered any of the lads from school, Jim?"

"Only Reni, really."

"Right. Well, when we were in the third year, there was a lad in the second year called ghost."

"Ghost?"

"A ginger-haired kid who lived in Wardle close flats next door to Reni. He was so white; he'd disappear in the daylight," Simon laughed.

Jimmy began laughing out loud, and when Alison remembered the lad they were talking about, he *was* really white; she began laughing hysterically.

"We were in the middle of the hall, nearer the back ghost was near the front. The lights on the ceiling in the hall had massive white glass globe shades on 'em, and *you* noticed the one high up above ghost's head come loose and slip," Simon explained.

"Did I?" Jimmy asked.

"Yeah. The hall had a really high ceiling, and we watched it drop all the way down and hit ghost on 'is head. *DONK*! Knocked him out cold, and the shade didn't even smash. Ghost's head had taken all the pace off it, and it just rolled next to him, lying spark out on the floor."

"Fuckin' 'ell," Jimmy exclaimed.

"Every kid in the hall started laughing, but it didn't last. Chemney and Sweeney were screaming from the stage for us to shut up."

"Who?"

"Teachers Jim."

"Right. Was ghost, OK?"

"Yeah. He got carried out by two other teachers. We saw him that afternoon. He was fine."

Alison enjoyed watching the two lads chat and reminisce; her worries eased, no aggression at all from Jimmy. She was glad she'd convinced Simon to do the right thing and come with her. She felt his presence was helping Jimmy remember even more. Living with them had to bring back Jimmy's memories, whether happy memories or sad ones, and the prospect of that uncertainty terrified her.

#

Chapter 25

Alison was convinced Jimmy had been touched by the hand of God. Surviving the accident and long-term coma, he had a lot to be thankful for, despite brain injury and paralysis. She'd seen with her own eyes how much he'd improved as a patient at Farley Hall Hospital for Brain Injuries.

She made her way across the forecourt to her vehicle, Jimmy cruising slowly alongside her in his chair. Mr Davies and the rest of Jimmy's care team came out onto the gravel forecourt in front of the 18th Century hall. Alison thanked them again for what they'd done for Jimmy. After she opened the back of her vehicle and lowered the ramp, the consultant handed her a large brown envelope containing Jimmy's discharge notes. Before Jimmy drove his chair up the ramp into Alison's vehicle, each one of the care team stooped over and gave him a hug. He was crying. He couldn't help it. She knew he was prone to tearful outbursts because of his brain injury. Mr Davies had told her, and she'd witnessed it herself on more than one occasion over the last two months. She guessed he was just grateful for all they'd done for him. She hugged Mr Davies once she'd strapped Jimmy into her vehicle. He'd reached out to shake her hand, but she couldn't stop holding him close, sincerely thanking him for everything he'd done. The entire care team were waving as Alison drove away from the hospital. She made eye contact with Jimmy in the rear-view mirror, a sadness in his eyes; he was still lost.

He slept in his chair for most of their journey down to London. She could keep her eye on him through the rear-view mirror. Driving along the motorway quietly listening to *The Smiths*, the last song *I Won't Share You*, from their final album *Strangeways Here We Come*, began to exude softly from the speakers.

I won't share you.

No, no, no, no.

I won't share you.

She'd listened to this album from start to finish as Jimmy slept. Together again, after unfortunate circumstances had brought him back into her life. For years she'd tried to forget him, yet now he was all she was thinking of. She sighed, comforted by the sound of Morrissey's voice.

#

It was almost four in the afternoon when they eventually arrived in Highgate. Alison was thankful Jimmy's upper body strength had returned as he negotiated himself from his electric chair just outside the front door of their home into a manual fold-away wheelchair Simon had purchased, parked on the doormat at the front door. He just about managed it with her assistance, and she pushed him into the dining area before briefly heading through the front door to put his electric chair in the garage and lock her vehicle.

When Alison returned, Jimmy was the first to speak.

"Wow. This place is amazing, Ali."

"It's lovely, isn't it. Mum and dad bought it for us a few years ago. D'ya fancy a brew?"

"Please."

"Shall I put some music on?"

"Yeah. I've been listening to the CDs you gave me. Put some Happy Mondays on."

"OK. I've got their first album on vinyl."

Alison stepped across to her music collection, reaching for; *Squirrel and G-Man Twenty-Four Hour Party People Plastic Face Carnt Smile (White Out)*. She put the vinyl onto the turntable and placed the needle at the start of the record. As the song *Kuff Dam* began, Jimmy smiled as Alison walked past. They could communicate and see each other across the open plan living space, and she returned his smile as she stood at the kitchen island whilst flicking the kettle on to boil.

They listened to music together for two hours before Simon arrived home. Alison spent most of it in the kitchen preparing the evening meal. She'd kept the music at a sensible volume so she could talk with Jimmy as she worked away in the kitchen, occasionally going over to the lounge to turn the record over or play a different one.

When Simon arrived home from work, he showered quickly, and the three of them sat down to eat. They laughed together as they ate their meal. Both Alison and Simon were enjoying reminding Jimmy of his past. Seeing the elated look of joy on his face as he remembered some of these things for himself gave Alison a warm feeling they'd definitely done the right thing.

After the meal, they spent the evening in the lounge listening to music. Alison thought it was the right thing to do; she knew the music was helping Jimmy to remember. They'd thrived upon it as teenagers and twenty-somethings. Sharing the same taste in music and loving the same groups. Simon had to be up at six, so he went upstairs to bed at eleven, leaving Alison and Jimmy alone, listening to music.

"Shall we listen to The Smiths?" He asked her when she came in carrying two mugs of tea.

"Why don't I put something on? I haven't played you yet? Something we both used to love? It might spark more memories for you."

"Yeah, like what?"

"Oh, I don't know. I'll have a look."

She put the tea mugs down on the coffee table and stepped over to her her wide selection of vinyl, sliding out her copy of *Recurrence* when she spotted it.

"Do you remember The Railway Children? They're from Wigan."

"No, I don't think so?"

"Tony Wilson sent us a tape of their first album in the post, suggesting you'd love them. You did. You bought me this album for my birthday."

"Did I? Is it good?"

"Oh yeah. It's fantastic if you like guitar music."

Jimmy was staring at the back of the sleeve as the first song began playing. "Hey, this is called Somewhere South. It's great, isn't it?"

"Yes. We both loved this record. Now we've both ended up somewhere south, haven't we?"

Jimmy laughed; it made her smile and warmed her heart as she sat on the sofa facing him in his chair. He'd finally said goodbye to that hospital. She knew he would feel comfortable here, knowing he'd be sleeping in a real bed instead of the hospital bed the circumstances of his life had forced him into. His laugh subsided, and he smiled at her as the guitar introduction they both loved started the second song, *A Pleasure*. As she stared into his eyes, that guitar riff made her stomach tie in knots and her heart flutter. Those blue eyes hadn't changed, and that face around them hadn't changed; she couldn't help herself; she knew she'd never stop loving him.

Fuckin' 'ell! She screamed in anger inside as she smiled at him.

The juxtaposition within her was obvious, and Alison knew she had the decision to make. A decision that could be made for her when she told Jimmy everything. He was different from the one she'd known and loved for so long. She had no idea how he was going to react.

#

Throughout December, Jimmy quickly got used to living in their home in Highgate. He wouldn't see Simon until six thirty in the evening. Alison had intentionally avoided booking any work during December. She knew it was a full-time job caring for someone with a brain injury who'd lost the use of his legs. She didn't want to mother him and was keen to ensure he kept a degree of independence. They were great days. They were happy days. They were days filled with music and memory recollection. The mnemonic for Jimmy was the guitar groups from Manchester and Salford the three loved so much. She'd played him a *Joy Division* album, and he'd remembered the first night he spent with her. She'd played him *The Smiths*, and he'd remembered the time they moved in together and went to see them play at The Free Trade Hall.

To avoid any sensation of cabin fever or feeling trapped inside their home, she made sure she took him on regular day trips. An opportunity for fresh air and different surroundings, albeit in a part of the country he'd never lived. She made sure she watched him carefully when they were out together. The fear he could explode emotionally toward somebody was constantly on her mind. Keen to defend Jimmy, she was always ready to apologise for his behaviour or the things he said. It was embarrassing and humiliating at times, but she never had any feelings of regret that Jimmy had come back into her life.

The three friends were close over Christmas. They spent time together in the home and began to enjoy the festivities. They had discussed where to celebrate the start of a new century and the difficulties of having Jimmy with them wherever they decided to go. After much discussion, they decided to drink in the local pub, followed by a walk home. The pub was packed, as were most that night, so they left around eleven thirty. Alison wanted the three of them to be together at home when the clock ticked past midnight. Simon had promised to avoid taking cocaine, but he broke that promise when they arrived home, and his wife started to roll the first of many joints. He carefully chopped out a few lines with his bank card, bringing in the New Year as he always did.

Jimmy cried; Alison knew he thought what could have been. He would have been celebrating the New Year alone in that hospital. Yet now, he was with the two most familiar faces he knew. Two people he'd spent decades growing up with. No disagreements or conflicts anymore, just three best friends happy to be together.

As winter became spring, when Jimmy spent quite a few weeks living with them in their home, Simon never suggested it was too much. That having his wife's ex-husband living downstairs was causing problems. The closeness of Jimmy and Simon growing up together was the saving grace.

It meant a house filled with laughter as both Simon and Alison did their best to help their friend remember his past.

#

Chapter 26

The telephone rang one Saturday morning in May. Alison wasn't expecting a call from her best friend, Tracy. She'd yet to introduce her to Jimmy; she'd been working overseas for the first five months of this year.

"Hello?"

"Ali, it's Trace. You OK?"

"Tracy, hi. I'm good, thanks. How was the trip?"

"Great. Nice to be back home, though. How's Jimmy doing?"

Alison was sitting on the sofa holding the white, wireless handset to her ear; she smiled at Jimmy, who was in the armchair.

"He's doing really well. Got a lot of his upper body strength back, and he's telling us his memories a lot more often. Instead of the other way around."

"That's brilliant. Have you been out with him much?"

"Yes, quite a few times. I'm going to take him to Brighton this summer."

"Fantastic. Hey, there's a Cindy Sherman exhibition on at The National Portrait Gallery next week. I thought you and I could go with Jimmy."

"Oh, right. Yes, she's terrific; I'd love that. Hang on, I'll ask him."

Alison rested the handset on her shoulder and gave Jimmy her full attention.

"Do you fancy a trip to a photograph gallery next week with my friend Tracy?"

"Photographs? What of?"

"It's an exhibition of photographs taken by an American photographer called Cindy Sherman. Tracy and I really like her work."

"Yeah, why not."

"Great. I can introduce you to Tracy."

"Where d'ya know her from?"

"From a photography conference a few years ago. We've been good friends ever since."

She turned her attention back to the phone call with Tracy. They settled on Tuesday next week to attend the exhibition, agreeing that it would be easier to get on the tube instead of attempting to drive into the city.

#

Alison and Tracy had travelled on the London Underground a lot. Up and down countless staircases that took you from street level down into the belly of the underground. Neither of the girls had needed to use the lifts before, until now. They used the lifts at the St. Michaels' Church stop, where they boarded and at Charing Cross Station, where their journey ended.

The bright spring sunshine was beaming down onto the London streets as they made their way along Charing Cross Road and entered the National Portrait Gallery. Alison was conscious this was the first time she'd been out in a busy public place with Jimmy. It terrified her that he may say something offensive to someone. She was glad she had her friend Tracy with her for support. She'd warned her about his verbal outbursts or the sexually suggestive comments he sometimes made. It made her feel embarrassed when he behaved in this way. Alison hoped that it wouldn't happen today in front of her friend. During Alison's first visit to the hospital, Mr Davies had said:

"Part of Jimmy's brain damage is to his frontal lobe; as a consequence, he exhibits a range of emotional and behavioural difficulties, which is termed *executive dysfunction*."

Yesterday, Alison forwarded an email to Tracy that she'd received from Mr Davies on the subject. She felt it necessary to inform her friend of Jimmy's behavioural problems. When she'd witnessed it up at the hospital, it was a shock to hear Jimmy make sexually suggestive comments to some of those nurses. It seemed so out of character.

After the three of them had spent some time looking around the photography exhibition, Jimmy spotted the gift shop and wanted to look around. They served hot drinks there, so the two girls bought a coffee and sat at the tables inside, leaving Jimmy alone to browse.

"It's weird, Trace. Hearing Jimmy say some of the things he says."

"I guess the brain injury has changed him?"

"Yes. The consultant told me about it the first day I went to see Jimmy. His inhibitions are reduced. It's like a guy having a few pints before chatting you up. Ya know, Dutch courage."

"Right, I see."

"He's not a hurtful or arrogant guy, Jimmy. He never has been. There's no malicious intent when he says these things."

"I get that, Ali. From the way you've described how he was before the accident. There's a sweet guy in there somewhere."

"Exactly, Trace. Couldn't have put it better myself."

Alison smiled at Tracy, glad her best friend seemed to completely understand Jimmy's communication problems.

"Has Si been alright with Jimmy living with you?"

"Yes, he's been great. They grew up together, didn't they? I'm just worried Jimmy may remember they hated each other when we split up."

"It'd be better coming from you that, wouldn't it?"

"Exactly. That's what I keep telling Si. I'll tell Jimmy when I think the time's right."

"Good idea."

"Hey, I didn't tell you, did I? Simon, and I had a meeting with Mr Davies, Jimmy's consultant, before we left the hospital."

"Really, what about?"

"Oh, Simon was worried we would have to pay Jimmy's hospital bills and the cost of his electric wheelchair."

"Oh, is Farley Hall a private hospital then?"

"Yeah. We asked Mr Davies he said Jimmy's medical bills had been taken care of."

"Taken care of? Who by?"

"We don't know. He said the benefactor wanted to remain anonymous."

"Anonymous? Yer jokin'?"

"No, I'm not. It's frustrating. I wanted to thank them."

"Have you told Jimmy?"

"No, he's got enough to worry about."

"I guess so."

"You wanna come back to ours? He'll sleep for a couple of hours. We can have a chat then. You can have tea with us if you want?

"OK, that'd be great."

Both girls were alert when they heard a young woman raise her voice angrily. Alison quickly stood up and raced to the cashier's desk where Jimmy was, leaving Tracy dumbfounded.

"What's happened?" Alison asked.

"Is he with you?" The young girl asked.

"Yes. Has he said something to you?"

"Said something? He slapped my arse and said, *nice arse, love.*"

Alison didn't smile when she looked at Jimmy, who stopped smiling immediately.

"I'm so sorry. He doesn't do it on purpose. He has a brain injury from a car accident."

"Brain injury?" The young girl asked, looking confused toward the girl behind the cash register, who looked just as confused.

"Yes, he can say and do things without thinking, that's all. Embarrassing, I know. Sorry. You shouldn't say things like that, Jimmy; you'll get into trouble," Alison explained.

The relief on the young girl's face was obvious, but Jimmy didn't understand why it was wrong.

"Oh, I never realised. I'm sorry I snapped at him."

"It's OK. You weren't to know," Alison said, smiling at the two young ladies.

#

As Alison helped Jimmy into the single bed they'd put in the sitting room for him, she noticed he was crying.

"Jimmy, what's wrong?"

"Nothing."

"Tell me. What's on your mind?"

"That girl in the gift shop. Why did I do that? Why did I say that to her?"

"Oh, Jimmy, it's not your fault. Don't cry."

She sat on the bed and held him close, his upper body propped up against the pillows.

"But it is. I shouldn't have slapped her bum or said that. I feel really bad for her now, but I'll never see her again to say sorry, will I?" Jimmy wailed, weeping into Alison's shoulder.

"It's happened now, Jimmy and you're sorry; that's all that matters. Put it out of your mind. Just try and be more controlled next time."

"I'm an arsehole."

"You're not an arsehole Jimmy. That isn't how you behave. It's the brain injury, remember."

"But I feel like shit now. I want to go back and undo it, but I can't. I hate myself."

"Jimmy, don't say that. Those two young girls understood once I'd explained. Yeah?"

They parted their embrace, Jimmy wiping his tears away with the bed sheet.

"I guess so. I'm tired, Ali. I need to sleep."

"OK, darling. You rest. I'll check on you in a while, OK?"

"OK," he said, smiling as she stood up.

Alison closed the curtains. Jimmy was very tired and fell asleep before she even left the room. She went into the kitchen to prepare the evening meal and make two mugs of tea, one for her and one for Tracy. They settled in the lounge for a chat until Simon arrived home.

"Is he OK?" Tracy asked.

"He's fine. He's a little upset with what went on in the gift shop earlier."

"Really?"

"Yes, it always happens like this."

"How d'ya mean?"

"He'll explode at a stranger in public for whatever reason, then hours later at home, he'll start crying about it. Delayed embarrassment at his behaviour toward a stranger."

"Oh, right. At least he understands it's wrong, and he's apologetic. Maybe that'll help him to rein it in, in the future?

"I thought that. He's so unpredictable, though."

"It must be strange for you, Ali, how much he's changed."

"Yes, but it's still Jimmy, isn't it? The first day up at the hospital, when I saw him, that recognition in his face when he saw me. It melted my heart, Trace."

"I bet. How long were you two together?"

"Sixteen years. Well, thirteen, really. When dad got a job, and we moved down here just before Christmas in seventy-nine, I didn't see Jimmy again until eighty-three."

"You moved in together after that, didn't you?"

"Not straight away. I had to contact Manchester University about finishing my photography degree up there and face my parents with the news that I was moving back to Manchester."

"Were they OK with that?"

"Not really. They wanted me to stay in London. More opportunities for work and wealthier potential boyfriends. They never liked Jimmy all that much."

"Really? That's a shame."

"I know, but they didn't understand how I felt about him."

"Maybe you were destined to be together?"

"Jimmy thinks so. You know our birthdays are on the same day?"

"Really?"

"Yes. Jimmy always used to say to me, *we're part of the same soul.*"

"Aw, that's lovely. You don't know how he'll react when you tell him why you split up?"

"No, and it's the only unknown I have about him now. It's obvious how he feels about me. We kissed back at the hospital. It was incredible," Alison said.

"Really? I'm guessing full-on snogging?"

"Completely full on. It felt like it used to."

As Alison turned her head to gaze into the back garden through the large glass doors, she made a determined decision. On Friday morning, when her husband was at work, she would tell Jimmy why they split.

#

Chapter 27

Alison needed a break. The last eleven months had taken their toll on her patience. The stress of her visits to the hospital in Cheshire. The convincing her husband needed before he'd let Jimmy move in with them. The task she'd taken on in caring for him, his emotional outbursts, and fiery temper. It had all become too much for her to deal with. Though she didn't want to admit it to herself, she needed a break from Jimmy.

She felt a humidity still prevalent in the air as she stepped onto the decking in the back garden through the opened bi-folding glass doors. After torrential rain all morning, the clouds were now clearing. Bright summer sunshine had sufficiently dried the rain, so she sat on one of the chairs and placed her work diary and cup of tea on the table.

After a busy morning and another angry verbal outburst, Jimmy was asleep in his single bed in the sitting room, his room. She believed he was childlike when he said the wrong things without conscious regard for who was listening, coupled with the tiredness he felt every day. Many of his verbal outbursts directly reacted to her continued refusals. He only wanted to talk about being married and moving back to Manchester. She understood it was his brain damage making it difficult for him to understand she was married to Simon or to accept the word 'no' as an answer. Still, his stubbornness was starting to frustrate her.

Simon had told them at the office he would be at work on Monday and then off for three days until Alison arrived on Thursday evening. He would return to work on Friday morning.

She was taking time out in the sunshine to plan tomorrow's journey; check again she had everything organised for the two-day wedding shoot in Reading. She lit her third cigarette. She was particularly stressed out with Jimmy's behaviour.

#

When Alison was expected to return on Thursday evening after Jimmy had slept for a couple of hours, Simon needed a drink. Safe in the knowledge his wife would be home at some point this evening to look after Jimmy. Regardless of the fact he had to be up at six, he pulled a half-empty bottle of single malt from the kitchen cupboard to finish it before he went to bed.

When Jimmy and Simon retired to the lounge and sat down after eating, Jimmy was the first to speak up, watching his friend sip through what was left in that whisky bottle.

"Roll us a joint, Si?"

"Yeah, no worries. Have you not sussed it yet?"

"No, it's difficult. Ali's been showing me."

"You used to roll 'em no problem back in the day."

"Where's Reni these days?" Jimmy asked.

"Fuck knows. I heard he'd moved to America. He got off the booze and drugs as well."

"Didn't we used to take another drug when we went out? I remembered it the other day Si."

"Yeah, we used to take ecstasy pills when we went out together, the three of us. What an amazin' drug that was. You remember when we tried our first E?"

"E, yeah, that's it. I *think* I can remember the first time we tried it. Didn't we buy our first ones in The Hacienda?"

"There was no 'we' Jim. You bottled it. I bought 'em in that alcove underneath the DJ in The Hac., where the scallies used to hang out. I bought us one each off them. I had to approach those Salford head cases myself," Simon revealed.

He laughed as he finished rolling the joint, tapping the end on the coffee table before sealing the end and passing it to a smiling Jimmy.

"Ta. What year was that, Si?" Jimmy asked.

"What year? Fuckin' hell, mate. It was about three years that. Big part of our lives going to the Hacienda. Eighty-eight, eighty-nine and ninety. I'll put some tunes on they used to play."

"Who's they?"

"The DJs. It was always either Dave Haslam, Mike Pickering or Graeme Park playing records when we went to The Hac."

"Is it still open, the Hacienda?"

'Nah. It shut three years ago, Jim. They went fuckin' bankrupt, ran out of money. Amazing place, though. I'll stick Voodoo Ray on; hopefully, you'll recognise it. You fuckin' loved that tune, Jim. We all did."

"Did I? Voodoo Ray? Is that a singer?"

"Nah, that's the name of the tune. It's by A Guy Called Gerald. Gerald Simpson. He's from Hulme Jim. Near the Factory Club. You don't remember, do you?"

"Nah. What did ecstasy feel like when you took it?"

Simon stood up from the armchair and wavered. He stumbled over to the turntable and vinyl collection before answering Jimmy.

"Oh, it's amazing, Jim. The media started calling it the *hug drug*."

Simon ran his finger across the spines of the record collection, his eyes struggling to focus as the effects of the single malt really started to take effect.

"The *hug drug*? Why?"

"It makes you feel so happy, mate. They reckon that's why lads stopped fighting at the football in the late eighties, because of this new drug."

"Really?"

"Oh yeah. Even Reni and his older brothers packed in the fighting at United once they started taking E."

"Did they?"

"Oh aye, we even saw him and his brothers in the Hacienda a couple of times, but I think they were only in there sellin' E."

"Really?"

"Yeah, they always went to the Thunderdome on Oldham Road, on the north side of town. Too dodgy for us that place, Jim. Full of hooligans and criminals."

"Yer jokin?"

"Nah, I'm not, mate. Reni liked telling us about it; he thought it made him look like the hard man. Loads of 'em from The Thunderdome always went onto Hulme in the early hours."

"I think I saw Reni when I was older," Jimmy said.

Simon was beginning to get so drunk that he didn't acknowledge or really hear what Jimmy said, preferring to continue telling him tales of the past.

"Apparently, someone had demolished the adjoining wall between two flats and turned it into a club called The Kitchen. We never went. Sounded a bit mental. I think Bez and the rest of the Mondays went there a lot."

"Cool, put that record on, Si. I'm dying to hear it."

"Alright."

He found their copy of the Voodoo Ray record. He slipped the vinyl from its cover before placing it onto the turntable. As the opening crackles from the vinyl emanated from the large speakers in the lounge, he turned to face his friend. As soon as the song started playing, Jimmy smiled. This period of their past had been lost to him because of the accident.

Jimmy began making shapes with his arms, bouncing up and down in the armchair. He plucked the joint from his mouth so he could shout, trapping it between two fingers of his hand.

"Fuckin' 'ell I remember this, Si. Turn it up, man."

"Oh, aye," Simon shouted, smiling; reaching toward the stereo, he turned up the volume.

They continued to listen to records Simon remembered from the Hacienda, the pair of them lost in memories of hedonism. Jimmy recognised and remembered almost all the records his friend had played. They were helping him remember a past the accident had taken away.

Simon was very drunk by this time; he finished what was left in the whisky bottle.

Drunk, remembering hedonistic nights taking ecstasy, he managed to roll Jimmy a final joint.

"Here you go, mate. I'm goin' bed."

"Nice one Si. Cheers."

Simon stumbled across the lounge.

Jimmy put the joint between his lips and lit it.

He watched his friend drunkenly misjudge the doorway's position to the hall, walking straight into the door frame with a loud bang. He swore and shuffled off through the hallway, slowly climbing the stairs before collapsing onto the double bed, fully clothed.

Jimmy lay on the sofa in the lounge in silence with all the lights out, enjoying that last joint as his mind meandered. He tried his best to remember how he felt just over a decade ago, under the influence of this drug they took whenever they went clubbing together.

It had happened to him.

His best friend had just described it.

He'd just heard all the music he used to dance to when he'd taken ecstasy.

He wanted to remember those times for himself.

The moonlight through the windows enabled him to see what he was doing as he placed the half-joint he had left in the ashtray on the floor. He looked out across into the back garden through the windows and lay on the sofa still, silent, and thinking. His brain desperately tried to unravel and unlock something nagging away at him. The memories kept swirling away after he'd grabbed at them, like water disappearing down the plughole of a sink. When his best friend had drunkenly described their past to him earlier, he felt a specific memory returning. An unhappy memory. A memory agonisingly blurred and out of focus. A memory that made him feel anger toward his friend. Perhaps tomorrow, when I'm not stoned, I'll remember, he thought before closing his eyes and drifting off to sleep.

It was very late when Alison finally pulled onto the driveway at home. She opened the front door quietly; there was absolute silence inside. She stepped softly across the polished oak floor and spotted Jimmy asleep on the sofa. Fetching a blanket from a cupboard and laying it over him, she went upstairs and found Simon asleep, fully clothed, on their bed. She left him sleeping and returned downstairs to make a cup of tea before retiring to the sitting room and the single bed they'd put in there for Jimmy. She went upstairs to use the bathroom, then came downstairs and went into the sitting room, flopping onto the single bed; exhausted, she fell asleep almost immediately.

#

Chapter 28

A lison was awakened just before eight when she heard Jimmy struggling to get into his chair from the sofa. She wondered why he hadn't shouted at her for help. She jumped out of the single bed in the sitting room, dressing quickly into her t-shirt and jogging bottoms. Walking briskly through the dining area, she made eye contact with him.

"Morning Jimmy. You, OK?"

He ignored her, clicking the joystick on his chair forwards, moving out of the lounge into the dining area toward her. She knew something was wrong, intentionally standing in his way.

"Jimmy?" she declared, making direct eye contact again.

"What happened between you and Simon?"

"What?"

"Not now. I don't know when. When you both went to The Hacienda without me."

"What's he told you?"

"Oh, so something did happen then?"

He looked up at her with tear-glazed eyes.

"Jimmy, it's complicated."

Judging by his sombre and unaggressive demeanour, he hadn't remembered much.

"Complicated!?" he barked.

"Yes!" She hollered, angrily turning away from him.

She left him and went to put the kettle on. He followed directly behind her, steering his chair towards the kitchen island. Alison stood staring at the blue light on the kettle as the water began to heat up. She knew she was on a razor's edge; say anything here that could fill out what Jimmy had obviously remembered, and he would hate her all over again. She didn't want that; she didn't know what it would do to him, what it would do to her. It didn't get any bigger than this, and she knew it.

"I told Simon I was going to speak to you today."

"Yeah, he said that last night."

"So, he did say something then?"

"Yes, but I remembered for myself. Simon was drunk."

"He was what!?" she angrily interrupted, looking up from the kettle to stare at him.

"Yeah, he was drinking whiskey. I think the records he played triggered my memories. I was thinking about things on my own on the sofa after he went to bed."

She'd been plunged into an awkward situation. Knowing it was inevitable, he'd remember the divorce for himself at some point. It didn't make it any easier for her now. The gravity of what went on between them when they divorced wouldn't be lost to Jimmy forever; she knew that.

Having to describe a situation of unfaithfulness and the consequences of it to a man she'd always loved wasn't going to be easy for her. She'd wanted to tell him gradually on her own terms and in the right place. The family home of her and her husband definitely wasn't the right place.

"Right, hang on. I'm gonna ring him," she stated angrily.

What the fuck has he said to Jimmy? She wondered as she stood in the hallway. Pausing to think, she lit a cigarette to her lips. She sighed as she exhaled from that first drag before putting her cigarette down in the glass ashtray on the small table next to the telephone.

She rang the direct number to his office; he answered the call after only a couple of rings.

"Simon Wilson."

The confident sound of his voice exasperated her; she was in no mood for a pleasant chat.

"What the fuck have you told him?"

"Oh, good morning to you an' all love. What time did you get in?"

"Never mind that. Why did you have to get drunk?"

"Why? Because I had to put up with him! Fuckin' hell, he's a nightmare. He's like a child 'avin fuckin' tantrums. He's stressed me out these last two days. I needed a stiff drink."

"Right. So why did you tell him about us going out taking E's?"

"He remembered it! Anyway, I was pissed."

"I TOLD YOU I was going to tell him everything today," Alison screamed angrily.

"Don't panic. He doesn't know owt."

"He does. He said the records you played last night triggered his memories. He's just asked what went on between me and you in The Hacienda?"

"You said you were gonna tell him today anyway."

"Yes, I know, but it needed handling carefully because of his brain injury."

"This isn't my fault Alison. You cheated on him."

"Yes! With you! Right, I'm gonna sort it," Alison angrily shouted.

She decided instantly where she needed to go to get Jimmy away from this house.

"What d'ya mean you're gonna sort it?"

"Don't expect us here when you get in. I'm taking Jimmy to Brighton for a couple of days."

"What? Now?"

"You shouldn't have told him."

"Oh, fuck off, you're married to me. You're not married to Jimmy anymore. Right, well, if you're goin' away, then I'm goin' out this weekend."

"Now there's a surprise. Cocaine and the other two twenty-four-hour party people."

"Yeah, so fuckin' what?"

"Oh, do what ya want!" She shouted, exasperated with him.

She slammed the telephone receiver down and almost broke it. *Arg*! She screamed inside because of her husband, his arrogance, his indifference towards Jimmy and his problems. I've had enough; I need to get away, she decided, walking back into the kitchen.

Carrying two mugs of tea with her, she sat at the table and passed one to Jimmy. She put her cigarette to her lips, lighting it and offering him one.

"Ta. What did he say?"

"Nothing. Forget about him. How do you fancy going to Brighton and staying for a couple of days? We need to get away from here, Jimmy. We can book into a hotel on the seafront, and I can explain everything. There is so much to this."

"Why can't you just tell me now?"

"No, I can't, Jimmy. Not here."

"I know something big happened. I want to know NOW!" He screamed, almost crying.

"NO. NOT HERE," she screamed back at him.

Intimidated by the forcefulness of her reply, he backed down.

"OK," he mumbled.

She walked away from him and stood before the bi-folding glass doors. She took a drag from her cigarette, sighing as she exhaled with her back to him.

"This isn't easy for me, you know. Having to explain to you the circumstances of me cheating on you, the consequences of me cheating on you, and the loss we suffered after that is fucking horrible, Jimmy."

She turned to look at him; his face changed from upset anger to desperation and fear. He didn't question her when she said *consequences*. Whether it was the long-term coma or the brain injury, she didn't know. She didn't care. In a way, she was thankful he was so lost, and he couldn't put two and two together. She had to take him away from here, from her home. To explain the whole story to Jimmy *here* in the open-plan living space where the child had previously played just wouldn't be right. And she knew she wouldn't be able to handle it.

She looked at him and sat in his chair open-mouthed as she approached. "We've always talked about Brighton anyway. Can we not get settled in a hotel there and relax? You have a lot to take in. I don't wanna overwhelm you."

He didn't answer straight away, confusion on his face. He was in fear and worried.

"Jimmy?" Alison asked as she stood in front of him.

He looked up at her like a lost sheep.

"I'm scared, Ali."

"Please don't be scared. I'll go and pack a few things for us, and we'll hit the road. You can sleep on the way to Brighton. I will explain everything to you later today, but it's a lot to take in. Just don't keep pestering me about it, OK."

"OK," he sighed, a faint smile appearing at the corners of his mouth.

She raced upstairs to pack a few things for them both. He wasn't happy this morning, and it was obvious why the poetic daydream he'd been living since she'd come back into his life shattered to pieces. She hoped she could repair the damage by being completely honest with him. She didn't want Jimmy to hate her all over again.

#

Chapter 29

Alison had always wanted to stay at The Grand Hotel in Brighton. She just wished it could have been under happier circumstances. The telephone conversation with her husband had infuriated her, so when she stood in the hallway booking the hotel, she paid for it from their joint bank account. When she pulled out of their driveway at home, Jimmy was still pestering her to tell him, so she raised her voice, shouting at him and terrifying him into silence again. He slept for the whole of the journey. When she parked her vehicle and approached the hotel with him, she was relieved to see the long wheelchair ramp at the front. They checked in just before one o'clock, and Alison arranged with the concierge to take their bags to the room. A double room. She thought Jimmy could sleep in his chair; he's used to it.

They left the hotel to buy fish and chips on the seafront. She was thankful his hunger had deflected the constant questioning. She sat at an old, weathered bus shelter on the promenade across the road from the hotel. They were inside a piece of Brighton's history, and she wanted to explain their own history together until Jimmy said something that put it all into perspective for her.

"We were happy together; I know because I've remembered. Why did you have to spoil it?"

She looked down at the flaking blue paint on the metal bus shelter she was picking at, just as she'd been doing with her memories when helping Jimmy to remember. Picking at them. Being selective with what she'd chosen to tell him. Yet now, she was vulnerable and exposed. To hear him say that, she knew she had to tell him everything. He had a right to know, and she knew it.

"I didn't want to tell you. I didn't want you to hate me all over again."

"So? You have to tell me now."

"I know, but it will take time, Jimmy. When we go back to the hotel. You need to rest first."

"But I want to know why?"

"I know. I know," Alison said softly, smiling and making eye contact.

"Tell me more about us. Being together, in love. I don't wanna talk about Simon."

"OK. Well, you know, after our first night, we started seeing each other every weekend. Mainly in your bedroom listening to records?"

"Did we? Which records?"

"Oh, loads. That's why we got on so well. We both loved the same groups. You know all about Joy Division; I told you when you were in hospital."

"Yeah, and Elvis Costello."

"Of course, because you sang Alison to me."

"Yeah. Didn't we go to see him play a concert?"

"Elvis Costello? Yes, we did. Do you remember where?"

"Not really. I remember it was a big place inside though."

"Yes, the Free Trade Hall. January seventy-nine. The place where we saw The Smiths play after we moved in together in eighty-four."

"Is that in the centre of town?"

"Yes, near the central library."

"That big round building?"

"Yes. The Midland Hotel is opposite. That's where I stayed when I visited you in hospital."

"Was it?"

"Yes. Once we were living together, we travelled the country to see groups play. We spent most of our money on concerts and records."

"Really?"

"Yes. Dexy's in Birmingham, Big Country in Scotland, Blur in London, Ride in Oxford."

"Wow, all those names sound familiar to me, Ali. How did we find out about these groups?"

"In the music papers, we'd buy. Or from Tony Wilson. You remember Tony, don't you?"

"Yeah, I love him. He always talked posh; I love that."

"Yes, you did. We'd watch Something else every Saturday at your house, which was his television programme for young people about music. They didn't just have local groups on either. We saw The Jam on that show. On the same episode that Joy Division were on."

"The Jam?"

"Yeah, we loved them. They're from London. They're fantastic. I think…"

"Paul Weller," he bellowed.

She smiled when he interrupted, knowing he remembered this group himself.

"Yes, that's right. He was the singer and the songwriter. There were three of them in the group. Bruce played bass guitar, and Rick played the drums."

"Yeah, I remember. We went to see them, didn't we?"

"Yes, not long after we'd seen them on the television one Saturday in November seventy-nine. You bought us tickets to see them in Manchester at the Apollo."

"That big theatre near a roundabout?"

"Yes, that's right. They played Eton Rifles on that TV show, which was their new single."

"Oh, I remember that."

"Brilliant song. It went to number one."

"Eat some trifles. Eat some trifles," Jimmy chorused to her.

"Ha, ha. You always used to sing it like that, Jimmy," Alison responded, laughing with him, glad the conversation about music had moved his focus away from discussing her night with Simon.

"I bet they were good in concert, The Jam. I remember I loved that group."

"They were Jimmy, and yes, you did love them. A proper group getting to number one."

"That was when you went away, though, wasn't it?"

"Yes, it was, unfortunately. Not long after that concert in November. My dad got a job in London, and we all had to move. My parents wouldn't let me give you their 'phone number or address. They wanted us to split up."

"I didn't want you to leave."

"No, neither did I. I had no choice, Jimmy. I was only fifteen at the time. You OK?" she queried, noticing his eyes closing.

"I'm just tired, Ali."

"Let's go back to the hotel. It feels like it's been a long day already. You need to sleep."

"OK."

They'd both finished eating their fish and chips; Alison stood, scrunching up the papers they'd been served in and dropped them into the bin at the shelter. Jimmy clicked the joystick on his chair forwards, and they made their way across the main Promenade Road in front of the hotel. She was glad she'd successfully managed to placate his anger for now. She wanted to tell him about when they were together, happy, and in love, but it would only be putting off the inevitable.

Explaining to him why they had to split up.

On the way up to their room, she sensed he wanted to stay awake and was fighting it. It was obvious he deserved an explanation. He didn't understand, but she didn't think he wanted to understand. She knew that he didn't want to accept it. He was drifting off to sleep sitting in his chair in the hotel room. She left him sleeping in his clothes. She couldn't sleep herself, nor did she want to. She thought about where to go with the conversation later. What to tell him next? How to 'soften the blow' before she admitted everything.

#

Jimmy slept for a couple of hours. When he awoke, he began questioning her straight away.

"When you told me that we lived together in Manchester, and we went to see The Smiths together at The Free Trade Hall, it made me so happy. Why did you spoil that?"

"Oh, it wasn't in the same year. I know that's no excuse. It should never have happened."

"What happened?"

"You don't understand."

"Tell me."

"It just happened, Jimmy. You know how close the three of us were. Ecstasy pills make you feel so sexually charged. As soon as it happened, I regretted it. You weren't there."

"What happened?"

"It was in the middle of October nineteen ninety."

"Why did you go to the Hacienda and take those pills without me there?"

"You'd already had three days off work, Jimmy. We'd planned that weekend for ages, but you were so poorly with the flu. You couldn't come out with us. I left you in bed in the flat."

"Right."

"I should have stayed at home with you and cancelled the night out."

"Then why didn't you?"

"I wanted to, but Simon had been really looking forward to it. He'd got hold of some good pills. Jon Da Silva was DJing that night."

"So? What happened?"

"We ended up having sex in the Hacienda. Simon didn't plan on it happening. Neither of us did, and I'm so sorry, Jimmy."

Done.

She'd told him.

It was all out in the open.

She felt she'd said enough about the night in question. He didn't question her about protection or pregnancy; it was the only time she felt thankful he had a brain injury. Or maybe it was the long-term coma? She didn't care. She wanted to deflect his thought processes away from the fact she'd cheated on him. One mistake that, years later, she had to explain again. Jimmy looked confused.

"So, you only did it once, then?"

"Of course, it was a mistake, I told you. I regretted it as soon as it happened."

She watched his every move from her position as she sat on the bed. She knew he could be prone to angry and violent outbursts because of his head injury. It was the thing she feared most about admitting this to him.

"I guess it's in the past, but I still love you," he declared humbly, smiling back at her.

"Oh, Jimmy, I love you," she fawned back at him, reaching out so they could hold hands.

He clasped her hand in his and didn't let go. She'd managed to confess she'd cheated on him without triggering anything in his mind about conception or those years closest to the accident. She wanted to change the subject, focus his mind on something else.

"Do you remember our little holiday in Scotland?"

"Scotland? I think so. I remember going to visit some castles with you."

"Yes, that's right, we did. You loved it."

"When was that?"

"That was your treat for my twenty-first birthday. It was September eight five. You'd bought us two tickets to see The Smiths at Barrowlands."

"What's Barrowlands?"

"A big concert hall in Glasgow where groups play."

"Oh, I see. It's a long way to travel to see The Smiths isn't it?"

"Well, it is, yes. You'd booked us three nights in a hotel in Glasgow, so we could have a little holiday up there after the gig."

"Oh, I think I remember that concert. It was so hot inside that place. I remember that."

"It was pandemonium in there that night. Crazy. They were pulling people out of the crowd down at the front. People were getting squashed. I felt safe with you, though," she whispered, smiling, offering him an emotional olive branch.

"Will you help me to remember that concert, that holiday we had? I don't want to think about you and Simon having sex."

She felt warmed by his innocence and this desire for her to help him. Pleased he didn't want to hear more about her and Simon. Not pushing her on it. Even more pleased, he hadn't flipped or attempted to trash their hotel room from his sitting position in that electric chair.

#

Chapter 30

Jimmy didn't say anything during their evening meal in the restaurant; he was obviously hungry and focused on his food. Once they got into the lift up to their room, he chose to speak up.

"Did the Smiths play a lot of concerts?"

"Oh yes. All over the world. They were only together five years."

"Oh, did they split up?"

"Yes, they did, unfortunately. Nothing that good lasts forever, does it?"

"I thought we would," Jimmy mumbled sulkily.

The lift door opened; he steered his chair forwards, brushing past her into the corridor.

"Oh, Jimmy, wait. Don't say that," she said, catching up to him.

"You said we were part of the same soul."

"I think we are. I do," Alison countered.

She used the key card to open the hotel room door.

"Do you?" Jimmy retorted, rolling his chair slowly into their room.

"Yes. Shall I put the kettle on?"

"If you want."

"Open that window if you're having a smoke."

"OK. Why didn't you bring that portable stereo with you? I want to listen to The Smiths."

"Sorry. Shall I put the television on?"

"Nah, I'll just look at the sea."

"OK, darling," she responded.

He ignored her, turning his chair to face the window.

She would never forget the way he looked this morning. Absolute disappointment. His dreams shattered. Even though he still only knew half the story. She finished preparing their tea and stepped over to the window, placing his cup on the table next to his chair.

"How old was I when we went to Scotland?"

"It was my twenty-first, wasn't it. So, it was your twenty-second the same day."

"I wish I could remember it."

"The concert in Glasgow was on a Wednesday. You'd booked the hotel for that night, Thursday and Friday night."

"Good idea, I guess?"

"Yes, it was. We had a wonderful time up there. We met two Smith's fans on the train on the way up there. I'll never forget that trip."

#

September 1985

They boarded the train together at Piccadilly train station just after lunch on Wednesday. Jimmy carrying one large suitcase, shared between them for their three-day break. In his wallet were the return tickets for the train journey back home on Saturday and two tickets to see The Smiths at Glasgow, Barrowlands, later that evening. He'd saved enough of his wages, booking a double room for their stay at the expensive Grand Central hotel in the centre of Glasgow. It was grand, it was historic, and it was only a twenty-minute walk to Barrowlands. Reason enough to feel pleased he'd chosen that hotel. They took their seats as the train pulled away from Piccadilly station.

The break was Jimmy's treat for Alison, but they knew it was a treat for them both. Seven days ago, he'd celebrated his twenty-second birthday; she'd celebrated her twenty-first.

We're part of the same soul.

They both knew it; they both felt it.

A few minutes after the train had left the station, some passengers were still trying to find their seats. Jimmy and Alison's were window seats on either side of a table with an empty seat next to them. Jimmy put his portable cassette player on the table, with a handful of cassettes for them to listen to. Original cassettes of three albums from The Smiths and two compilation tapes he'd made of all their singles and B-sides they'd released so far.

Not too long into their journey, a young couple approached them. A dark-haired lad with thick eyebrows and his tall blonde girlfriend both wearing Smiths T-shirts.

Jimmy looked up from organising his cassettes as the lad spoke.

"Excuse me, are these seats taken?" the lad asked.

Jimmy and Alison smiled when they saw them.

"They are now. Sit down," Jimmy said, welcoming.

"Yes, sit with us. You're Smith's fans. Fantastic," Alison said.

"Oh, thanks. I think we were last to get on. We thought we'd be standing all the way to Glasgow, didn't we, Ian." The girl said as they sat down.

"Yeah. Hi guys, I'm Ian; this is my girlfriend, Vanessa."

"Alright, Ian, Vanessa. I'm Jimmy, this is my girlfriend, Alison. You two going to the Barrowlands gig?"

"Yes, is it that obvious?" Vanessa asked, laughing.

Jimmy pointed to his stack of Smiths tapes, and the four burst into laughter.

"I guess you two are going?" Ian asked.

"Yes. Have you seen them before?" Alison questioned.

"Yes. At the Free Trade Hall last year and the Palace Theatre in March this year."

"Oh, we went to both of those," Alison said.

"Are you staying up there, Ian?" Jimmy asked.

"No, we're getting the last train home after the gig. Can't afford a hotel room, we're skint. We're both students at Manchester University; it's how we met," Ian said.

"Right. Where are you from?" Jimmy said.

"Preston. Vanessa's from Warwickshire," Ian answered.

"Right. We're staying three nights at a hotel in Glasgow; it's only a twenty-minute walk to Barrowlands. We're having a three-day break up there. I'm a student, but Jimmy works full-time. It's a present from Jimmy for my twenty-first birthday," Alison said.

"Oh, happy twenty-first, Alison," Ian and Vanessa said.

"Thanks, guys. Are you looking forward to the concert?" Alison asked.

"Oh God yeah. We love The Smiths," Vanessa stated.

"Jimmy lived next door to Morrissey. Well, until The Smiths became successful. We always knew him as Steven. His mother still lives next door to Jimmy's mum."

"Oh wow. No way. Every single Smiths' fan will be jealous of you, Jimmy," Ian said.

"Yes, I bet," Vanessa agreed.

The extensive train journey north, through the country and up into Scotland, meant the two couples got to know each other quite well by the time they reached Glasgow railway station. They stuck together when Jimmy and Alison checked into the hotel and left their suitcase in their room, deciding they should find a place to eat near Barrowlands before the venue opened its doors. All four of them were hugely excited about the evening's concert.

#

The overture to Prokofiev's Romeo And Juliet bounced around inside the venue at ear-splitting volume. Everyone inside Barrowlands knew that music. In every venue *The Smiths* had played this year, it was the last song on the intro tape. Everybody knew what was coming. The loud classical music lasted for over a minute before the group emerged from the shadows and everyone inside the place began screaming. As *Morrissey* would always do, when the group mounted the stage before they began playing, he shouted a greeting into the microphone. Welcoming everybody into the world of *The Smiths*.

"*Hello,*" *Morrissey* said, and the entire crowd screamed hello back.

Mike Joyce, the drummer, clicked his sticks together in a rhythm the group could follow, and they began playing their first song, *Shakespeare's Sister*. There was a loud cheer of recognition, drowned out by the sound of the group coming from the stage. Almost immediately, Alison regretted pushing their way to the front of this raucous crowd. Everyone inside the place started bouncing along to the fast pace of this song and the sound of *The Smiths*.

By only the third song in, security guards at the front were pulling people from the crowd. There was a smell of stale beer and sweat pervading the air, and it quickly became stiflingly hot. As Alison looked across the crowd between songs, she could see steam rising from everyone. She couldn't believe how many people seemed overcome with emotion. Before the group had arrived on stage, she'd been chatting to a young teenage Scottish lad next to her called Stephen. He was crying. She couldn't believe it. She could see the impact this group from Manchester were having, bawling your eyes out wasn't something she thought Scottish lads did.

A few songs in, *Morrissey* decided to say a few words.

"*Due to excessive demand at Radio One, we have a new single out.*"

The crowd erupted into cheering and more screaming as Alison watched more people being pulled from the crowd at the front. She was still standing by Jimmy's side as he'd insisted; they held hands when the crowd began swaying, pushing, and shoving each other to stay upright and alive. They'd separated from Ian and Vanessa early on and hoped they would be reunited outside later when this throng of fans began leaving the venue after the gig.

"*It is called The Boy with The Thorn in His Side.*"

The group began playing the song with three clicks of the drummer's sticks. Alison could see the heat inside the venue begin to affect *Morrissey*. Wearing a white Smiths T-shirt with his face on it and a grey jacket over the top, his prominent quiff began to flatten under the intense heat inside the venue. When the group finished playing the song, the crowd began football, chanting *Morrissey's* name. Jimmy and Alison looked at each other, and they both smiled, knowing Steven had got what he'd always wanted. Adoration. To be loved by so many people.

The group left the stage after a particularly emotional rendition of *Meat Is Murder*, but everybody knew they would be back.

Cheers and screams were everywhere when the group came back onto the stage. Then *Morrissey* spoke to the crowd again.

"Thank you for all your kindness and generosity."

The group launched into their first encore.

The instantly recognisable guitar introduction from *This Charming Man* elicits screams and cheers from the crowd. The group left the stage again, returning to deafening shrieks from the crowd. They played their first single, *Hand in Glove*, as more and more people were pulled from the crowd, one or two actually making it to the stage to hug *Morrissey*.

They played their final song, *Miserable Lie,* and the concert ended. *Morrissey* sang the last two lines from the song before saying farewell as the band finished.

"I need advice, I need advice. Goodbye."

The place erupted again into cheering and screaming as the band left the stage, followed by boos when the house lights went up.

Outside the venue, there were hundreds of fans milling around. They spotted Ian and Vanessa quite quickly, who were in a desperate hurry to leave and catch the last train back to Manchester. The four knew it was only a ten-minute walk to the railway station in Glasgow; Jimmy and Alison offered to walk with them ensuring they made it to the train on time.

On their train journey back home to Manchester three days later, they discussed their short holiday and how much they'd enjoyed it. They'd been together for almost seven years and lived together for eighteen months. Alison thanked Jimmy for the time they'd spent away and the expensive hotel room where they'd stayed for three nights. He told her he'd been planning it for months. To take her away for a holiday and combine the two things he loved the most.

Alison, and The Smiths.

#

Chapter 31

August 2000

She didn't want to wake Jimmy from sleeping. She had no desire to use the telephone in the room to ring her husband either. Even at this hour, she knew he wouldn't be home. He'd be out shoving cocaine up his nose, with little thought for her and less for his friend of so many years.

Watching a brain-damaged paraplegic Jimmy Smith asleep in his wheelchair as she'd described their life together fifteen years ago was emotionally draining for her. She hated that he'd lost so much: his family, the use of his legs, his independence, virtually all of his memories. His damaged brain struggling to remember. His behaviour sometimes mirrors that of a petulant child.

Alison knew she couldn't possibly know how he felt. It took all her energy to step over to the ensuite bathroom, use the toilet and brush her teeth. She left Jimmy sleeping in his chair as she took off all her clothes before turning out the bedside light and climbing into bed.

With her head on the pillow, she turned her gaze and watched Jimmy sleeping in his chair. Since the first day she saw him almost a year ago, she'd worried he would hate her all over again when he remembered why they had split up. She was happy that despite his brain injury, he seemed to have accepted that it was all in the past, and she obviously couldn't undo it.

#

After breakfast, the following morning, they decided to explore Brighton. The sun was beaming down through an almost cloudless sky. Both accordingly wore t-shirts, light cotton trousers and sunglasses. Jimmy had been disappointed earlier because he wanted to go out and see the ocean. The wheels of his electric chair had struggled to negotiate the pebble beach. Sulking, he insisted they parade up and down streets looking in shop windows as they both enjoyed an ice cream cornet from a shop on the seafront. Jimmy shot ahead of Alison when he finished his ice cream. Something had caught his eye.

"Ali, look a record shop. Let's go inside."

She jogged up alongside him, trying to see where he was looking. She saw the shop he was contemplating across the road from where she stood.

"The Wax Factor. Yes, let's have a look inside."

"Yeah, come on," said Jimmy as he shot into the road.

"Jimmy, watch the road."

Checking for traffic in both directions, she crossed the road, stepping ahead as they approached the shop front.

"Hang on, let me hold the door for you."

He smiled a beaming grin up at her as she held the door for him, rolling past her into the record shop. She followed him in, gently pulling the shop door closed.

"Where will The Smith's records be, Ali?" he asked, looking up at her like a lost child.

She scanned the shop floor before answering. Pleased, the space between the racks was enough to accommodate Jimmy in his chair.

"Over there, Jimmy. Rock and Pop. They're alphabetically sorted; find the letter 'S' records," she suggested.

She followed him to the Rock and Pop section. He positioned his chair as close to the racks as possible before reaching over and flicking through the records in the 'S' section.

"I'll leave you looking while I have a browse, OK?"

He didn't look up to acknowledge her or answer. He was focused on looking at all the records he was flicking through. Pulling each record out and examining them front and back.

She began wandering around the store, not committing to browse through any particular genre of music. A record with a cover familiar to her caught her eye. She picked it up to look at it more closely. On the cover was an old painted scene of a woman opening a large five-barred gate, allowing through a horse and cart carrying a bale of hay. In large black capital letters in the top left corner of the record cover:

VAUGHAN WILLIAMS
THE LARK ASCENDING
FIVE VARIANTS OF "DIVES AND LAZARUS"
THE WASPS - ARISTOPHANIC SUITE.

She knew they used to own this record and how much they both loved this music. Lost in the euphoria of being on a sunshine-filled break with him, and without thinking, she impulsively decided to show him the record. She approached him, still browsing through records.

"Jimmy. Do you remember this record? We both loved this music."

He looked up and turned his chair to face her.

"I don't know; let's have a look," he said.

"Vaughan Williams, Jimmy."

She expected him to smile, perhaps even remember those two songs they'd listened to so many times. She wasn't expecting his smile to disappear completely and his face to drop into a stern and serious expression.

"Vaughan?"

"Yes. Vaughan Williams. We both loved his work."

"But Vaughan?"

She immediately regretted picking that record up and showing him. Why didn't she think? Nobody had said that name to Jimmy in the year she'd got to know him again. It had obviously triggered his memory. She should have known it would, cursing herself for being so stupid.

He clicked the joystick on his wheelchair and ignored her, spinning around quickly and heading for the door. He was distraught, and she knew that. Yet still, she just stood, frozen in shock.

In a strong Mancunian accent, he shouted at the couple in the doorway just entering.

"Hold that fuckin' door open and get out of my way."

He raced past them, running over the man's foot.

"Fuckin hell mate, watch it," the stranger shouted with a southern English accent.

Alison raced for the door herself, apologising to the couple on her way out of the shop. She raced into the street, chasing after him just as he disappeared through a crowd.

"Jimmy, wait. Let me explain," she screamed.

Alison ran after him, but she'd already lost him in the crowd. She stopped running and panicked, pacing around in a circle, wondering where he could have gone. On a hot and sunny day in Brighton, people are everywhere in a maze of unfamiliar streets. She asked a few people in the neighbouring streets, but nobody saw a man racing in an electric wheelchair. She sat on a wall, frustrated, taking a cigarette from her pack of twenty, putting it to her lips and lighting it. She exhaled and sighed, tearful because deep inside, she knew he'd remembered it for himself.

Why was that classical record staring me in the face earlier? Why did I have to pick it up and show it to Jimmy? That composer was the reason behind the boy's name. I should have known it was risky, she thought. She was frustrated with Jimmy but more frustrated with herself.

Alison spent the entire afternoon walking along every street and looking in every shop. She checked the seafront; he wasn't there. She checked back at the hotel; he wasn't there. She was growing more and more worried as each hour passed. What if he's said something to someone? He could get himself into trouble. A fight, perhaps? She was sick with worry.

When they were together, they'd never visited Brighton. He was lost in a place completely unknown to him. She felt stress and worry begin to take over her. She needed a cup of tea to stop and think for a moment. Other than the police, there was nobody she could telephone for help. Across the road from a large church, she spotted a coffee shop. She opened the door and stepped inside, ordering a mug of tea, then sitting at the window, hoping she might see Jimmy pass by. Sipping her tea and thinking, she contemplated her next move. The only thing left to do was call the police and register him as a missing person. Gazing up at a map of Brighton pinned to the wall, she realised she hadn't checked the beach. She'd covered all the streets inland; it was the only place she hadn't looked. He'd struggled so much with his chair on the pebbles this morning that she didn't think he would be there. Unless it was his intention to ride into the sea, she concluded worryingly.

Taking her last gulp of tea, she left the coffee shop, increasingly concerned about Jimmy's mind. Terrified something could have happened to him, she began to speed up her walk. Further ahead, she saw a large white Victorian building she assumed to be a hotel on the seafront. Beyond it, she could see the ocean. She had no idea if he would be on the beach or not. He must be back at the hotel if he wasn't here. Surely, he would have found solace indoors somewhere by now, she thought. The sun was dropping toward the horizon as she stepped from the promenade onto the pebbles. She looked across the beach and out to sea. At this time of the evening, it was almost empty. She spotted Jimmy straight away, sitting in his chair at least fifty yards farther out. She was impressed with how far he'd made it across the pebbles. As she got closer to him, she noticed he was sleeping. His face reddened from the hot summer sun that had been beaming down all day. She stepped in front of his wheelchair to face him and tapped him on the shoulder. A thousand thoughts raced through her mind, but she knew she had to be honest with him.

\#

Chapter 32

August 2000

He blinked his eyes open and stretched his arms above his head, his mouth opening wide in a gaping yawn as he leaned his head back against the chair's headrest. When it took him to realise where he was and with whom he was, Alison thought carefully about what to say to him. She knew he would be feeling betrayed, feeling she'd intentionally kept things from him.

"Jimmy? Have you been here all afternoon? I've walked along every street in Brighton looking for you."

He looked up at her as she spoke. He didn't reply straight away. The only two people on this part of Brighton's beach are in a moment of absolute silence.

"Why didn't you tell me we had a son?"

He looked lost, humble, and confused. She'd been his guide for almost a year, but she didn't think he would feel part of her soul anymore. She knew it, and she hated it.

"I told you it was complicated. Why did you have to leave me and disappear?"

She wanted to understand what he'd remembered. He looked away from her, out into the darkened ocean. She didn't say anything else.

"Since Simon got drunk the other night, I've remembered a lot."

The way he said it seemed threatening to her, but she knew that wasn't his intention.

After extensive conversations with Mr Davies at the hospital, she obviously had a better understanding of brain injury and knew how jumbled his memories were. She was the only person who could help him because she was so prevalent in many of his memories. She wanted to help him put things in a cohesive and chronological order, so his damaged brain could fully understand.

"Tell me what you've remembered, Jimmy."

"Why? So, you can say it didn't happen and lie."

It hit her in the heart when he said that. Whether with intent or not, he'd hurt her. She understood why he did it, but it didn't make it any easier for her to take.

"Jimmy. I've never lied to you. I've just kept things from you. I just didn't want to overwhelm you. On the advice of Mr Davies, we had to get you

settled into your new life with us at home, with a brain injury, with
paralysis. Then I would tell you everything about our past together. When
the time was right. It's hard enough for anyone to hear, even without a
brain injury."

She watched as he looked down around his chair. She knew his response
to an uncomfortable situation like this would be to click the joystick on
his chair and move away. That's what he was thinking about, but he
couldn't move. He couldn't do it this time.

"I'm not going back to your house. Not until you've told me everything."

"OK, OK. I understand."

Alison sat down on the pebbled beach next to Jimmy's chair, her
shoulders slouching from the mental and physical exhaustion his
disappearance had caused. As uncomfortable as it was, it was nice to sit
down after pacing up and down Brighton streets and in and out of shops
all afternoon.

"Memories of people and places have come back to me. I need you to fill
in the blanks. I'm so confused."

"That's what I'm here for."

"I know. I have a memory of the three of us going to see Oasis at The
Hacienda near your 30th Birthday. Reni was there too. I met up with him
early and bought two ecstasy pills off him. I remember we sneaked up
onto the roof and smoked a joint after the gig. Just me and Reni."

"I didn't know that. You loved Oasis, Jimmy. We all did. We went to see
them play a lot in ninety-three and ninety-four."

"Yeah, I can remember some of that."

"Jimmy, we need to go and eat. You can have a bath back at the hotel as
well."

He didn't refuse or demand answers; she knew he was tired and hungry.

"As soon as we've eaten, you'll tell me?"

"Of course. Come on, I'll give you a push across these pebbles."

"Well, you'd better tell me everything later. I've got the feeling I've been
cheated."

#

Dinner in the hotel restaurant was a mostly awkward silence. She knew
he was confused and hurting. She wanted to keep the conversation to a
minimum anyway, concerned about how he may react in public. As soon
as they'd finished eating, they made their way up to their hotel room.
Despite his brain injury and as angry as he was, she still felt safe with him

upstairs alone. They'd known each other for so long and been in love for many years.

She opened their hotel room door, stepping inside ahead of him. Reaching across the bed, she switched on one of the bedside lamps before stepping into the bathroom and leaning over the bath to put the plug in and turn on the taps, returning to the bedroom and sitting on the bed.

He sat staring out the window at sea in silence, without turning to face her when she sat down. After a short while, she went back into the bathroom to turn off the taps. The bath salts she'd tipped into the bath had produced lots of foam. She swirled her right hand around in the water, checking the temperature, before returning to the bedroom.

"The bath's ready. Come on."

"How will I get in?"

"It's OK; the bathroom has disabled access. There's a couple of handrails in there. You can use them to climb out of your chair and get your bum onto the tiled bit at the end of the bath, I'll swing your legs round, and you can slide in."

"OK, I'll give it a go."

Most hotel bathrooms are quite small, and this was no exception. He couldn't drive his chair into the bathroom, so he used the door frame and the sink to help him climb across to the tiled section at the end of the bath. His lifeless legs were dangling onto the bathroom floor as he unbuttoned his shirt and took it off, passing it to Alison.

"Thanks. I'll need to get your shoes and socks off, then your trousers and underpants. OK?"

"Yeah, if I press my fists down onto the tiles, I should be able to lift my bum up so you can pull them off."

"Yes, good idea."

It was the first time she'd seen him naked since he came back into her life. As his full-time caregiver, she would help him wash back in Highgate daily. Now, together and alone in a hotel bathroom, it felt different. She helped him swing his legs around, and he slid down into the bath, carefully lowering his body into the warm soapy water. Despite his opinion of her being somewhat skewed after parts of his memory had returned, he smiled at her as she took his position sitting on the tiling at the end of the bath. A momentary silence in the bathroom as Jimmy relaxed and lay in the bath. His head rested on her thighs as she broke the silence and spoke.

"That Oasis gig at the Hacienda was the launch party for their debut album. Do you remember?"

"Oh yeah. Definitely Maybe. What an incredible record. Makes me wish we'd brought a stereo with us. I'm so happy I can actually remember these things now, Ali."

"You've done so well since that first day we met."

"It's all the music you've played to me; it flicks switches in my mind. It's weird."

"It's not weird, Jimmy; it's fantastic."

"I think seeing you so much has also helped me with my memory. I knew it would."

"Good, I'm glad you have those memories again."

"So am I."

"Hey, we've never listened to Oasis together since we met up again, have we?"

"No. I know why now, don't I?"

"Of course. I knew I couldn't mention Oasis to you. I was terrified you'd remember because of what happened at that time. I told Simon not to mention that group either."

"Right. Now I get it."

"You don't get it, Jimmy. I never wanted to hurt you. That's why I've kept things from you this past year. It would be too much for you to take in. I'll explain things properly now."

"OK," he said softly.

She smiled at him as his head leant back almost into her lap. He lay there smiling up at her, her thin cotton trousers soaked through and stuck to her thighs.

She smiled. She knew he didn't hate her.

It made her feel completely in love with him, as she always had.

#

Chapter 33

Monday 5ᵗʰ September 1994

Jimmy had gone down early to the Hacienda. He'd arranged to meet Reni outside at half past six to get the pills. Later, walking down Whitworth Street, Alison looked forward to the Oasis gig. She was pleased Simon seemed to love them as much as she and Jimmy did. He'd been in their flat when *Johnny Marr* telephoned last September, excited about a group his manager was trying to get signed. He explained that they were playing a gig at the Canal Café Bar in town on the 14ᵗʰ. He'd arranged to get them on the guest list and introduced the three of them to the group before the gig.

"They blew us all away that night, Si."

"I know, they're gonna be huge this group Ali."

"Yeah, definitely."

The Hacienda came into view as they made their way around the slight bend in the road.

"Fuck me. Look at the fuckin' queue." Simon exclaimed.

Alison smiled when she saw how many people were milling around outside the Hacienda for *Oasis*. She smiled because she knew they wouldn't have to queue up to get into the place.

"It's OK. Liam's put us on the guest list."

"Oh, nice one," Simon said.

He pulled a bag of white powder from his pocket.

"Put that away. You'll get it taken off you."

"Chill. I won't. You want some?" he said, scooping out a quantity of the white powder from the bag with his little finger and snorting it up his nose.

"What coke? No ta. Jimmy came down here earlier and bought two pills off Reni. He's booked the rest of the week off work, and I've no lectures tomorrow. His mother's having Vaughan for a couple of days."

"Right. I didn't know Reni was coming down."

"Yes, but I think he's as much into selling pills and making money as he is Oasis."

"Yeah, probably. Queues moving; we should get in and get a drink."

"Yeah, you're right," Alison said.

Once inside, Alison and Simon squeezed themselves politely past pockets of people, spotting Jimmy near the bar.

Jimmy noticed Alison almost straight away, smiling and gesturing for her and Simon to come over. He stepped away from the bar area, embracing Alison, kissing her, nodding, and smiling at Simon.

"You get Vaughan to mam's all right?"

"Yes, he's fine. He loves spending time with his nanna. Did you get those pills off, Reni?"

"Yeah, he's in here somewhere. Shall we drop 'em? They're on at eleven."

"Yeah, get me a drink, and I will."

"Oh yeah. Hang on," Jimmy gestured, making eye contact with a guy behind the bar who knew him.

Jimmy stuck two fingers in a victory sign, and the guy behind the bar nodded. A moment later, the barman stepped over and passed Jimmy two cans of lager.

"Ta mate," Jimmy smiled.

He passed the cans to Alison and Simon, who took them and cracked them open. Simon coming up from the cocaine he'd just ingested, drank the whole can in one sustained slug. Jimmy passed Alison one of the pills and put the other one in his mouth, both taking a drink from their cans and swallowing. They had two hours to kill before Oasis was due onstage, but after about half an hour, when the effects of the ecstasy pills began to take effect, the time flew by. They were completely loved up, with each other and everyone else inside the place. Alison thought briefly about being here with Jimmy in November eighty-three, watching *The Smiths* play. Eleven years later, the same thing was happening again. The Hacienda was rammed full of people in the know who knew how incredible a group from their city were before the rest of the world caught on.

Five lads from Manchester stepped out onto the stage to raucous cheers and applause. The loudness of the guitars was the first thing Alison noticed when the group started with *Rock and Roll Star*. She watched her man by her side stare intently at Liam, arms behind his back with his wide, open-mouthed singing style. Every song they played was a loud annihilation of the senses. Liam barely moved. Liam didn't need to move. That voice he had was everything.

"You're loving this, aren't you, darling?"

"Fuckin' right I am. The best band in the world, off me tits on E, with the woman I love. It doesn't get better than this, does it?"

"No, it doesn't," she said, hugging him around the waist and agreeing.

As the group played the closing part of the song, Jimmy shouted, singing along with Liam.

"Yeah, yeah, yeah," he screamed, stretching his arms straight above his head and punching the air with both fists.

"Part of the same soul, babe," she said, making eye contact, and coming together for a full-on romantic kiss, as *Oasis* belted out one of their favourite songs.

After the gig, Jimmy wanted to hang with Reni and the Oasis lads. Simon had shoved all his coke up his nose, and Alison was starting to come down a little from her ecstasy experience; the pair wanted to leave. They left Jimmy in the Hacienda and walked back to the flat.

Jimmy had a quarter of weed shoved down his trousers for his ecstasy comedown. Just after one thirty in the morning, when Alison and Simon had left, he searched for Reni. He found him eventually, obviously pleased he'd managed to shift all the pills he'd brought with him.

"What you up to, man?" Jimmy shouted into Reni's ear over the music.

"Nowt."

"You wanna sneak up onto the roof of this place? Get us away from the idiots and skin up."

"Ha, ha. Yeah, man, good idea. Let's do it."

They managed to sneak away unnoticed backstage and up the concrete staircase, quickly reaching the top of the four-story former yacht warehouse. Both lads sat down, leaning back against the decorative stone balustrade that finished the top of the building. Jimmy put his cigarettes, cannabis and rolling papers on the dry roof between his outstretched legs, thankful it hadn't rained all weekend. He did his best to roll a joint, which he managed with only a gentle breeze blowing.

"Fuckin' blindin' gig that wan' it, Reni?"

"Yeah, mega. They're fuckin' great. Liam wants me to come on tour with 'em."

"Does he?"

"Oh yeah. I can sell drugs. I think I can make a fair bit of money shifting t-shirts an all. Cash on the hip while I'm away."

"Nice one. When you goin'?" Jimmy asked, taking successive drags on the joint he'd rolled.

"Thursday. Couple of days in Europe, then Japan."

"Japan? No way?"

"Yeah. It's gonna be wicked, man. You should come with us?"

"I'd love to, but I've got me job, haven't I? I can't leave Ali here with Vaughan either?"

"Nah, but Liam wants you to come out with us."

"Does he?"

"Oh yeah."

"Well, I'm not fuckin' twenty-one anymore like he is, am I? Listen, Reni. I wanna ask you summat. Here" he said, passing Reni the joint.

"Ta, what's on yer mind, Jim?"

"You know our Vaughan?"

"Oh, aye. Top lad."

"Do you think he looks like me?"

Reni's face dropped in shock, but he knew what Jimmy was getting at.

"Honestly? I don't think he looks anything like you."

"Right. I thought so."

"What d'ya mean?"

"I'm getting' a DNA test done," Jimmy announced, concentrating on rolling another joint.

"What? You don't think Vaughan's yours?"

"Nah. It's been on my mind for weeks," Jimmy said.

Lifting his head, he made eye contact with his friend.

"Where the fuck are you gonna get a DNA test from?"

"You remember Angie Tompkins? Our Vicky's mate?"

"Yeah."

"She's a sister at the children's hospital. I went to her house last week."

"Can she sort it?"

"Oh yeah. She told me; you get two swabs, one to swipe inside my mouth, one for Vaughan's mouth and then you seal 'em in clear plastic tubes they come in."

"Right. How long d'ya have to wait to find out?"

"A week."

"Have you not spoken to Si about it?"

"That's the thing. I think he might be the father."

"Fuckin' 'ell. Really? Why him?"

"He came down here with Ali at the back end of nineteen ninety. On E the pair of 'em an' all. I was in bed with the flu. Vaughan was born about nine months after that."

"Fuck off. And you reckon he fucked her when you were in bed with the flu? Nah. Ali wouldn't do that. Have you not spoken to her about it?"

"Yeah, right. I can't. What if I'm wrong? She'll go off her tits, man."

"Yeah, it's a risky one, init. If it's on yer 'ead, though, you wanna know, don't ya? But mate, if yer wrong and Vaughan's yours? Then what?"

"I know, mate. I've gotta find out, though."

"Just let me know what happens, will ya?"

"I will. Don't worry."

A short time later, they both stood up to get going. It was almost two in the morning, and they'd be closing the place in five minutes. At least Jimmy knew he'd have an answer by the end of this week. He would know if he was Vaughan's father. Or the unthinkable had happened, and Alison had cheated on him, with life-altering consequences.

#

Chapter 34

Saturday 17th September 1994

Outside Angela's house, DNA test results in hand, Jimmy wanted to find somewhere he could sit down privately and open the envelope. He didn't want to rush it; this was a big moment. He could walk to Longford Park in twenty minutes, so he could sit on the horizontal branch of that tree near the play area. A place where he'd spent so much time with Alison in the past.

During that long walk from Angela's house, he listened to the first album by *The Smiths* on his Walkman. He stopped to fast-forward side two when he stepped onto King's Road. He really wanted to listen to *Suffer Little Children* before he got to that branch in the park. It was *Johnny Marr's* guitar sound in that particular song he wanted to hear. After four clicks of the drumsticks, the song started. Jimmy listened intently through his snug-fitting headphones as he walked toward Stretford. He felt on the verge of tears because of those guitars and that unopened envelope. Perhaps it was the girl he could hear crying at the song's end or the feeling he already knew the inevitable answer inside that white envelope. All the way there, he wished he hadn't bothered organising the test in the first place. He hated being in this position, but it was a predicament he'd put himself into. The nagging doubt sent him paranoid. No doubt Alison's parents would blame the cannabis, but he couldn't care less about their opinion. His response usually told them to fuck off if they questioned his cannabis consumption. Perhaps they were right. Perhaps he was behaving unreasonably. He hated them even more in case they were right.

He stopped his cassette player and dropped his headphones around his neck. Sitting down on the branch, he put a cigarette to his lips and lit it before stuffing his cigarettes and lighter into his coat pocket. As he exhaled that first drag, he looked up, surveying from left to right, taking everything around him. He was glad it was cold, and all the children were in school. Not a soul in sight. He looked down at the plain white envelope; no little plastic window, no text, no label printed on it, just Private & Confidential - Angela Tompkins, written in blue ballpoint pen across the front.

Jimmy turned it over, carefully peeling it open, watching the adhesive cling to the back of the envelope as his fingers prized it open. The last few strings of glue peeled away and lost the battle; the envelope was open.

Inside he could see what looked like one A4 piece of paper, professionally folded in two places. The paper opened easily, and he began to study it carefully.

Two wide columns of information took up most of the page.

One column is headed: the child. Another headed: the putative father.

"Putative father?" he questioned aloud.

He'd never seen *that* word before.

Thin horizontal strips are made up of hundreds of tiny, coloured vertical lines.

Rows and rows of numbers meant nothing to him.

Jimmy took another drag on his cigarette before gently exhaling as he saw that word again in a closing sentence at the bottom of the page. He didn't know the word's meaning, but he suspected he knew what it meant when he absorbed it. He read the sentence aloud and slowly, just to confirm to himself that he understood it.

"The putative father is NOT the father of the child."

He looked down at the paper, read the sentence again and started crying.

"The putative father is <u>NOT</u> the father of the child."

He held onto the paper with a shaking left hand, and his shoulders sank. His right elbow resting on his right knee, he dropped his forehead onto the palm of his right hand. Tears of sadness flooded him; he couldn't stop them. He didn't know what to do. He was numb. He could only see Vaughan's face, which made him cry even more. Only now, with confirmation, was he sure. Only now he could say: I was right. Vaughan's hair is exactly like Simon's, and now I know why; I have proof. When he thought about Simon, the empty retching in his gut tightened into knots. The sadness turned to anger, to hatred.

Jimmy had intentionally left his cannabis at home when he'd set off for Angela's. There was no way he wanted that stuff chilling him out. He was angry. Now it all made sense. The night at the Hacienda four years ago when he couldn't go, the pregnancy announcement when they'd always used protection, and the child's hair colour all added up to only one conclusion.

Jimmy wasn't Vaughan's father. Simon was Vaughan's father. How could he do it? How dare he break our trust? Someone I'd known since I was only three years old, he thought as the tears began to flood out of him again. Wiping both eyes with his sleeve, he stood up, putting the test result back into the envelope, then slipping it into the inside pocket of his jacket.

He sat there for ten minutes, upset, hurt and vulnerable, every thought welling into hatred toward Simon.

Jimmy slowly walked away from that horizontal branch, stunned and in shock. He needed music. It was his escape. It was why he had his *Walkman* with him. He wanted to hear music that would give him self-confidence and readiness for a confrontation. *Oasis* always did that for him. He found a compilation tape he'd made of all their singles and B-sides in his coat pocket. He knew the first song on the tape was *Cloudburst*, a song from his *Live Forever* CD single. He was angry and knew this music was perfect for his mood. Liam's voice and those guitars always made him feel like he could take on anyone. When the song started, he began walking with a stride that aped *Liam Gallagher's*, fists clenched down by his side. The sadness, weakness and slump in his posture had gone, replaced by tension, walking tall and striding with anger and hate.

When he reached Simon's front door, he knocked much more firmly than usual. His friend was thirty years old but still lived with his mother in the only house he'd ever lived in. When his friend opened the door, he was the first to speak.

"Fuckin' 'ell Jim. I thought it was the police. What's up?"

Jimmy just stood there. Angry. Constantly thinking of Simon and Alison. That night. Of all places inside the Hacienda. It had happened once he could cope with, but not when it produced a child who, for three years, he'd thought was his own flesh and blood.

"You comin' in or what, mate?"

He had to ask him. Despite really wanting to hit him, Jimmy wanted to know why.

"Mate? Why d'ya do it?"

"Do what? Aren't you gonna come in?"

"Answer the fucking question first! October 1990, Jon DaSilva. AT THE HACIENDA!"

"Woah. Chill man. As I remember it, you were in bed with the flu. You couldn't go."

That answer from Simon just infuriated Jimmy even more. The cockiness.

"I've done a DNA test on Vaughan."

It was out in the open, and Jimmy studied his friend's face closely to look for any reaction. In a split second, Jimmy could tell the penny had dropped. He could see it in the face of a man he'd known virtually all his life. When you look at someone, you can see they're thinking and rapidly going over things in their mind.

They both looked directly into each other's eyes; it was enough to tell Jimmy that his best friend knew exactly what he was getting at. Even before Simon spoke, Jimmy's blood was boiling over, and he knew he wanted to attack.

"No, what happened was...," Simon pleaded, but it was too late for talking."

Jimmy stepped into Simon's house, grabbed his friend by the throat with his left hand and began pushing him. Striding forwards, using all his body weight and not letting up on his throat, Simon was forced back through the hall into the kitchen, falling back against the sink. Jimmy swung a right hook in his direction using the most force he'd ever been able to muster. The punch caught Simon square in the jaw, flinging his head backwards and his body following suit. As he fell against the cooker, he slumped onto the floor. As Simon stood up slowly, Jimmy grabbed his shirt and jumper at his chest with his left hand, pushing him against the back door.

Whack! Whack! Whack! Whack!

Fuelled by hatred, he cracked Simon hard in the face four times. The only time he'd ever hated his best friend. The blood splattered from his nose onto the back door, the walls and Jimmy's jacket. His friend's left eye was cut and bleeding. His nose was broken, pouring blood onto his clothes. Jimmy's hatred didn't dissipate; he didn't want to let up on his friend. Simon had ruined everything. Alison had ruined everything, but he couldn't hate her. Somebody had to pay for the hurt he felt inside because of this. Again, Jimmy punched him in the face.

Whack! Whack! Whack!

With three more blows, his friend's face was a distorted, bloody mess.

Simon was weakening, his legs wobbling. Jimmy could feel his friend slipping downwards as he gripped him by the scruff of the neck with his left hand. As he let go, Simon's legs completely gave way. Jimmy had knocked him out, his back sliding down the back door until he slumped on the floor. Head in the corner, with his eyes closed.

Jimmy bent over and screamed into Simon's silent face.

"ARG!!!"

His friend was out cold. The volume of the scream into his face didn't wake him.

#

Chapter 35

Sunday 18ᵗʰ September 1994

The following morning, warm and comfortable but awake under his duvet, Jimmy heard his mother open the front door, barely hearing her gently close it as she left for church. He smiled, knowing she didn't want to wake him. He climbed out of bed and stood up, opening the curtains, watching his mother stride up King's Road seeking divine intervention. It saddened him because he knew how hurt she must be feeling. When they'd cried together yesterday, he thought about suggesting they share a joint. He immediately thought better of it, grateful enough that his mother at least allowed him to smoke joints in her back garden. He grabbed the tray he had in his bedroom. On it; was a small bag of cannabis, cigarette papers and his packet of twenty cigarettes. He sighed as he began to build a joint, knowing circumstance was forcing him toward his vice so early in the morning. As he'd gotten older, it was something he enjoyed with Alison in the evening, never during the day and never before at such an early hour. Jimmy was hurt. He needed to escape. He wanted his mind to wander away from thoughts of parenthood, Vaughan, and Alison. Sat on his bed in his old bedroom; it was his thirty-first birthday today, but he was in no mood to celebrate.

He made his way downstairs without consideration for washing or dressing; he slumped slowly through the lounge into the kitchen. Still in his pyjamas, dressing gown loosely tied at the waist, he flicked the kettle to boil. He dropped a tea bag into a clean mug from the cupboard and unlocked the back door, opening it wide to let some fresh air in. He pulled a kitchen chair to the back door, made himself a mug of tea and sat down. He put his mug onto the kitchen side next to him before putting the joint to his lips and lighting it. He took a long drag and then slowly exhaled, sighing, and slumping into the chair, as the thick smoke around him slowly began to escape into the back garden. Escape. It was all he was thinking about. It was all he wanted to do.

Had this situation happened differently with another man, he knew it would have been Simon consoling him, offering him support. Yet here, all alone, Jimmy hated him. Hated Simon for what he'd done. Only his mother offered solace and succour, but Jimmy didn't want to see her in that state. Her grandchild had been taken away. As if he'd just died. Lost to her. Gone. Forever.

The only people Jimmy could turn to for support, Reni, Liam and the rest of Oasis, were in Japan. He'd always turned to the music groups he loved. They were his real friends. They just sang and played to him. No mither. No disappointment. They never let him down. In *Liam Gallagher* and *Oasis*, he'd found so much more. They were friends. Making music that he loved. Lads that he loved. Lads that always had time for him.

Just after six in the evening in Stretford, Isobel's telephone rang at home. She answered the call, and when Jimmy took the telephone from his mother, he could tell Reni was pretty out of it. It was 2am at the hotel in Japan, and Jimmy told his friend what had happened. Reni was shocked at what he heard. He couldn't believe it. Jimmy asked about joining them on tour.

"The last Japanese gig is on Monday, mate. You'd be better meeting up with us in America. They're playing in Seattle on Friday. I think our flight's on Wednesday. I'll find out which hotel in Seattle we're staying at, and bell ya. Meet us there."

"Right, OK. I'll see you over there, Reni. I'll get a plane ticket tomoz."

"Sweet. I'm sorry, man. I wasn't expecting this to happen. Am I alright letting Liam and the rest of the lads know?"

"Yeah, man. Tell LG I said hello, and I'll see you out there, mate. Laters."

"See you soon, man. Keep yer 'ead together."

#

Monday 19th September 1994

The first thing Isobel did when she got up was telephone Jimmy's boss at work. He reassured her that under the circumstances, her son should take two weeks' holiday and not worry about working at a time like this. Lay in bed, Jimmy could hear her on the telephone when he woke not long after eight. He considered immediately getting out of bed, going to the bathroom and splashing cold water onto his face. He needed to go into town and buy a plane ticket to America. The warmth underneath that duvet, the familiarity of those four walls around him, were like a comfort blanket after what had happened on Saturday. Simon was in the hospital with a broken nose and jaw; his mother, Mary, had telephoned Isobel last night. It was a difficult position for them both to be in; they'd been friends for so long.

As Jimmy lay there, he only had one thing on his mind; he needed to escape. To escape a situation that had been involuntarily placed upon him. Forced upon him because of his own decision. A choice he had made himself. Get a DNA test done.

He was glad he had a well-paid job and savings in the bank; he would need the money. By the time he'd convinced himself to get out of bed, brush his teeth, get washed and dressed, it was almost nine o'clock when he came downstairs.

"Morning, love," Isobel uttered as Jimmy walked into the kitchen.

"Alright, mam."

He sat with his mother at the table, accepting a cigarette from her and lighting it.

"You wanna brew love?"

"I'll do it, mam. You want one?"

"Aye, go on."

Jimmy stood up to flick the kettle on to boil and prepare two mugs of tea.

"Mam, I'm goin' town in a bit."

"What for?"

"Plane ticket. I'm getting a flight to America, aren't I?"

"Oh, you're still going through with it, then?"

He turned to face her, placing both mugs of tea on the table.

"I've got to, mam. I need to get away, and I wanna meet up with Oasis they're touring."

As he sat down, his mother patted the back of his left hand reassuringly.

"OK, son. I'll be fine here. I'm going to pop next door and see Liz while you're out."

"Good idea. You shouldn't be on your own."

#

Jimmy had just withdrawn most of his savings from the bank. Having paid cash and got a good price for a plane ticket, he still had a few hundred pounds tucked in the inside pocket of his coat alongside his ticket. As he walked into town from the travel agents towards the Arndale, he had his headphones on. Whenever he was out by himself, he always had his *Walkman*. Today was no different. He needed to flee into music. Stop himself from thinking about what he once had. Three years of being a father; were wasted, pointless and irrelevant. Living a lie. As he walked into the Arndale Centre, listening to *Oasis*, he didn't feel like he could take on the world as he always would when he listened to them. At the moment, it felt like life was pointless and irrelevant.

As he stepped into the lift alone, he looked at the floor numbers on the keypad and decided he would head to the open car park on the top floor. He'd been up there in the past with Simon when they were younger. You get a great view of Manchester from up there.

Walking towards the edge of the car park in the sunshine, still listening to *Oasis*, he stopped next to a large yellow plastic salt bin against the steel fencing surrounding the rooftop car park. He leant over the fencing, peering down to the pavement a few hundred feet below.

Watching a small boy hold his father's hand as he crossed the road, Jimmy felt lost and alone inside. He pushed with as much force as he had left, slowly moving the grit bin away from the fence so he could sit on it and look across Manchester. The city he'd been born and raised closest to. The city that had given him so much music, so many guitar groups. He lifted his feet up, resting them on one of the steel bars as he sat there. He fished for the cigarette packet in his coat pocket, taking out the small joint he'd rolled at home, lighting it and taking a large drag. He leant his body forwards over the fencing, exhaling smoke toward the pavement below.

Jimmy started to weep.

He watched his tears under the force of gravity race downwards out of sight.

He thought about how fast his body would travel, how hard his head would hit the grey concrete floor. How long would it take for him to die?

My son is dead. The child of my loins does not exist. He never existed.

I didn't do this.

She did it. Selfishly, sharply slicing our souls in half.

Part of the same soul, my arse.

What is there to live for now? I have no one?

Whether subconsciously with intent or by accident, the song *Live Forever* began playing.

The whistle at the song's start and that drum introduction saved him. Made him think twice. The thought of what it would do to his mother rescued him. The thought of seeing Reni, seeing Liam and that group play live again protected him.

He wiped his eyes with his sleeve and sat there, slowly smoking the joint. Jimmy continued to listen to a group he loved from a city he loved. A group he knew that he could refer to as his friends. He really needed fucking friends now.

#

Chapter 36

August 2000

He'd actually drifted off to sleep in the bath. Alison knew she ought to help him into his chair, so he could sleep. He opened his eyes with his head still resting in her lap. He looked up at her. She didn't realise how much he'd heard her say, but when she looked at him, he wasn't smiling. She suspected she knew why, even despite his inability to remember. Before she'd even suggested she should get him out of the bath, he hit her with a barrage of questions.

"So, I did a DNA test on Vaughan? What happened? Where is Vaughan now? Am I his dad?" he questioned her, confused.

"Oh, Jimmy, let's get you out of the bath, shall we? So, I can explain everything."

"Everything?"

"Yes. Everything. This isn't easy for me, Jimmy."

"OK then. Help me out."

"Of course. Come on, lift yourself up onto here. It's getting late."

When she suggested he sleep in the bed, he smiled.

"No, Jimmy. So, you can get a good night's sleep. I think we both need it."

Alison knew what was on his mind. She knew that regardless of his brain injury and partial paralysis, he was still a red-blooded male.

It had gone midnight by the time Jimmy had successfully climbed into bed. Sitting in the armchair by the window, she thought about how difficult it would be to 'fill in the blanks' for him. She'd spent the last couple of years trying to forget the pain she'd been through with Vaughan, but now she had to go through it again. Jimmy didn't know what had happened. His response to the DNA test result back then was to beat Simon up and put him in hospital, then get a flight out of the country. He didn't know what had happened to Vaughan after that. He couldn't care less about a child that wasn't his.

With a cigarette between her lips, she took the first drag and burst into tears.

"Ali, what's wrong?"

Using both hands, he pushed himself up and sat upright in bed.

Alison couldn't stop herself from crying. Minutes ticked as she ignored his continued pleas to join her in bed. Impatience brought on by his brain injury eventually made him speak.

"Where's Vaughan?" he asked innocently.

She ignored him, choosing instead to look down at the bedroom carpet. She looked up at him, trying her best to speak.

A word and then a sob. Another word. Another sob.

"You've no idea…...what Simon…...and I went through."

"What happened?"

She paused for a moment breaking eye contact with him, staring again at the hotel room carpet. She looked up at Jimmy and began to explain.

"We were in London on a Saturday in ninety-five."

"Yes."

"This is really hard, Jimmy," she sobbed.

"What happened, Ali?"

"Vaughan ran into the road and was hit by a bus."

"Oh no," Jimmy said.

"The driver didn't see him. He couldn't see him."

Her sporadic sobbing turned into floods of tears. Jimmy's memory loss forced her to think back and remember a day she'd spent a long time trying to forget.

"I'm so sorry, Ali. I don't know what to say?"

For a brief moment, he'd thought he was a father, but with her help, he remembered the DNA test. He didn't know how to feel, but he was saddened to see her so upset.

"There's nothing you can say, Jimmy."

"How old was he? When I found out?"

"Three."

"So, for three years, I thought I was his dad?"

"Yes, I thought you were. The DNA test result was as much of a shock to me as it was you."

"Bollocks. You just thought nobody would find out Vaughan wasn't my son."

"Jimmy, that's not true. I didn't know. I wouldn't do that to you."

"You had sex with Simon. You admitted it."

"I know what I did, Jimmy. You don't have to keep reminding me. You and I had sex a lot. Why would I think one mistake with someone else would produce Vaughan?"

She was looking directly at Jimmy. Trying to gauge how he felt. It was hard for her. She felt almost as crushed as she did when the bus hit Vaughan. Living with that sadness for so long had only partially diluted her pain. It isn't something she was ever going to forget. It was the only stain on a relationship they both felt was perfect.

Part of the same soul?

Adultery was a stain that discoloured many relationships. Raising a child you assumed to be your own flesh and blood was considerably worse. She knew that. Convincing him, she didn't know Vaughan was not his child was going to be difficult.

She'd not lied to him. Like Jimmy, she'd assumed that having a child together was the cherry on top of the icing on top of the cake and that they were indeed part of the same soul.

"Whether you believe me or not, it doesn't really matter now, does it? Vaughan has gone."

"Come and sit here?" he asked.

She moved up to the bed and sat alongside him. She'd put her soaking wet cotton trousers in a carrier bag, instead now wearing casual jogging bottoms and a t-shirt. She leaned back against the headboard and looked at Jimmy.

"It doesn't matter to me, Ali. It makes me sad to see you this upset. Now I know why. You lost your son. That doesn't make me hate you. How could it? We're part of the same soul."

"Oh, Jimmy. I honestly didn't think he wasn't your child. How could I? I love you so much. I've always loved you. I didn't want us to ever split up."

He turned to look at her, directly in her eyes, as he spoke.

"Ali, I love you so much."

He moved his face toward her, and they kissed passionately, their faces touching. A moist sheen of tears covering both their faces, Alison briefly pulled away from him to slip out of her clothes and join him under the duvet.

They embraced again, kissing more and more passionately as the moments ticked by. When Jimmy touched her between her legs, she could feel his penis hardening against her thigh. She thought briefly about the conversation she'd had with Tracy about sex, happy that he didn't seem to be paralysed down there. She pulled her face away from his before gently whispering.

"I want you so much, Jimmy."

"Oh Alison, I've always loved you. I want you too."

That was all she needed to hear.

"Lie down, Jimmy," she suggested.

He took the cue and, using his upper body strength, slid down the bed on his back until his head was resting on the pillow. She climbed on top of him, and Jimmy entered her gently. Allowing her backside to slide down onto him, her full body weight supported by his groin. Up and down slowly she went as they continued to kiss passionately.

"You're my guide," he said, smiling at her as they both paused to come up for air.

"Oh, I love you so much, Jimmy."

"Part of the same soul we are."

He began to rapidly thrust his groin upwards as best he could with his paralysed legs.

Faster and faster until he came.

She could feel him explode inside her, pushing her over the edge. She came with her own shuddering orgasm as he was still thrusting; her body weakened, her legs wobbling like jelly. She collapsed on top of him, exhausted and lost in the moment. She was too drained to move and lay beside him until he softened inside her. She swung her right leg over and lay on her back next to him, her head on the pillow. She was satisfied but breathless, as was he.

Still panting together, neither of them said anything for a moment. Until Jimmy smiled and broke the silence.

"Wow. Was it always that good, Ali?"

She smiled back at him. At that moment, nothing had changed. No split. No, Simon. Just the two of them united and in love. Making love. Part of the same soul.

#

Chapter 37

Alison was awake before Jimmy; she slid out from under the duvet, determined not to wake him. He was asleep, so she dressed silently and pocketed her cigarettes and lighter. She put her coat on and zipped it up before gently opening and closing their hotel room door. She needed some time alone, away from Jimmy, away from everybody.

Without speaking to anyone downstairs, she walked straight out of the hotel and crossed the road. She stepped onto the pebbled beach and checked her wristwatch. It was just after seven thirty in the morning, and the beach was empty. She looked up at the cloudless bright blue sky; it would be another warm and sunny day today. Sitting down on the pebbles and taking a long drag on her cigarette, she sighed as she exhaled. She didn't want to think this was all she'd wanted when Jimmy returned to their lives. It wasn't fair on Simon. She thought back through her relationship with her second husband. How it had been completely on the rebound from Jimmy when she'd run into Simon's open arms. The attentive way she'd supported Jimmy over the past year had driven a wedge between them and driven her husband to booze and cocaine as his way of dealing with it.

Was her marriage over because of Jimmy?

Because of what had happened last night?

Because of how she *really* felt inside her soul.

She dropped the end of her cigarette between the pebbles and immediately lit another. She wasn't looking forward to facing her husband. She wasn't looking forward to it because Simon had been right all along. She'd *always* been in love with Jimmy regardless of what had happened. She didn't think she'd ever stopped loving him.

Alison felt stressed and had several problems only she could deal with. The onus was on her to resolve the situation. Should she try and repair the damage to her marriage? Take off those rose-tinted spectacles and stop assuming things would be just like they used to be with Jimmy. He was disabled. He had a brain injury. Life would be different now. Could she handle that?

She knew she would have to treat each day as a new day, a new challenge. Jimmy's behaviour and verbal outbursts were so unpredictable.

Absolutely anything could trigger him to explode. She'd witnessed it but had always been ready with an immediate apology and a polite explanation of his brain injury. She could do it. She wanted to do it. She didn't want to hide him away at home. Facing social situations with Jimmy was the way to help him improve. Practice. Help him become more aware of how his behaviour impacted other people. She looked out to sea, watching the tide slowly going out. There were only a few metres of beach exposed, and for a moment, she thought she could just stand up and walk into the sea.

The pressure of everything was finally getting to her. She knew she could end it right here, right now and avoid facing up to the problem. Tears began to stream down her face, trapped inside a decision she *had* to make one way or the other. She lit a third cigarette, drawing in smoke, lost and alone with no one to turn to. The responsibility was hers, and she knew it.

Alison just sat there on the pebbles, smoking that third cigarette.

Sobbing, inhaling.

Sobbing, exhaling.

The Smiths felt like Jimmy and Alison's group, though she knew all their fans would claim that. As a fan, the music of that group is *always* with you. It was one of the many things that united Jimmy and Alison and made them part of the same soul. She thought about some of their songs and how she would always associate them with Jimmy, whether he was by her side or not. The song *Hand in Glove* playing over and over again in her head since last night's lovemaking, the lyrics at the forefront of her mind. She knew it was the greatest love song ever written. She knew how much it meant to her and Jimmy.

We have something they'll never have.

She'd felt incredible making love with him last night, despite his disabilities. She knew hand on heart that it had never felt like that with Simon. Staring intently at the horizon, where the pale blue sky met the darker blue ocean, she concluded that it was Jimmy and only Jimmy she'd always wanted to be with. When she did it with Simon one night under the sexually charged influence of ecstasy, that had been bad enough. Creating a child that everyone assumed to be Jimmy's for the first three years was inexcusable, and she knew it. Vaughan had been killed in a road traffic accident, Jimmy's memory had been completely wiped, and it felt like a clean slate for her. She winced at that thought. A clean slate? She'd lost her son and spent three years dealing with it; the slate was far from clean. She'd accepted Vaughan was gone, lost forever, but Jimmy's memories weren't lost; they were all in there somewhere, and he'd remembered so much in the year she'd spent rehabilitating him. She knew it wasn't a clean slate, a clean break. She had to face her husband and tell him it was over, but she wasn't looking forward to it. Pulling a packet of tissues from her pocket, she dried her eyes and wiped her face. She checked the time on her watch, just after eight, shocked at how quickly time passed as she'd sat there contemplating her future.

On that beach, the decision naturally came to her. She could only love Jimmy in the way she could ever do. He was right. They were and are part of the same soul. Always.

I need to go and wake him, she thought as she rose to her feet. I'm not putting off the inevitable any longer. She made determined and confident strides from the beach across the road to the hotel to go and wake Jimmy. She *really* needed to go home and talk to her husband.

Opening their hotel room door gently and quietly to avoid waking him, she stepped inside. He was still sleeping. She threw her coat onto the chair by the window and approached the bed.

"Jimmy, wake up," Alison said, gently pushing his shoulder.

It took him a moment to realise where he was. When he eventually opened his eyes, he smiled at Alison before speaking.

"Good morning, beautiful," he exclaimed.

"Oh, Jimmy, good morning. I love you."

"I love you too. Last night was incredible."

"Yes, it was. I should never have run to Simon after the DNA test just because you left the country upset. I should have tried to reach you. Talk to you. Tell you how bad I felt. I'm so sorry."

"Stop apologising and forget about it. It's in the past, isn't it? I'm only interested in what happens now. You're dressed. Have you been out?"

"Yes, I went to the beach," she replied, kicking off her shoes and climbing onto the bed.

"Why?"

"I just needed time alone to think. I have a big decision to make, don't I?"

"What do you mean?"

"Oh, come on, Jimmy. I have to tell Simon."

"Really? You mean you want to be with me?"

"Of course, Jimmy. We should never have split up."

Jimmy started crying, which Alison had expected, knowing how emotional he'd become since acquiring the brain injury. She held him close as he wept into her bosom.

"It's OK, darling. We're together again."

"I know, I know, and I love you, but I feel really bad for my friend."

They separated their embrace, and Alison wiped his eyes with a tissue.

"It's not your fault Jimmy. It's not Simon's fault, either. The accident, everything. I think it was meant to happen, to bring us back together. It must have been written in the stars."

"Really?"

"Yes. I intentionally tried to hide my feelings from you last year. Only because I didn't know how you felt about me. Or how you would feel about me when you remembered Vaughan."

"I'm still in love with you, Alison. I always will be. We're part of the same soul."

"Oh, Jimmy, let's go. We should get a bite to eat downstairs and check out. Head back home. Though Simon might not be there."

"Why? Did he go out over the weekend?"

"He did, yes. The advertising company where he's Creative Director secured a big contract on Friday. They all went out to celebrate. God knows where he's ended up."

"Right. Does he do a lot of coke, Simon?"

"Yes, and booze, too much. It's changing him, Jimmy."

"He'll probably still be off his head."

Having spent two full days and nights in Brighton, she thought about how her husband had spent the weekend. What state he would be in when they arrived back home.

#

Chapter 38

Throughout the journey back to Highgate, Jimmy kept insisting they should move back to Manchester. Alison had to calm down his excitement and explain they had to speak to Simon first. His best friend for so many years took his girl back from him. It would hurt Simon's pride; she knew that. All the way back home, she had to keep insisting to herself she was doing the right thing.

In the early afternoon, when she pulled onto the driveway parking next to her husband's car, she breathed a sigh of relief he was home. Once she'd locked her vehicle and reached the front door, Jimmy parked his chair next to her. When she unlocked the front door and stepped into the hallway, she was shocked at what she saw. Takeaway food wrappers, pizza boxes and empty beer cans everywhere. It was obvious Simon had brought the party back home with him. She grabbed the wheelchair from the hallway, and Jimmy climbed into it. She pushed him into the dining area.

"Someone's had a big party," he said.

"Looks like it, doesn't it. Simon?"

Silence and no response.

"He'll be asleep in bed. His car's outside."

"Can I have a brew, Ali?"

"Yeah, sure, I'll go and wake Simon," she said, flicking the kettle on to boil.

Alison ran upstairs, only moments later coming back downstairs confused.

"He's not in bed."

"Is he not?"

"No."

"I'll have a look round. By the state of the place, he'll be wherever he's dropped."

"OK."

"I'll check his man cave first."

"Right."

She walked through the hallway, and when she reached the study door, she slowly opened it. The first thing she noticed was Simon's mother's regency dining chair on its side on the floor, as if it had been thrown against the radiator in anger. As she opened the door fully, she saw him. Simon had used the chair to stand on, a mains extension cable tied around his neck wrapped around one of the solid oak beams in the ceiling. The weight of his lifeless body on the ligature had forced his head forward. His chin was into his chest, and his head bowed; she couldn't see his face. Just the top of his head and his lifeless body hanging there, not moving, feet dangling a foot from the floor. Her mouth opened wide, face warped with emotion. She began to shudder and shake, not knowing what to do. Slowly walking towards him, she stopped, reaching out and touching his stone-cold, lifeless left hand. Looking up at his face, she could see the soul of Simon was gone. His face was a translucent grey, with eyes fixed in a stone-cold stare. She collapsed onto the floor, hurt, frustrated, upset, and confused. She began to cry, wailing, sobbing, and bawling loudly. Her energy sapped, and she shrank herself into a ball, covering her head with both hands. Beads of perspiration on her forehead as she shivered. She wanted to scream, and she did so. She couldn't hold the hurt in any longer. "NO!" She screamed so loudly it made the study windows rattle.

She was still weeping uncontrollably as she heard Jimmy approaching in his chair.

"Ali, what's up?"

She heard his concerned question from the hallway.

"Jimmy, do NOT come in," she sobbed on the floor.

Curiosity drove him to the open door. Alison turned when she heard him in the doorway.

"Fuckin' 'ell," he said.

Wincing, he turned his face away. He couldn't look. Jimmy was confused. His damaged brain either didn't understand or didn't *want* to understand what had happened.

"He's dead, Jimmy. Come on, let's leave him. I need to call the police," Alison stood up, wiping her tears away.

"What's happened? I don't get it?" Jimmy said.

"COME ON! OUT!" She screamed at him.

Jimmy nervously reversed his chair out of the room, and Alison followed him. As she closed the door behind her, she couldn't look back at Simon. On the way through to the dining area, Alison picked up the wireless telephone handset from its cradle in the hall. She sat at the dining table to make the call. Jimmy followed her and parked his chair next to her as she sat down. She dialled 999 and waited for an answer. Jimmy just watched her. They were both in shock.

"Police, please."

A pause as the operator connected her call.

"I've just returned home from a two-day break. I've just found my husband…...he's hung himself at home," she mumbled, struggling to get the words out.

A pause as the operator spoke.

"No, he's stone cold."

The emergency services took the address details and confirmed they were on their way.

"Thank you," she said, pulling the handset away from her ear and ending the call.

Alison was inconsolable and couldn't stop crying. Jimmy didn't know what to do other than hold her close and be there. He'd lost his best friend, and she'd lost her husband, but after the time with Alison last night, he wasn't sure how he should feel.

Struggling to remember all the times he'd spent with his best friend, he was still hurting inside. His best friend, his soul brother, was gone. Alison and Jimmy continued to sit silently, smoking their way through Alison's packet of cigarettes.

A few minutes later, they heard the noise of vehicle engines as flashing blue lights from outside began bouncing around the hallway walls.

"Right, they're here. You stay here."

Alison had to deal with it; she couldn't leave this to Jimmy. He was disabled, he had a brain injury, and she had to be strong for him. His best friend had just killed himself.

"OK," he mumbled.

She opened the door to two police officers and two paramedics she had invited into her home.

"He's in there," Alison said, pointing to the study door.

"OK, we'll let the paramedics take care of him. Can we sit down with you and have a chat? Take some details?" The female police officer asked her.

"Yes, come through."

They walked slowly through to the dining area, sitting together at the table. The policewoman began to take notes as Alison gave her Simon's date of birth and all the other necessary details about her husband.

The two paramedics reappeared with solemn looks across their faces.

"He's on our stretcher now," they said to the police officers.

"OK, thanks," both officers replied.

The paramedics turned and left through the front door, closing it behind them.

"The funeral will have to be in Manchester," Alison blurted out.

"Alison, don't worry about anything at the moment. The Coroner will take Simon to the chapel of rest shortly, and I'll contact Greater Manchester Police, OK?"

"Oh, OK. Thank you."

The officer placed her hand on Alison's shoulder.

"You don't have to thank us. We're here to help."

Alison remained sitting at the dining table, numb and in a state of shock; she didn't move. When the time was right, she stood and went to the front door with Jimmy as everyone left, and they watched as the coroner's vehicle drove their friend's body away. She turned in silence and walked towards the kitchen, Jimmy following behind, pushing at the wheels of his manual chair to move him forwards.

"I'll make us something to eat," Alison suggested.

"OK," Jimmy responded, parking his chair next to the dining table.

She didn't feel like eating but forced herself by preparing sandwiches for her and Jimmy. She made two mugs of tea and put them on a tray with the food, carrying them to the dining area as she sat down.

"Here. Corned beef on brown Jimmy. You hungry?" She asked.

"Not really, but I'll eat it. Thanks, Ali."

"No, me either. We need to eat something, though."

"Yeah," he said just before taking the first bite of his sandwich.

Alison began chewing her first mouthful, staring across the room through the glass doors into the garden at nothing in particular. She was hurting, she felt in some way responsible, and she was terrified by the thought of having to face Simon's mother back in Manchester.

"I drove him to it, Jimmy," she said, turning to face him.

His face had a look of shock. How could she say such a thing?

"You did not! He did that!" Jimmy shouted as he pointed towards the study.

She looked at him, her eyes swollen and red from crying so much. She tried to smile at him, but she just couldn't. She felt it was the booze and cocaine that drove Simon to that place to that state of mind, but she still blamed herself. Knowing she would fall completely in love with Jimmy again was inevitable. What she never expected was this. She could have handled another divorce. The messiness of it, the arguments. Not this, though.

Why? Why did he have to do it? Take his own life. He had everything. The job, the house, the money, the lifestyle. But it was the lifestyle that killed him. Cocaine seems alright when you're in the throes of it and 'on it'. But what about when you stop taking it? How does the human brain handle that? The human brain makes decisions and controls what we do and who we are.

She was back with Jimmy, but he was paralysed and had a damaged brain. She never tried to dissuade Jimmy from smoking cannabis with her because of his brain injury. If anything, she felt it helped him. Stopping stress levels in him from rising would always lead to a temper tantrum. Besides, she was fairly confident cannabis or coming off it, could never drive anyone to do what Simon had done.

Once they'd eaten their sandwiches and drank their tea, Alison's sombre mood and Jimmy's paralysis drove her to think about a song she wanted to listen to. She stood up and spoke to Jimmy as she walked over to her record collection.

"I'm putting that Ride song on. I've got Nowhere on vinyl."

"Paralysed," he said as he pushed the wheels on his chair forward to the lounge.

"Yes. It's on side two. Hang on."

Alison pulled her copy of the album out. She dropped the vinyl onto her turntable, carefully placing the needle at the start of the song she wanted to hear. She turned the volume up quite loud; she knew this song's sombre, haunting, gothic sound perfectly suited the circumstances. They spent the rest of the evening sitting in the lounge, listening to music. Nothing too uplifting, just music that would keep Alison down here, feeling sorry for herself and what had happened. The only thing that stabilised her and gave her hope was Jimmy was back in her life. Two parts of the same soul reunited.

#

Chapter 39

The following day she composed herself sufficiently to ring Mary Wilson, Simon's mother. Greater Manchester Police had contacted her yesterday, so she knew what had happened to her son. It didn't make the call any easier for Alison to cope with. It was awkward, and it was tearful. Mary's constant questioning of why he did it didn't bring her closer to understanding why her son had taken his own life. Alison didn't have the answer, and Simon didn't leave a suicide note. Her husband was dead, and she would never have the answer. She thought it best not to mention the rekindling of her relationship with Jimmy. Still, she told Mary he was back in their lives and had moved in with them in London, describing Jimmy's brain injury and partial paralysis. Mary's brother Albert was making the arrangements for her son's funeral, and she insisted Alison use her car so she and Jimmy could be part of the funeral cortege.

She hated making that call but knew it would have been pretty ill-mannered to wait for Mary to ring her. Facing her parents with Jimmy would be much more difficult to handle. Both Simon and Alison had agreed to keep Jimmy's accident, his hospitalisation, his paralysis and brain injury, and the fact he now lived with them in London secret from both their parents. They didn't need to know; they wouldn't understand. Only Alison knew this was the way it was meant to be.

Mary rang during the week with a date for the funeral, Friday the 25th of August 2000, one o'clock at their local church on Edge Lane in Stretford. The day before, Alison went to see her best friend Tracy in Crouch End and cried. She went to visit her parents in Chelsea and cried. She had to re-introduce them to Jimmy, which was awkward. They didn't understand how Jimmy could be back in Alison's life. They thought it wrong their daughter announced her love for Jimmy so soon after what her husband had done. They didn't know how close Alison and Jimmy had become over the last twelve months. She left her parents' home infuriated; she'd had enough disapproval of her relationship with Jimmy. Another reason to move back to Manchester.

Alison thought a lot about Simon and what they'd once had. How bizarre circumstances had changed it all. Was it disrespectful to think that since Jimmy had come back into her life, it just confirmed she'd been on the rebound with Simon all along? A shoulder to cry on when she needed it in ninety-four. She was never a woman to dwell on the past, and even after the death of someone close to her, life had to go on. She knew that. She was determined to use her role as a freelance photographer to make plans to move north. Alison's parents had bought her a house in London. She owned it and had no mortgage payments to worry about. She didn't want to live there anymore; she had too many memories. She intended to sell the house and buy a home in Manchester.

#

Marston Road, where Simon had lived with his mother all his life, was already full of parked cars when Alison and Jimmy arrived. She parked around the corner on King's Road, opposite Jimmy's old house. The hearse was parked outside Simon's mother's home. Words inside the hearse around the coffin spelt out in flowers:

Simon – Son – Soul Brother.

As Jimmy and Alison approached the house, they saw the flowers, and he burst into tears. Alison stopped her strident walk to the front door. She turned, leaned over, and held Jimmy close to her, whispering into his ear. "It's OK, darling. Think about all the things you've still got to remember about him. All the times you spent together, and the things you got up to. Yeah?"

"I was enjoyin' him tellin' me, Ali," Jimmy sobbed like a lost child.

"I know, I know. We've just gotta get through today. Then we'll head back, OK?"

"Yeah, OK."

She stood straight, grabbed a tissue from her handbag, and wiped his face dry.

Mary came to the front door knowing Jimmy couldn't reach the doorway in his chair. All Alison could do was hold Mary close and apologise.

"I'm so sorry, Mary."

"It's not your fault, love. It's not Jimmy's fault, either. It's nobody's fault. We just have to crack on," Mary said, her voice gravelly and splintering with emotion.

Alison noticed Jimmy staring at Mary's staircase when she parted her embrace with Mary.

"Are those stairs helping with your memories?" Alison asked.

"Yeah, they are."

"That's grand Jimmy," Mary said, leaning over to embrace her son's best friend.

Mary wanted to sit in the front passenger seat of Alison's car, and her brother Albert took the one remaining seat in the back next to Jimmy's electric wheelchair. The people attending the funeral started engines and slowly made their way to the church behind the hearse. It was a lovely sunny day in Stretford for the funeral; the religious people in the congregation would no doubt claim it was Simon's doing. The church was on the other side of Edge Lane, only around the corner from where Jimmy and Simon used to live. Alison pulled into the car park, driving slowly behind the hearse, the other five cars in the cortege pulling in slowly behind her. She parked and stepped out of her vehicle, lowering the ramp for Jimmy to reverse his chair. Dressed respectfully in a black trouser suit, black heels and black handbag, she'd helped Jimmy dress in a black suit she'd had to buy for him last week. Dressing Jimmy in one of Simon's suits wouldn't have been right. They both knew that. The congregation spilt out from their cars, slowly making their way into the church.

"You OK, Ali?" Jimmy asked, looking up at her as she walked alongside him

"Yes, I'm fine, darling," she answered, forcing a smile.

For over an hour, the priest provided a remembrance service for Simon Wilson. Mary, his mother, was inconsolable. Alison and Jimmy sat together at the front next to her. Mary's brother Albert doing his best to stay strong. As Jimmy patted and rubbed her back, Alison cried through most of the service. It was all he could do as tears streamed down his face thinking about his best friend, now that three best friends had become two.

As the congregation made their way to the graveyard to bury the body, Alison and Jimmy drifted away from Mary, allowing her to be with her brother and her close friends. She was too upset to function. She was struggling. The anguish of losing her son was too much to bear.

After Simon had been laid to rest, Mary hugged Alison before leaning forward to hug Jimmy as he sat in his chair. Mary thanked them for travelling many miles to attend her son's funeral. The pair watched Mary, and the rest of the congregation get back into their cars and head for the social club. With their memories of Simon, Alison and Jimmy wanted some time alone anyway, declining to attend the wake as they had to travel back to London.

Alison lit two cigarettes and passed one to Jimmy. Neither of them were smiling.

"Here."

"Thanks, Ali."

Jimmy sat staring at that hole in the ground, exhaling smoke from his cigarette.

"I'm gonna miss him," he said, sighing.

Alison turned to Jimmy and leaned over to hug him.

"I know. Me, too. I love you," she sighed into his ear.

"I love you too, Alison," Jimmy answered.

#

Chapter 40

Once everyone had left the churchyard, Alison crouched next to Jimmy in his wheelchair by Simon's grave. The noise of a loud car engine diverted their gaze towards the car park behind them. They looked on as a silver Ferrari came to a stop. A man in a hat and sunglasses climbed out. He locked the car, walking slowly over toward them.

"Jimmy? Alison?"

Jimmy manoeuvred his chair to face the man as Alison stood upright.

"Andrew?" she questioned.

"All right, Ali? How ya doing?" Reni replied, removing his sunglasses.

"Good, thanks. We didn't think we'd see you here."

"I had to come; I knew you two would be here."

Jimmy smiled when he recognised that voice.

"Reni? Is that your car?"

"Nah, I'm leasing it, Jimmy, while I'm over here for a few days. Good to see you, man."

Smiling, he lowered himself to hug his friend as he sat in his wheelchair.

"What do you mean over here?" Alison asked.

"I live in America now, Los Angeles. I made a shit load of money selling drugs and Oasis merchandise over there. I'm nearly a millionaire now."

"Fuckin' hell, Reni. Nice one!" Jimmy said loudly.

"Never mind that. I feel bad for you, Jimmy. Brain injury and paralysis. I'm so sorry, man."

"Wait a minute Andrew. How come you know about Jimmy's accident?" Alison asked.

"How come? You mean Jimmy's not told you?"

"Eh?" Jimmy said.

"The accident wiped Jimmy's memories."

"You're joking? He doesn't remember anything?"

"Nah. My memories are fucked, Reni," Jimmy moaned.

He turned to face his friend, baffled, saddened he had no memory of them in America.

"You mean you don't remember all those Oasis gigs we went to in America, Jim?'

"Not really. It's all still a bit of a blur."

"Fuckin' 'ell man. Liam was fuckin' distraught after yer accident. He wanted to go home and fuck the tour off. He said you're like the older brother he wished he'd always had."

"Really?"

"Oh, aye. Me and you saw Oasis play loads of times in America. Access all areas passes at every gig. It was fuckin' great, Jim. I think it got up Noel's nose how much Liam loved you."

"He's unbelievable. Best rock and roll singing voice on the fuckin' planet."

"You always used to say that to him."

"Did I. It just came to me automatically 'coz I was thinkin' about him."

"Right. Well, he used to buzz off it. It was the last thing anyone said to him before he went on stage. You saying that to him and him replyin' with, 'you fuckin' know it, Jim!'"

"Wow," Jimmy said, smiling proudly.

"You don't remember the gig in Philadelphia? When that car shot past the venue and mowed you down. It nearly took me with it an' all."

"No, I don't remember," Jimmy complained.

"You mean you were with Jimmy when the accident happened?" Alison asked.

"Yeah. We met up in LA in the January at the first gig on the Oasis American tour. I was on the bus with 'em; Jimmy had a ticket for the gig. He told me what had happened with Vaughan. Liam was fuckin' heartbroken for him. Jimmy looked so lost out there on his own; Liam insisted he got a pass for the whole tour and a seat on the bus next to him." Reni explained.

"Right. This is all news to me, Jimmy. The reason you left England was because of me. What's going on, Andrew? Did you pay Jimmy's medical bills and buy his chair?"

Reni stood there and pulled his cigarette packet and lighter from his coat pocket. He put a cigarette to his lips and lit it, smiling; he exhaled that first drag.

"No, I didn't. Hang on," he answered

With his mobile phone in his hand, he speed dialled a number waiting for an answer.

"Liam? What? Right, OK," Reni said into his phone.

He looked at Alison and Jimmy before speaking again.

"He wants me to put him on loudspeaker."

Alison looked quite surprised; Jimmy just smiled.

"What? Who?" Alison asked, confused.

"Fuckin' buzzin'," Jimmy shouted.

Through that mobile phone, Reni held out in front of him an instantly recognisable voice. Instantly recognisable to Jimmy and probably most people across the world.

"Jimmy! How's it goin', man?" Liam shouted.

"LG, you fuckin' legend. I'm all right considerin' ya know," Jimmy shouted back.

"I was sorry to hear about what happened with Si," Liam stated.

Jimmy looked at Alison; he didn't know what to say, so she took over.

"Thanks. Funeral's over init. I'm driving us back to London now. Liam? Did you pay Jimmy's medical bills and buy his chair?" Alison asked him.

"Yeah, I fuckin' did. He was out of it in a coma over there. No way was I gonna leave him with no money to pay those fucking' bills. So, I got Marcus, our manager, to sort it."

Alison was shocked; she looked at Jimmy crying. She stooped down to hold him close.

"Babe, it's OK, don't get upset. Thank you, Liam. I'll never be able to pay you back."

"LG saved me life. I can't fuckin' believe it," he wailed.

"I don't want paying back, and don't cry, Jim, it's embarrassing," Liam said, smirking.

"I'm sorry, Liam, he get's really upset because of his brain injury," Alison said.

"Sorry Ali, I shouldn't laugh. I had to help him. He's like the older brother I wished I had and not the dickhead I have to deal with."

"Who, Noel?" Alison asked.

"Yeah. He didn't wanna pay the bills. He knew it'd be millions. He's a greedy cunt r kid."

"Wow. Thank you so much, Liam. I don't know what Jimmy would have done without you."

"I had to, Alison. He'd have done the same for me."

"Oh, aye. Defo LG. Best rock and roll voice on the fuckin' planet!" Jimmy shouted, the euphoria he now felt calming his tears.

"You fuckin' know it, Jim. Why don't you stop off at Reading, Alison? Come and see the gig. You can stay in the hotel where we're staying. I'll get Marcus to sort it."

"Yeah, defo!" Jimmy shouted before Alison had a chance to think about it.

"Are you sure, Jimmy? You know how tired you get," Alison sensibly reminded him.

"Yeah, but a fuckin' Oasis gig Ali! I want to watch them play," Jimmy pleaded with her.

"OK, we'll come down, Liam," she announced.

"Nice one, Ali. I'll sort passes out for ya. Get me number off Reni, give us a ring in a bit."

"OK, Liam. Thanks again," Alison said to him happily.

"No worries, man. Laters."

The line went dead, and Reni stuffed his mobile into his coat pocket. Telephone conversation over, now they knew the identity of the mystery benefactor.

"I'm in shock, Reni," Alison stated.

"Well, I knew all that anyway, I helped Marcus make sure everyone got paid over there, and Farley Hall got paid. I didn't wanna spoil the surprise. Liam told me he wanted to tell you guys."

"He's incredible, Reni. I'll never be able to thank him enough," Jimmy said, smiling.

"No, we won't, Jimmy. We'll be able to see him in person once we get to Reading, though. That should spark your memories a little. You coming down, Reni?" Alison asked.

"I'd love to, Ali, but I've gotta get this car back to the leasing company this afternoon and get to the airport. I'm flying back tonight," Reni said.

"Oh, OK. Well, give us yours and Liam's number. When me and Jimmy have moved up here, I'll give you a ring. See if you're able to fly over for a bit of a housewarming. What do you think?"

"Yeah, sounds great."

Reni wrote down the two telephone numbers on a slip of paper and passed it to Alison.

"Jimmy, you take care, man. I've gotta get going," he said, hugging his friend in his chair, then turning to Alison and giving her a hug.

"Thank you so much for coming today and for putting my mind at rest. I wanted to thank the person who'd bought Jimmy his chair and paid all his medical bills," Alison said.

"Well, you'll see Liam soon. You can thank him in person. Have fun down at Reading."

"Thanks. I'm sure we will," Alison said, smiling.

"Nice one Reni," Jimmy shouted to him, but he was already walking toward the car park.

They both looked on as he unlocked the Ferrari and climbed into the driver's seat. When he fired up the engine, it was loud. Alison could feel the low resonating rumble through the floor, and Jimmy felt it in his chair as he sat there. Reni accelerated out of the church car park and onto the main road, the wheels of his car squealing on the tarmac road out of sight.

"Fuckin' 'ell. Liam Gallagher. I knew we were close, but I never thought it was him who paid for me Panzer and all me medical bills." Jimmy was smiling.

"I know. What an amazing guy. Those medical bills will have run into millions of pounds whilst you were in that coma."

"Ya reckon?"

"Definitely, yes."

"How far is Reading from here, Ali? How long will it take to get there?"

"Well, it's not far from London, about four hours it the traffic is not too bad."

"Have you got any Oasis on tape in your car Ali?" Jimmy asked.

"Oh yes," Alison happily responded.

"Ace. Let's go. I wanna see LG. I wanna see Oasis. I haven't been to a concert since my accident, have I?" Jimmy happily responded, bouncing on the seat of his wheelchair.

"OK, I know. Let's go, Jimmy. We'll stop on the way down for something to eat."

"Fantastic," Jimmy announced, clicking the stick on his chair forwards.

Alison began walking toward her vehicle in the car park, Jimmy idling alongside her.

It was a sad day, they'd both lost their friend, and she'd lost her husband but been reunited with Jimmy a year ago. They were returning home to London, but not before meeting up with *Liam Gallagher* at Reading Festival and watching *Oasis* play a gig tonight.

The mystery benefactor. *Liam Gallagher.*

A man nine years younger than Jimmy, they'd been inseparable during that tour of America during the latter part of ninety-four and the early part of ninety-five. Liam knew it, Reni knew it, but Jimmy had forgotten everything. Alison had been completely unaware of what happened to Jimmy when he left for America after ingesting the DNA test result. He couldn't tell her about it; he couldn't remember those memories so close to the accident. An accident that ruined everything. Jimmy had a lot of missing memories, and he needed Liam to fill in the blanks.

He had just watched his best friend's body being lowered into the ground. The best friend he ever had as a child and a teenager. Tonight would be like that time in America, watching the best friend he'd ever had as an adult sing those songs incredibly well. Songs his older brother had written. Back then, he *hated* Alison because of what had happened; she'd ruined everything. Now, despite being paralysed, despite that brain injury, tonight, watching *Oasis* with Alison by his side again, he knew he would be the happiest man alive. His soul reunited with the missing half.

#

THE END.

About the Author

Steven Anthony Lomas

Steven had a retail management career, it ended in a car accident when he was 32 years old on 7th of Feb. 2004. It left him with frontal lobe brain damage. Perhaps it is the traumatic brain injury that has unleashed his creative side? Steven spent from 2012 until 2018 in education, he now holds two degrees and a master's in creative writing. In the Spring of 2014, a story came out of the ether, and he started writing. He named the novel Decades after the Joy Division song. The first 10,000 words was his dissertation for a master's in creative writing, which he passed with merit. The story is about a man from Manchester with a brain injury, his life before it, marriage, paternity fraud, and divorce. They do say the first novel is autobiographical.

Milton Keynes UK
Ingram Content Group UK Ltd.
UKHW012251291123
433483UK00006B/431

9 789360 168681